OPERATIVE WITCHCRAFT

"In our postmodern world, appearances often upstage matters of real substance, and people freely adopt new personae as they please—witness the plethora of contemporary witches, many of whom share little in common with the sorts of rural figures that bore the name in earlier times. Nigel Pennick's *Operative Witchcraft* is an unromanticized 'warts and all' survey of the real history and lore of witchcraft in his native England and elsewhere. This treasure trove of seldom-seen material encompasses topics ranging from toadmen and horsemen to weird plants and darker folk traditions, including a fascinating chapter on the syncretic links between British witchcraft and West Indian Obeah religion. One could not ask for a more knowledgeable and sympathetic guide through these shadow-filled realms than Nigel Pennick."

MICHAEL MOYNIHAN, COAUTHOR OF LORDS OF CHAOS AND
COEDITOR OF THE JOURNAL *TYR: MYTH—CULTURE—TRADITION*

"*Operative Witchcraft* is a fascinating, wide-ranging, and detailed work that acknowledges and tackles the complex nature of British witchcraft. The book discusses the powers of the witch, how witches have been portrayed, and the persecution of them through legislation and unofficial violence borne of ancient fears. The comparison with West Indian Obeah highlights the repetition of old patterns of persecution in Britain's former colonies. Nigel Pennick has long been a leading authority on this subject, and *Operative Witchcraft* is another excellent work, shining new light not only on the history of witchcraft but also on how it has been practiced over the centuries. This beautifully written and authoritative work, which is both accessible and academically rigorous, should grace the bookshelves of folklorists, historians, practitioners of witchcraft, and those with a general interest in this enduring aspect of our culture."

VAL THOMAS, HERBALIST, PRACTITIONER OF WITCHCRAFT
AND NATURAL MAGIC, AND AUTHOR OF *A WITCH'S KITCHEN*

"While most historians of witchcraft have focused on the early modern and Renaissance era (myself included), Pennick goes beyond the great conflagrations of Europe to show how magic and witchcraft survived into the twentieth century. *Operative Witchcraft* offers one interesting tidbit of forgotten magical history after the next—not a page went by that I didn't stop and say, "Wow!" Well written, well researched, a fantastic addition to any witchcraft library."

THOMAS HATSIS, AUTHOR OF
THE WITCHES' OINTMENT
AND *PSYCHEDELIC MYSTERY TRADITIONS*

"Nigel Pennick stands with one leg in the eldritch world and one in the mundane, as all who know him can attest. After a lifetime of dedication to these ancient mysteries, both in theory and in practice, there is no one better qualified to lead the reader through the highways and byways of operative witchcraft."

IAN READ, FORMER EDITOR OF
CHAOS INTERNATIONAL AND *RŪNA* MAGAZINES,
LEADER OF THE RUNE-GILD IN EUROPE,
AND FOUNDING MUSICIAN IN THE BAND FIRE + ICE

"Yet another generous offering from Nigel Pennick! In *Operative Witchcraft*, Pennick's extensive knowledge of British folk magic tradition builds a richly furnished mansion from the presumed molehill of its textual and material traces."

DANICA BOYCE, PRODUCER OF *FAIR FOLK* PODCAST

"In this intriguing book, Nigel Pennick gives numerous examples of operative witchcraft—witchcraft as it was actually practiced and documented by earlier researchers. It also includes details of the techniques and practices he personally learned from traditional practitioners over a period of more than forty-five years."

ANNA FRANKLIN, AUTHOR OF
THE HEARTH WITCH'S COMPENDIUM
AND *THE SACRED CIRCLE TAROT*

OPERATIVE WITCHCRAFT

Spellwork and Herbcraft
in the British Isles

NIGEL PENNICK

Destiny Books
Rochester, Vermont

Destiny Books
One Park Street
Rochester, Vermont 05767
www.DestinyBooks.com

Text stock is SFI certified

Destiny Books is a division of Inner Traditions International

Cataloging-in-Publication Data for this title is available from the Library of Congress

ISBN 978-1-62055-844-7 (print)
ISBN 978-1-62055-845-4 (ebook)

Printed and bound in the United States by Lake Book Manufacturing, Inc. The text stock is SFI certified. The Sustainable Forestry Initiative® program promotes sustainable forest management.

10 9 8 7 6 5 4 3 2 1

Text design and layout by Debbie Glogover
This book was typeset in Garamond Premier Pro with Rockeby Semiserif, Rotis Semi Serif, and Gill Sans MT Pro used as display typefaces

All photographs by Nigel Pennick. Artifacts in Nigel Pennick's collection and archive engravings courtesy of the Library of the European Tradition. All Botanical illustrations/photos are in the public domain except for fig. 6.4 and fig. 6.18, which are courtesy of Creative Commons.

To send correspondence to the author of this book, mail a first-class letter to the author c/o Inner Traditions • Bear & Company, One Park Street, Rochester, VT 05767, and we will forward the communication.

THANKS AND CREDITS

To those both living and now departed, for various and sundry assistance over the years, discussions and information that contributed in one way or another to this book, I thank the following: Ivan Bunn, Michael W. Burgess, Andrew Chumbley, Michael Clarke, Frances Collinson, Jess Cormack, Ben Fernee, Anna Franklin, Tony Harvey, Brian Hoggard, Tim Holt-Wilson, Chris Jakes, Pete Jennings, K. Frank Jensen, Linda Kelsey-Jones, Patrick McFadzean, Rupert Pennick, Mike Petty, Sid Smith, Val Thomas, John Thorne, and Genevieve West in addition to the staffs of various libraries, archives, and record offices in England, Scotland, Wales, Switzerland, and Germany.

The popular image
of a witch

In a dirtie Hair-lace
She leads on a brace
Of black-bore-cats to attend her;
Who scratch at the Moone,
And threaten at noone,
Of night from Heaven to rend her.

A-hunting she goes;
A crackt horne she blows;
A' which the hounds fall a-bounding;
While th' Moone in her sphere
Peepes trembling for feare,
And night's afraid of the sounding.

ROBERT HERRICK, "THE HAG"

Contents

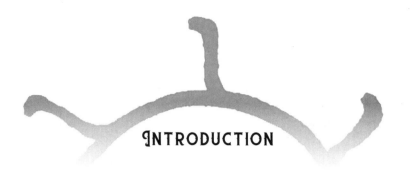

The Many Names
of Witchcraft

This book is about witchcraft in the British Isles, a subject that has generated a large body of literature and opinion. The history of witchcraft has been approached from many angles: religious, sociological, political, speculative. Witchcraft has been described in terms of pagan survival, devil worship, spiritualism, shamanism, early feminism, peasant resistance against ruling-class oppression, folk medicine, veterinarianism, agriculture and horticulture, folk meteorology, fortune-telling, finding lost property, the exercise of unknown paranormal powers, fraudulence, confidence trickery, and extortion. Perhaps individual people deemed witches in the past did fall into one or another of these categories, but as a broad and complex historical subject, witchcraft cannot be labeled conveniently as just one or another of these.

This work on operative witchcraft deals with the early modern and modern periods in Great Britain, from the late sixteenth century to the early twenty-first century. Until 1735, witchcraft, as defined by the law, was a heavily punishable offense that carried the death penalty for certain charges. Of course the law never succeeds in totally extirpating those offenses that it creates; it often acts as a recommendation for those who feel a need to transgress. In the absence of internal documentation—that is, accounts written or told by the practitioners

1

themselves—we are dependent on a history that derives from almost random anecdotal accounts. This is a history that emphasizes accounts that are usually secondhand. Here, there is a hierarchy of credibility; the absurd allegations from witch trials, following the motifs that were expected at the time, tell us more about the beliefs of the witch hunters than about those of the people accused of witchcraft and labeled as witches. Accounts of witch trials are not necessarily sound or objective. It is probable that most of the words we have from the alleged practitioners were put into their mouths by their accusers.

These accounts infer motives, but they are not the direct record of the practitioners themselves, alleged or otherwise. Many historical accounts appear to be fabricated, perhaps written after the event with the objective of justifying the necessity of the witch trial and the punishment of those deemed guilty. Sensationalized accounts existed long before the advent of the tabloid press. Equally, we cannot take for granted the speculations of the twentieth-century witchcraft writers Margaret Murray and Gerald Gardner. In actuality, there are enormous gaps in the recorded historical evidence of what practitioners did. We are presented with disconnected fragments from which we must attempt to construct a plausible and relatively coherent picture.

Witches, imaginary or real, were viewed as being transgressors and deviants, people whose way of life lay outside the acceptable norms of society. From a more modern viewpoint, the witches can be seen as people who contested the generally accepted social constructs of reality. In an era when a particular worldview was considered by those ruling the land to be the single reality, pluralistic realism, the possibility that numerous, equally authentic truths can coexist, was not even considered. Religious belief was enforced with draconian rigor, and political debate was strictly controlled.

Witchcraft was classified as a crime. The history of operative witchcraft is that of the struggle between preventive actions and the continuance of covert practices. It is clear that, like any human culture, witchcraft has evolved and changed over the years. In earlier times, publication of the information read out at witch trials clearly provided recommendations for the activities of deviants, activities that in turn were guaranteed to attract disapproval and punishment. At the center of the witch trials stood the figure of the devil, supposedly controlling the actions of witches, recruiting new ones, and egging them on to commit destructive, antisocial actions. The claim that witches were part of an evil conspiracy bent on the destruction of society, a claim recognizable in the early twentieth-first century in its new guise as the "war on terror," was no longer taken for granted as the function of witchcraft.

Before the middle of the eighteenth century, works about witchcraft gave accounts of what tortured prisoners had told their tormentors, having been prompted by the received opinions of what witches did to provide accounts that fitted in with expectations. After the middle of the eighteenth century, with the abolition of the legal belief in witchcraft and the judicial killing of those arrested, accounts of what people were actually doing, their artifacts, and performances began to be written down. Although still called witchcraft, the magic was now seen as operative and practical. The publication of articles and books describing recipes and remedies, as well as "what witches do," clearly influenced the practice of witchcraft from the late eighteenth century. A feedback loop was created by these publications: those who considered themselves witches got ideas from them, and in turn were reported as performing these rites and remedies. After the repeal of the Witchcraft Act in 1951, witchcraft emerged as a religious practice, a new stage in its development that in many instances took it far from its operative roots. In this work I give numerous examples discovered by earlier researchers and published in folklore books and journals. I also include details of techniques and practices that I have learned from practitioners over a period of more than forty-five years.

Nigel Campbell Pennick
Cambridge

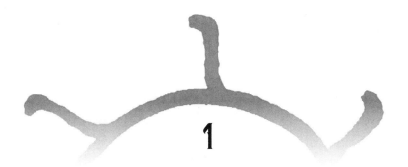

Operative Witchcraft

DEFINITIONS AND PRACTICES

Magicians strive not to be counted among the could have beens,
The would have beens and the should have beens.

Magic is an integral part of culture. It has often been ignored by historians who, not believing in its efficacy or even recognizing that in the past many people did believe, have dismissed any belief in it as beneath mention. Alternatively, magic and the occult sciences, when they have been mentioned, have been portrayed as worthless superstition or irredeemably diabolical and evil, unspeakable rites to be shunned, lest they taint the reader. But to present magic as a dangerous subject that ought to be censored lest it seduce the reader into criminality is unhelpful, for it pushes students of magical history into a ghetto when students of human depravity and violence, such as war and crime, are welcome in the mainstream. Magic played a significant part in shaping people's lives. Magic is an integral part of our cultural heritage, ancient skills, and wisdom and a perennial response to universal situations and problems.

The expression "ancient skills and wisdom," which was coined in Cambridge in 1969 by John Nicholson, describes the knowledge, the abilities, and the spiritual understanding of how to do things according to true principles. The ability to practice these ancient skills and wisdom requires an understanding of one's personal place in the continuity of one's culture over thousands of years. It necessitates being present in one's own tradition based on place and the accumulated knowledge and skills of countless ancestral generations as well as being open to new things and how they can be harmonized with the old. Ancient skills and wisdom are timeless because they are based on universal principles, and these basic essentials of existence and of human nature do not change. Western occult philosophy embodies these ancient skills and wisdom. It has an enormous corpus of interconnected traditions and currents that have been expanded, developed, and refined through time, as has the definition of what witchcraft is and who are the witches. Some of those called witches were people who knew particular techniques—ways of doing things and the tricks of the trade that were unsuspected and unknown by most people. These techniques are comparable to those of the art and activity that were transmitted through apprenticeship to members of craft and rural fraternities, but they were less obviously useful than the crafts of the shoemaker, the seamstress, the miller, or the ploughman.*

Practitioners of vernacular magic were readily accessible in seventeenth-century England, despite the Witchcraft Act of 1604 (see chapter 5, page 32). In 1621, Robert Burton wrote in his *The Anatomy of Melancholy,* "Sorcerers are all too common; cunning men, wizards and white-witches, as they call them, in every village, which, if they be sought unto, will help almost all infirmities of body and mind" (Burton [1621] 1926, vol. II, i, I, sub. I, 1926 ed., v. 2, 7). Burton was, of course, totally disapproving because he believed that these practitioners were using forbidden powers, so it was not lawful to resort to them for cures, under the principle "evil is not to be done that good may come of it." But people who had no recourse to any other medical or legal assistance

---

*Because the proper names for Plough Monday and the Confraternity of the Plough use the British spelling of the word *plow,* the British spelling has been retained for this word and its variations in all instances. All other words with alternate British spellings have been Americanized.

Fig. 1.1. Seventeenth-century image of a witch

were, of course, clients of white witches, cunning men, wizards, and quacks, whether or not they were officially legal.

In the second edition of his *A Glossary of Words Used in the Wapentakes of Manley and Corringham, Lincolnshire* (1877), Edward Peacock gives the entry: "White Witch: A woman who uses her incantations only for good ends. A woman who, by magic, helps others who are suffering from malignant witchcraft." (Those who practice beneficial magic are, however, generally called wise women or wise men). A working definition of the various kinds or functions of witches was in use in the West Country of England in the nineteenth century. In her *Nummits and Crummits* (1900), Sarah Hewett published the distinction between three recognized categories of witchcraft: black, white, and gray. The black witch was malevolent, bringing every known evil on others; the white witch, in opposition, employed countermagic against black witchcraft. White witches, however, made money out of their craft: they charged their clients to take off the spells.

The third category was the gray witch, which Hewett considered worse than either the black or the white, for the gray witch has the power to put spells on people, to use the evil eye, to curse, and to bring bad luck. But also she has the power to heal and bring benefits. Writing about the same region in 1899, H. Colley March defined a wise man or wise woman as one who, without fee or reward, tells folk how to overcome witchcraft. This fee is the subtle distinction between the wise woman and the white witch inferred in Peacock's definition. Perceptions, of course, have never been fixed. Writing about Devonshire charmers in 1970, Theo Brown noted that charmers of warts and so forth would never accept payment because to take money would deprive them of their power. Brown observed that this was a modern development, as the white witch of old was always a professional and charged considerable fees (Brown 1970, 41).

In addition to the overt practitioners of what is considered to be witchcraft proper, the name *witch* is given to certain men from the Confraternity of the Plough in their Plough Monday disguises. Thus, in Northamptonshire, "Witch-Men, *n*. Guisers who go about on Plough-Monday with their faces darkened." In Northamptonshire, Plough Monday had the alternative name of Plough Witch Monday (Sternberg 1851, 123).

Witches and witchcraft are not necessarily synonymous. Some labeled the magic performed only by those labeled as witches to be witchcraft, while those not labeled as witches were seen to be practicing magic against the machinations of the witches. More confusingly, those performing countermagic against witchcraft were sometimes also considered witches, as in the case of white witch versus black witch, but others performing the same countermagic, both professionals and amateur individuals, clearly did not consider themselves to be practicing witchcraft at all. In 1705, in his *Discourse on Witchcraft,* John Bell warned his readers to "guard against devilish charms for men or beasts. There are many sorceries practiced in our day. What intend ye by opposing witchcraft to witchcraft, in such sort when ye suppose one to be bewitched, ye endeavour his belief by burnings, bottle, horse-shoes and such-like magical ceremonies" (Lawrence 1898, 113). The definition of witches as people belonging to a secret organization confused the issue of the forms of folk magic that permeated the whole of society, with specific practitioners having their own specialized forms of magical practice.

Recorded instances of British traditional practitioners from the seventeenth century onward who used at least some magical techniques in common with that of operative witchcraft describe them by various names, many of which are generic, while others focus on a particular characteristic or skill: black, white, or gray witch; wise woman; old wife; handywoman; charmer; cunning man; clever man; doctor; wise man; wizard; warlock; magus; magister; magician; professor; mountebank; lijah; conjuror; conjuring parson; planet reader; quack doctor/doctress; wild herb man; root digger; root doctor; herbsman; toadman/toadwoman; toad doctor; tuddy; horse doctor; cow doctor; seventh son of a seventh son; boggart seer; skeelie folk; and so on.

These categories are in addition to those of a more organized and speculative kind, from Christian mystics, astrologers, thaumaturges, Jewish mystics, kabbalists, and others whose expertise lay outside the bounds of orthodox religion and, later, science. Society has always been pluralistic in terms of belief, doctrine, and practice, even in times when authorized worldviews were imposed by force with the sanction of violence on violators.

Equally, society has always been full of forbidden and unrecorded activities, rule breaking, illicit practices, fiddles, rackets, scams, hokkibens, confidence tricks, bribery, and corruption. Practitioners of these activities always deny all knowledge when suspected; they are always uncooperative with those who ask questions. Those with specialist knowledge, which gives them a livelihood, power, or both, are always covert and secretive about their knowledge and know-how. It is worth keeping quiet and not letting on. This air of mystery simultaneously attracts customers and frightens people. Catherine Parsons, a folklorist from Cambridgeshire, noted in 1952, "Witches liked to be credited with the power of evil so that the credulous would pay for protection and people's misfortunes would add to their reputation"

(Parsons 1952, 45). But the opposite could happen too, with people getting the blame for misfortune when they never claimed to have powers. Henry Laver, writing in 1889 about Essex half a century earlier, remembers Mother Cowling, "an old harmless woman at Canewdon who was credited with the possession of fearful powers and was blamed for others' ills" (Laver 1889, 29).

The charter among villagers was never to talk about witches and their activities, but the research work of the folklorist is to investigate. In 1925, an old woman in whom the Norfolk folklorist Mark Taylor was interested, put the toad on him (Taylor 1929, 126–27), and in 1952, Parsons noted, "I flouted the witches in 1915 by reading a paper on witchcraft before the Cambridge Antiquarian Society at some risk to my well-being for one should never talk about witches if one wants to keep free of their craft" (Parsons 1952, 45).

Fig. 1.2. Toad mummified in wrapped bundle,
Cambridgeshire

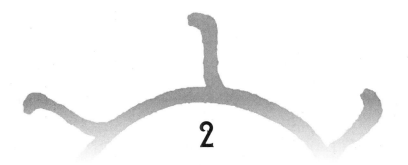

2

Witchcraft, Fortune, and Misfortune

The protection racket operated by some witches has already been mentioned. Witchcraft and its related vernacular magic gave special opportunities to commit other crimes, especially the ability to steal without getting caught. In the fens of Cambridgeshire and Lincolnshire, "no door is ever closed to a toadman" is a saying (Pattinson 1953, 425). (For more on the power of the toad, see chapter 11.) A head horseman at King's Lynn in 1911 was always said to be able to make locked doors fly open by throwing his cap at them (Randall 1966, 110–11). In 1953 it was said of a certain pig farmer in the Peterborough region who always had enough in the days of wartime shortages, "Pig feed rationing in the war meant nothing to him: he was a toadman" (Pattinson 1953, 425). In 1933 a magical formula for stealing extra corn to feed one's horses was taken from a wagoner at Digby in Lincolnshire. It involved catching a frog, killing it, and cutting its heart out. The body of the frog was then buried, and the wagoner carried the heart. It gave him the ability to pass through the small holes cut in barn doors for cats to come and go. In this way he could steal extra corn (Rudkin 1933, 199). One of the powers of the toadman or toadwoman is to be able to travel "out of the sight of people," which literalists interpret as becoming invisible. But this is not the invisibility of standing in front of someone who can see through you. It is the invisibility of not being noticed, not being seen. The Herefordshire clever man Billy o' Dormee from Pembridge "could charm the taties out o' the stacks and nobody'd know, till they went to get 'em out; they'd be gone, and no sign. . . . You canna keep nothin' with folks like that about" (Leather 1912, 56).

Those who knew the secrets of animal control, and toadmen and toadwomen are the most celebrated examples of such people, could use their powers for good or ill. There are many instances of people controlling horses by means of secret techniques that were often classified as witchcraft (see especially "The Horse Witch" section in chapter 10, page 98). Those who put on shows with horses, such as circus performers, could make them do things that amazed the onlookers. Members of horsemen's fraternities sometimes made their horses perform as demonstrations of their power to others. Other animals could be controlled similarly by those in the know. A woman near Ross in Herefordshire was said to be able to make pigs dance when she whistled (Leather 1912, 55). It is interesting that the Pig and Whistle is a traditional pub name. Miss Disbury of Willingham in Cambridgeshire, who was an old woman in 1900, was noted for her uncanny power over cattle (Porter 1969, 175).

Near-universal belief in witches and their powers was prevalent in country districts until well into the twentieth century. James John Hissey, writing about Lincolnshire in 1898, recalled a meeting with a clergyman he met on a journey there "who confided in me" and said, "To get on in Lincolnshire, before all things it is necessary to believe in game, and not to trouble too much about the Catholic faith." He further assured Hissey as a positive fact that both devil worship and a belief in witchcraft existed in the county. He said, "I could tell you many strange things of my rural experiences." And he did: how the devil is supposed to haunt the churchyards in the shape of a toad, how witchcraft is practiced, and so forth. "You may well look astonished," he exclaimed, "at what I tell you, but these things are so; they have come under my notice, and I speak advisedly from personal knowledge" (Hissey 1898, 223).

Accounts with any detail show how women who practiced as witches were marginalized and socially excluded and numbered among the most impoverished people in their respective villages. An 1888 description of Old Judy, the "witch of Burwell" in Cambridgeshire, tells that she lived in the most northerly of the squatters' cottages, which were "half a dozen primitive one-storeyed hovels built of wattle-and-daub with clunch chimneys thatched with sedge and litter" (Porter 1969, 161). The Horseheath witch, Daddy Witch, was described as "half-clothed in rags" and "lived in a hut by the sheep-pond at Garret's Close" (Parsons 1915, 39). The theory of Reginald Scot in *The Discoverie of Witchcraft* that "the Divell exhorteth them to observe their fidelitie unto him promising them long life and prosperitie" could hardly have been more wrong (Scot [1584] 1886).

Although frightened of witches, people also showed curiosity. There are examples of the funerals of reputed witches being attended by large crowds of people. The funeral of Susan Cooper at Whittlesford in 1878 was accompanied by large crowds who expected strange phenomena to occur. After her interment, the children of the village school trampled on her grave "so that the imps couldn't get out" (Porter 1969, 175). Similarly, the funeral of a witch known as Mrs. Smith in Cambridgeshire in 1880 drew "such crowds of people at her funeral, they pushed each other right into the grave, expecting she would burst her coffin" (Wherry and Jennings 1905, 189).

People would travel long distances to visit magical practitioners; for example, "a man living in the neighborhood of Chichester, whose children and grandchildren are much afflicted, has twice taken a journey of upward of a hundred miles, with different members of his family, to visit a cunning man in Dorsetshire, who professes to be in possession of the charms. The month of May is the only month when they will work, and the sufferers, to have any benefit therefrom, must have their eyes fixed on the new moon at the time when they are presented with a box of ointment made from herbs gathered when the moon was full" (Latham 1878, 45).

The shoemaker James Murrell of Hadleigh in Essex (1812–1860) was known widely as Cunning Murrell. His specialty was to treat sick animals with herbal remedies, to recover stolen horses or cattle, and to perform countermagic against those whom his clients believed had bewitched them (Howe 1956, 138). After his death, letters were found written to him by people from as far away as Suffolk and London, asking for advice (Howe 1956, 139). In Lincoln in the 1840s, around the same time that Murrell was practicing in Essex, a man known as the Wizard of Lincoln traded on his ability to find stolen goods and the thieves who had taken them (Gutch and Peacock 1908, 84). Also in the nineteenth century, a Herefordshire cunning man called Jenkins was known to have the ability to find lost property and to identify thieves (Leather 1912, 57–59). In 1891, the Reverend J. C. Atkinson noted, "The most lucrative part of the Wise Man's 'practice' seems to have been connected with the recovery of stolen or otherwise lost goods" (Atkinson 1891, 120).

There are numerous recorded tales of misfortune following the slighting of a witch and various ways of dealing with it. Here are three accounts from nineteenth-century Oxfordshire. In 1902, Percy Manning recounted a story told to him by ninety-one-year-old Mrs. Cooper from Barton, near Headington. She remembered that when she was a child, a woman named Miriam Russell, known as Old Miriam, had the reputation of being a witch. One time, she went to the Powell family, her farming neighbors, to ask a favor but was rebuffed. She said she would remember them. A few days later, the cows and calves all suddenly ran about as though they were going mad, and several calves were found at last on top of a thatched barn. Old Miriam made it known that this was her work. The Powells then willingly gave her what she wanted, and then the cows were quiet and the calves came down off the barn.

Manning also writes of another "notable witch," Dolly Henderson, at Salford near Chipping Norton, who was active in the 1860s. A woman called Ann Hulver believed that Henderson had bewitched her and went to a cunning man to have the spell removed. Henderson was eventually attacked with a thorn stick and died soon after. Another incident in the same village in 1875 involved a man who was convicted of manslaughter for using a pitchfork to stab an old woman. His defense, rejected by the court, was that she was a witch and he was attempting to break her spells (Manning 1902, 290).

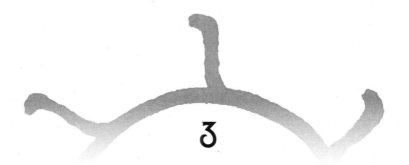

3

Power and the Powers of Witchcraft

Everyone who follows a religious or magical pathway can feel some kind of energy or power that comes through and into them but that clearly has its source outside them. Whatever their pathway, all believe that there *is* a power that can be accessed and used through the performance of a set of practical techniques. What this power is, and where it comes from, has several interpretations, some of them incompatible. There are theories that come from the Christian worldview that the witch's power comes through God. The witch's power may come through the power inherent in nature, which in Christian terms is an imperfect, fallen creature of God, but in some pagan interpretations the witch's power is a direct manifestation of nature divine, numinous in its own right. Another source of power may be channeled through autonomous spirits that can be good, bad, or neutral to humans. These spirits must be contacted by rites and ceremonies that either supplicate or command them. This can involve making a pact or deal with the spirit, as in the Christian witch hunters' interpretation of witchcraft, or compelling the spirits to perform the operator's will, commanding them with words of power, often Jewish or Christian in origin, accompanied by the appropriate rites and ceremonies at the proper place and time. Another means of gaining and using power may involve the operator becoming temporarily possessed by a spirit, as in shamanism.

Christian dualists promoted the theory that all power comes from God, who created everything in existence and is exclusively good. By that theory, everything that goes wrong or is of bad intention cannot possibly come from God. Yet clearly "badness" exists and must come from somewhere. So, according to this theory, everything bad must come indirectly or directly from a source of evil, which the clerics personified as a rather human entity or intelligence, the devil. In 1972, Bishop Robert Mortimer's church commission on exorcism defined evil and its origin as a distortion of right orderliness that proceeds from created, intelligent wills, either human or demonic. These may act independently or in some form of collaboration. The exorcists claimed that human beings may accept demonic temptations, while black magicians sometimes actively attempt (perhaps with success) to obtain the assistance of demons (Mortimer 1972, 17).

Fig. 3.1. Witchcraft in the seventeenth-century imagination

Certain Christian sects asserted that only ordained clergymen could deal with spiritual matters and that anyone performing any kind of unauthorized spiritual procedure for good or ill therefore had a power that emanated from the devil. An extension of this is that because the church insisted on its members being baptized—that is, undergoing a magical ritual to bind them to the Christian god—those practicing magic must also have undergone a comparable ritual to bind them to the devil. In ancient and medieval times, initiation rituals were universal for the membership of craft and trade guilds and rural fraternities, so it was unthinkable that someone could gain knowledge and power without undergoing one. In former years the theory that witches and magicians sold their souls to the devil to gain knowledge and power was popularized by stories and plays about Doctor Faustus. Modern practitioners of pagan witchcraft subsequently removed all of the Christian elements and references to the devil that once were present from much of traditional witchcraft. On the other hand, those who believed in and actively worshipped the devil restyled themselves as Satanists. We are all active participants in the construction of meaning.

In his *The Anatomy of Melancholy,* Burton expressed all the fears of the age ascribed to the horrendous power of witches. In a section titled "Of Witches and Magicians, How They Cause Melancholy," he wrote of the powers and activities ascribed to witches.

> Many subdivisions there are, & many several species of Sorcerers, Witches, Enchanters, Charmers, &c. They have been tolerated heretofore some of them; and Magick hath been publickly professed in former times, in *Salamanca, Cracovia,* and other places, though after censured by several Universities, and now generally contradicted, though practiced by some still, maintained and excused . . . that which they can do, is as much almost as the Devil himself, who is still ready to satisfy their desires. . . .
>
> They can cause tempests, storms, which is familiarly practised by Witches in *Norway, Ireland,* as I have proved. They can make friends enemies, and enemies friends, by philtres . . . enforce love, tell

Fig. 3.2. *Death and the Devil Chain the World,*
a symbolic painting in a monastery at Fussen, Germany

any man where his friends are, about what employed, though in the most remote places; and, if they will, bring their sweethearts to them by night, upon a goat's back flying in the air . . . hurt and infect men and beasts, vines, corn, cattle, plants, make women abortive, not to conceive, barren, men and woman unapt and unable, married and unmarried, fifty several ways . . . make men victorious, fortunate, eloquent . . . they can make stick frees, such as shall endure a rapier's point, musket shot, and never be wounded . . . they can walk in fiery furnaces, make men feel no pain on the rack or feel any other tortures; they can staunch blood, represent dead men's shapes, alter and turn themselves and others into several forms at their pleasures. . . .

I have seen those that have caused melancholy in the most grievous manner, dried up women's paps, cured gout, palsy, this and apoplexy, falling sickness which no physick could help, *solo tactu,* by touch

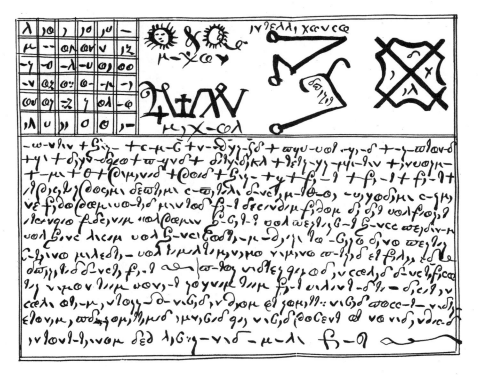

Fig. 3.3. Formula for exorcism found beneath a brass plate on a tombstone in Lancashire in the nineteenth century

alone . . . one David Helde, a young man, who by eating cakes a Witch gave him . . . began to dote on a sudden, and was instantly mad. . . . The means by which they work, are usually charms, images, as that in *Hector Boethius* of King *Duff;* characters stamped on sundry metals, and at such and such constellations, knots, amulets, words, philtres &c. which generally make the parties affected melancholy. (Burton [1621] 1926, vol. I, ii, I, sub. III, 1926 ed., v. 1, 231–34)

It appears that some people known as witches did follow the Faustus stories and create rituals in which they believed that they had sold their souls to the devil. If we are to believe the testimony of a folklorist-clergyman, the Reverend R. H. Heanley, at least one wise woman, Mary Atkin, believed on her deathbed that the devil was coming to take her. This is the classic tale of the end of one who has sold her soul. Heanley wrote:

It fell to my lot in 1885 to attend old Mary on her deathbed. In fact, she sent for me from another parish "to lay the Devil," whom she believed to have come for her. If nothing else had come, the hour of an evil conscience had undoubtedly arrived. She, at all events, firmly believed in her own powers, and, had it not been for the greater presence which she asserted was in the room, would, I fear, as little have regretted the use she had made of them. Her last words to me were: "Thou hast fixed him, Master Robert, for a bit, as firm as ivver I fixed anny; bud he'll hev' me sartain sewer when thou art gone." [Standard English: You have fixed him, Master Robert, for a while, as firm as I ever fixed anyone, but he will have me for certain, sure when you have gone.] And she died that night shrieking out that he had got her. (1902, 13–17)

Catherine Parsons, in her accounts of witchcraft in and around the Cambridgeshire village of Horseheath, stated:

In Horseheath witchcraft is by no means a lost art. One is told that the chief difference between a witch and an ordinary woman is, that if the latter wishes her neighbour misfortune, her wish has no effect, but the same wish in the mind of a witch has effect, because the witch is believed to be in league with the Devil, she having made a contract to sell her soul to him in return for the power to do evil. (1915; 1952)

But there is a tricky liminal way out of this if one sells one's soul to the devil, for "if a person sells his soul to the Devil, to be delivered at a certain specified time, the vendor, if wary, may avoid payment by putting in the contract 'be it in the house or out of the house' and then when the time arrives, sitting astride on a window sill or standing in a doorway" (Peacock 1877, I, 84).

The matter of who the devil was in these cases complicates our interpretations of witchcraft and magic, for at secret initiations into rural fraternities, such as the Millers' Fraternity, the Horseman's Grip and Word, and the Confraternity of the Plough, a man personating the devil officiated. In one recorded horseman's initiation is the question "Who told you to come here?" and the answer was "the Devil" (Singer 1881; Rennie et al. 2009, 86). Perhaps the terrified candidate believed that he had seen the *real* devil, but it was one of the leading members of the fraternity who had terrified him. Similar confusions over the identity of "a black man" and "the devil" exist in American traditional rituals at crossroads (Hyatt 1974). Devil characters such as Beelzebub and Little Devil Doubt also appear in mummers' plays (see chapter 12).

The Huntingdonshire folklorist C. F. Tebbutt observed that one form of witchcraft with no menace to others was used in the Horsemen's Guild. Members of this guild or cult had the power to control horses and claimed that it came from the devil. This power gave them great advantages as farriers or horsebreakers (Tebbutt 1984, 86). When he was personated in a rural fraternity's initiation ritual, the devil's reported name describes a role, not an actual name of power. Of course, this

Fig. 3.4. Symbols of horsemanry in pargetting work at Thaxted, Essex

character was invariably assumed by the clergymen who heard about it to be the ecclesiastical devil, and thus the guildsmen were always misinterpreted as being devil worshippers. It is likely that the question "Have you ever seen the devil?" is a rural fraternity watchword that asks for a particular answer (Randall 1966, 109–10). Every secret fraternity has ambiguous questions that must be answered with a proper form of words that assures the questioner that the other person is an initiate. A wrong answer shows that he is not a member.

It is clear that when an immaterial entity is being referred to rather than a guiser (a person in disguise), this figure is a conflation of perhaps a number of pagan deities with the ecclesiastical principle of evil. The epithet *old* (*auld* in Scots) prefixes many of the names given to this being: Old Nick, the Old 'Un, the Old Lad, Old Scratch, Old Ragusan, Old Sam, Old Horny, Old Bargus, Old Bogy, Old Providence, the Auld Chiel, and the Auld Gudeman. *Old* is clearly a reference to something ancient, most likely the belief in a god of the elder faith. Sometimes this being is the Halyman, the Black 'Un, or without the epithet "Old," as Nick, Samuel, Bargus, Him, and Daddy. The possible origin of these names for pagan deities is further confused by the common practice of never saying "devil." Fear of using this name is present in folk custom all over Great Britain. "Talk of the devil, and he will appear" is an old adage that warns us of the consequences of so doing. But different districts had different levels of prohibition. In Lincolnshire, it was not strong; indeed, there is a tune in a 1780 music manuscript by Thomas Dixon from Holton le Moor in that county called "As Sure as the Devil's in Lincoln." In the city of Lincoln is the tradition that at the cathedral, the devil has the wind waiting outside for him. The expression "as sure as the Devil's in Lincoln" means a certainty, and certain clumps of trees in that county are called "the Devil's Holts."

Certain villages have a reputation for witchcraft. In Essex, the village of Canewdon is called "the Village of Witches," where there are said to be always living six (or nine) witches (Howe 1952, 23), and in Cambridgeshire, Horseheath has a similar reputation. The infamous witch trials at Warboys in Huntingdonshire are commemorated by a weather vane in the form of a witch riding a broomstick, and so it is said there is always a witch in Warboys. A commonly told story is that "the office of witch" is a permanent one and must be handed on to a successor before the incumbent can die, however old she is. This is told at Horseheath and Bartlow (Porter 1969, 161). The power is sometimes said to be passed from father to son and mother to daughter, but this is by no means a universal principle (Howe 1952, 23). Although these are often dismissed as mere stories with little if any substance, they may be told from some knowledge of local realities, especially in places where the population has remained stable for a long time and knowledge and practices of many things are handed down in families. Those who claim to be members of hereditary witchcraft families will assert its truth. According to E. W. Lidell, who wrote under the pen name Lugh and claimed to be a hereditary witch, George Pickingill, who died at Canewdon in Essex in 1909, founded nine covens of witches in East Anglia and southern England (Lugh 1982, 3; Gwyn 1999, 19). Pickingill is said to have been an influence on the prominent twentieth-century magician Aleister Crowley (Lugh 1982, 5–6) and also on contemporary Wiccans, but this, like much about the transmission of witchcraft, is disputed.

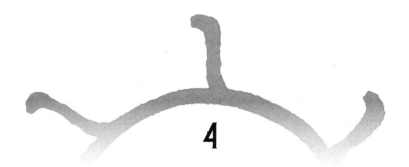

4

The Gamut of Witchcraft

AN EARLY FICTIONAL PORTRAYAL

From the late sixteenth century, witchcraft was a popular subject for writers and playwrights. William Shakespeare's three witches in *Macbeth* are among his most famous characters. It was not Shakespeare but his contemporary Ben Jonson who wrote the most detailed dramatic scene containing witches. In 1609 he wrote *The Masque of Queens,* a dramatic performance for and by the court of King James I, designed and staged by Inigo Jones. Masques, of which many were staged in the reigns of King James I and King Charles I, were courtly performances for royalty and the court, not performances in a public theater staged for paying spectators. The masquers were members of the royal family and lords and ladies close to the king. They were distinguished from actors in that they had no speaking parts: that was beneath them. They wore gorgeous costumes designed by Jones and danced at appropriate places. Actors were employed for the speaking parts and any action that took place in the masques. The masques of Jonson and Jones were divided into two sections: the masque proper, in which the aristocrats personated virtuous noble and divine characters symbolizing idealized order, and the antimasque, in which professional actors presented a contrasting world of vice, disorder, and chaos. There was a transformation scene where the chaotic world of the speaking actors was overcome and superseded by the harmonious order of the court.

The Masque of Queens is of significance to the present study, for the antimasque featured a convention of witches whose activities and paraphernalia were drawn from an erudite knowledge of writers' works on antique and contemporary witchcraft and demonology. Jonson published an annotated text of the masque in quarto in 1609 and in the folio of 1616. Jonson's published masque, with its comprehensive annotation much longer than the actual text, serves as a source for information on operative witchcraft of the period, or at least what observers saw as its practices. The masque was written for King James, who had signed an act against witchcraft into law and had published the book *Demonologie: In Forme of a Dialogue,* whose subject was witchcraft. The symbols, paraphernalia, and *materia magica* written about by Jonson are immediately recognizable from recorded accounts of operative witchcraft from the seventeenth century to the present day. Jonson noted that his description of the various items used by the witches in the antimasque

> is also solemn in their witchcraft, to be examined, either by the devil or their dame, at their meetings, of what mischief they have done: and what they can confer to a future hurt. . . . But we apply this examination of ours to the particular use; whereby, also, we take occasion, not only to express the things (as vapours, liquors, herbs, bones, flesh, blood, fat, and such like, which are called *Media magica*) but the rites of gathering them, and from what places, reconciling as near as we can, the practice of antiquity to the neoteric, and making it familiar with our popular witchcraft. (Jonson [1609] 1816, vii, 127)

In his introduction to *The Masque of Queens,* Jonson tells us that he "therefore now devised, that twelve women, in the habit of hags, or witches, sustaining the persons of Ignorance, Suspicion, Credulity, &c. the opposites to good Fame, should fill that part; not as a masque, but a spectacle of strangeness." Jones designed a stage set of hell, "which flaming beneath, smoked unto the top of the roof." The witches appeared

with a kind of hollow and infernal music. . . . First one, then two, and three, and more, till their number increased to eleven; all differently attired: some with rats on their heads, some on their shoulders; others with ointment-pots at their girdles; all with spindles, timbrels, rattles, or other venefical instruments, making a confused noise, with strange gestures. The device of their attire was Master Jones's, with the invention, and architecture of the whole scene, and machine. Only I prescribed them their properties of vipers, snakes, bones, herbs, roots and other ensigns of their magic, out of the authority of ancient and late writers.

These eleven witches beginning to dance (which is the usual ceremony at their convents or meetings, where sometimes they are also vizarded and masked) on the sudden one of them missed their chief, and interrupted the rest with this speech,

HAG: Sisters, stay, we want our Dame;
      Call upon her by her name,
      And the charm we use to say;
      That she quickly anoint, and come away.

1 CHARM: Dame, dame! The watch is set:
      Quickly come, we all are met.
      From the lakes, and from the fens,
      From the rocks, and from the dens,
      From the woods, and from the caves,
      From the church-yards, from the graves,
      From the dungeon, from the tree
      That they die on, here are we.

      Comes she not yet?
      Strike another heat.

2 **CHARM:** The weather is fair, the wind is good,
Up, dame, on your horse of wood:
Or else tuck up your grey frock,
And saddle your goat, or your green cock,
And make his bridle a bottom of thread,
To roll up how many miles you have rid.
Quickly come away;
For we all stay.

Nor yet! Nay, then,
We'll try her agen,

3 **CHARM:** The owl is abroad, the bat, and the toad,
And so is the cat-a-mountain,
The ant and the mole sit both in a hole,
And the frog peeps out o' the fountain:
The dogs they do bay, and the timbrels play,
The spindle is now a turning;
The moon it is red, and the stars are fled,
But all the sky is burning:
The ditch is made, and our nails the spade,
With pictures full, of wax and wool;
Their livers I stick, with needles quick;
There lacks but the blood, to make up the flood.
Quickly, dame, then bring your part in,
Spur, spur upon little Martin,
Merrily, merrily, make him sail,
A worm in his mouth, and a thorn in his tail,
Fire above and fire below,
With a whip in your hand, to make him go.

O now she's come!
Let all be dumb.

At this the Dame entered to them, naked-armed, barefooted, her frock tucked, her hair knotted, and folded with vipers; in her hand a torch made of a dead man's arm, lighted, girded with a snake.

The witches pay reverence to their dame, who then calls them one by one,

DAME: But first relate me, what you have sought,
Where you have been, and what you have brought.

1 HAG: I have been all day, looking after,
A raven, feeding on a quarter;
And, soon, as she turned her beak to the south,
I snatch'd this morsel out of her mouth.

2 HAG: I have been gathering wolves' hairs,
The mad dog's foam, and the adder's ears;
The spurging of a dead-man's eyes,
And all since evening star did rise.

3 HAG: I last night lay all alone
On the ground, to hear the mandrake groan;
And pluck'd him up, though he grew full low;
And, as I had done, the cock did crow.

4 HAG: And I have been choosing out this skull
From charnel houses, that were full;
From private grots, and public pits;
And frighted a sexton out of his wits.

5 HAG: Under a cradle I did creep,
By day; and when the child was asleep,
At night, I sucked the breath; and rose;
And pluck'd the nodding nurse by the nose.

6 HAG: I had a dagger: what did I with that?
  Kill'd an infant to have his fat.
  A piper got it, at a church-ale,
  I bade him again blow wind in the tail.

7 HAG: A murderer, yonder, was hung in chains,
  The sun and the wind had shrunk his veins;
  I bit off a sinew; I clipp'd his hair,
  I brought off his rags that danced in the air.

8 HAG: The screech-owl's eggs, and the feathers black,
  The blood of the frog, and the bone in his back,
  I have been getting; and made of his skin
  A purset, to keep Sir Cranion in.

9 HAG: And I have been plucking, plants among,
  Hemlock, henbane, adder's-tongue,
  Night-shade, moon-wort, libbard's-bane;
  And twice, by the dogs, was like to be ta'en.

10 HAG: I, from the jaws of a gardener's bitch,
  Did snatch these bones, and then leap'd the ditch:
  Yet I went back to the house again,
  Kill'd the black cat, and here's the brain.

11 HAG: I went to the toad breeds under the wall,
  I charm'd him out, and he came at my call;
  I scratched out the eyes of the owl before,
  I tore the bat's wing: what would you have more?

DAME: Yes, I have brought, to help our vows,
  Horned poppy, cypress boughs,
  The fig-tree that grows on tombs,
  And juice that from the larch-tree comes,

The basilisk's blood, and the viper's skin:
And now our orgies let us begin.

In the heat of their dance, on the sudden was heard a sound of loud music, as if many instruments had made one loud blast; with which not only the hags themselves, but the hell into which they ran, quite vanished, and the whole of the scene altered, scarce suffering the memory of such a thing; but in the place of it appeared a glorious and magnificent building, figuring the House of Fame, the top of which were discovered the twelve Masquers, sitting upon a throne triumphal, erected in the form of a pyramid, and circled with all store of light. From whom a person by this time descended, in the furniture of Perseus, and expressing heroic and masculine Virtue, began to speak.

HEROIC VIRTUE: So should, at Fame's loud sound, and Virtue's sight,
All dark and envious witchcraft fly the light.

The aristocratic part of the masque followed, the witches having been banished by virtue.

(Note: The Sir Cranion mentioned in the spiel of the eighth hag is the giant crane fly, otherwise known in England as Daddy Longlegs. It was customary to keep a crane fly in a bag around the neck, either as a familiar or for therapeutic purposes. Daddy is a byname of the devil, as used by the famous Daddy Witch of Horseheath, Cambridgeshire.)

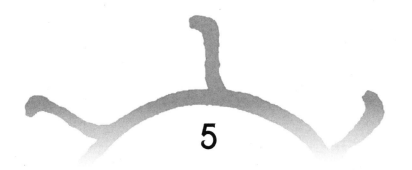

5

The British Laws against Witchcraft

The characterization of witchcraft and witches in Europe was formalized first in the witch hunters' bible *Malleus Malificarum,* written by the German monks Heinrich Kramer and Jacob Sprenger and published in the 1480s under the aegis of the Catholic Church. This was the era when popes were formally cursing comets and the dolphins in the Mediterranean Sea. The underlying thesis of the text, justified by reference to the Bible, was that women are mostly responsible for evil deeds because "all witchcraft comes from carnal lust, which is in women insatiable. See *Proverbs* xxx. There are three things that are never satisfied, yea a fourth thing which says not. It is enough; that is, the mouth of the womb. Wherefore for the sake of fulfilling their lusts they consort even with devils" (Kramer and Sprenger 1971, 47). The witch hunters claimed that this alleged uncontrollable lustfulness of women was compounded with weak-mindedness and gullibility, stating that "women are naturally more impressionable . . . there are more superstitious women found than men . . . they are more credulous" and that they are "more ready to receive the influences of a disembodied spirit" (Kramer and Sprenger 1971, 43, 44). *Malleus Malificarum* was the authorized text about witchcraft, explaining how to recognize a witch and detailing the authorized methods of torture to force her to confess

30

and reveal the names of her associates. From the recommendations of *Malleus Malificarum,* all the persecution, torture, and executions of the witch were dealt with by ecclesiastical law, which punished them as heretics. Henry VIII, in crushing hunts, followed.

In England, before the reign of King Henry VIII, witches were dealt with by ecclesiastic law, which punished them as heretics. Henry VIII, in crushing the power and influence of the Roman church, brought in an act against witchcraft in 1542, making it a criminal offense of the state, determining "that witches etc., who detest their neighbours, and make pictures [images] of them for many purposes, or for the same purposes made crowns, swords and the like, or pulled down crosses, or declared where things lost or stolen were become, should suffer death and loss of lands and goods as felons." Although *Malleus Malificarum* was, of course, a Roman Catholic text, its assertions and practices were taken for granted by this first Protestant monarch of England, who kept the title given him by the pope—Defender of the Faith.

In 1562 the Scottish Parliament under Queen Mary enacted the law against witchcraft called Anentis Witchcraft, and in the next year, 1563, Queen Elizabeth I's law against witchcraft, An Act against Conjurations Enchantments and Witchcrafts, was enacted in England. Witch hunting intensified after 1572, when Queen Elizabeth heard a sermon preached by Bishop Jewel that ranted against witches; he said, "The Schole of them is great, their doings horrible, their malice intolerable, the examples most miserable . . . these be the scholers of Beelzebub the chief Captaine of the Divels." The key act against witchcraft came shortly after England and Scotland were unified under the Scottish king upon the death of Queen Elizabeth I in 1603, as King James VI of Scotland, the new king of the United Kingdom of Great Britain, had taken a personal interest in the witch trials at Berwick in 1591. His book of 1587 (reprinted in 1603), *Demonologie: In Forme of a Dialogue,* was published to refute the claims of Reginald Scot in his *Discoverie of Witchcraft* ([1584] 1886). When he became king of the United Kingdom in 1603, James I (as he was now restyled) promulgated a new act against witchcraft that superseded the English law of 1563, but not the Scots law of 1562.

In 1604, the new law, the Witchcraft Act, extended the remit of what was considered witchcraft, and acts of magic deemed to have been performed with the intention of bringing death were to be punished with death.

> If any person or persons . . . shall use or practise or exercise any invocation, or conjuration, of any evil or wicked spirit, or shall consult, covenant with, entertain, employ, feed, or reward any evil and wicked spirit to or for any intent or purpose; or take up any dead man, woman or child out of his, her, or their grave, or any other place where the dead body resteth, or the skin, bone, or any other part of any dead person, to be employed or used in any manner of witchcraft, enchantment, charm or sorcery whereby any person shall be killed, destroyed, wasted, consumed, pined or lamed in his or her body, or any part thereof; then every such offender or offenders, their aiders, abetters and counselors, being of any of the said offences duly and lawfully convicted and attained, shall suffer pains of death as a felon or felons, and shall lose the privilege and benefit of clergy and sanctuary.
>
> And further, to the intent that all manner of practise, use, or exercise of witchcraft, enchantment, charm, or sorcery should be from henceforth utterly avoided, abolished and taken away, be it enacted by the authority of this present Parliament, that if any person or persons shall . . . take upon him or them by witchcraft, enchantment, charm, or sorcery to tell or declare in what place any treasure of gold or silver should or might be found or had in the earth or other secret places, or where goods or things lost or stolen should be found or become; or to the intent to provoke any person to unlawful love; or whereby any chattel or goods of any person shall be destroyed, wasted, or impaired, or to hurt or destroy any person in his body, although the same be not effected and done; that then all and every such person so offending, and being thereof lawfully convicted, shall for the same offence suffer imprisonment for the space of one whole year, without bail or mainprise, and once in every quarter of the said

year, shall in some market town, upon the market day or at such time as any fair shall be kept there, stand openly in the pillory in the space of six hours, and there shall openly confess his or her error and offence. And if any person or persons being once convicted of the same offences as is aforesaid, do eftsoons perpetrate and commit the like offence . . . being of any of the said offences lawfully convicted . . . shall suffer pains of death as a felon or felons.

Those convicted of witchcraft in England and Wales were not burned at the stake but instead hanged on a gallows. The punishment of burning at the stake was reserved for those who had committed "petty treason," which meant a woman who had murdered her husband. Those women burned as witches in England were killed that way because the charge had been that they had done away with their husbands by witchcraft. The punishment of burning at the stake for petty treason was abolished only in 1790, long after witchcraft had ceased to be a capital offense under the Parliamentary Act, which superseded that of 1604.

Enacted during the reign of King George II, the Witchcraft Act of 1735 repealed the earlier acts and the Scottish witchcraft act of 1562 of Queen Mary, Anentis Witchcraft, which had remained in force in Scotland when the 1604 act of the United Kingdom was brought in. The 1735 act abolished the death penalty for the practice of magic intended to cause death and also for the second offense of divination and love magic. It had a new approach to witchcraft; instead of enshrining in law the assertion that witchcraft worked, which made it necessary to extirpate it as contrary to the common good, the new act made it illegal to pretend to practice witchcraft, divination, the finding of lost goods by magic, and fortune-telling.

No prosecution, suit, or proceeding, shall be commenced or carried on against any person or persons for witchcraft, sorcery, enchantment, or conjuration, or for charging another with any such offence, in any court whatsoever in Great Britain . . . and for the more effectual preventing and punishing any pretences to such arts or powers as are before mentioned, whereby ignorant persons are frequently deluded and defrauded, be it further enacted by the authority aforesaid, that if any person shall pretend to exercise or use any kind of witchcraft, sorcery, enchantment, or conjuration, or to undertake to tell fortunes, or pretend, from his or her skill or knowledge in any occult or crafty science, to discover where or in what manner any goods or chattels, supposed to have been stolen or lost, may be found, every person, so offending, being thereof lawfully convicted . . . shall, for every such offence, suffer imprisonment by the space of one whole year without bail or mainprise, and once in every quarter of the said year in some market town of the proper county, upon the market day there stand openly on the pillory by the space of one hour, and also shall . . . be obliged to give sureties for his or her good behaviour, in such sum, and for such time, as the said court shall judge proper according to the circumstances of the offence, and in such case shall be further imprisoned until such sureties be given.

Fortune-tellers were prosecuted under this act, and it was found to be useful for the authorities in the perennial persecution of the Gypsies. A fortune-teller called Scotch Jenny who lived at Peakirk near Peterborough was called a "wise woman" by the local press when she was prosecuted under the 1735 act and was forced out of business. She died in 1798. Lucy Barber of Market Deeping was brought to court in 1822 and charged with obtaining money by foretelling the future. She returned the fee to her client, promised never to obtain money in this way again, and was discharged.

In 1824 the Vagrancy Act was passed to punish old soldiers who had served King and Country fighting in the Napoleonic Wars and who now found themselves destitute and homeless, forced to become beggars on the street. The act also targeted Gypsies and Irish immigrants who had come to Britain in an attempt to better their impoverished lives. The Vagrancy Act made it an offense to sleep on the street or to beg. It became a criminal offense to be homeless. A permanent police force was set up around this time, patrolling at all hours of the day and night on the lookout for criminal activity. Eventually, the police superseded the local officials whose job it was to persecute beggars, such as the beggar-banger employed by the Corporation of Brackley, whose job it was to "bang"—that is, expel by force—all beggars from the town. In Cheshire these officers were called bang-beggars (Sternberg 1851, 7). The Vagrancy Act is still in force in the early twenty-first century. The act defined what one had to do to be deemed a "rogue and a vagabond" and included sections intended to prohibit certain acts of fortune-telling. The definition of a rogue and a vagabond thus included "every person pretending or professing to tell fortunes, or using any subtle craft, means, or device, by palmistry or otherwise, to deceive and impose on any of His Majesty's subjects." This part of the Vagrancy Act was only repealed in 1989 as part of the Statute Law (Repeals) Act 1989.

The Vagrancy Act 1824 did not supersede the 1735 act and instead added more offenses that took in occultists and magicians. Shortly afterward, the rise of spiritualism as a practice brought its practitioners into conflict with the law. The 1735 Witchcraft Act remained on the statutes of the United Kingdom until 1951, when the Fraudulent Mediums Act repealed it and brought in new offenses. The last prosecutions under the 1735 act were of Helen Duncan, imprisoned for nine months in 1944, and, later in the same year, the last of all was Jane Rebecca Yorke, then aged seventy-two, who was found guilty on seventeen counts but was treated more leniently. Some Parliamentarians had been lobbying for the abolition of the 1735 act since the early 1930s, as it was seen to be anachronistic. So eventually it was superseded by the Fraudulent Mediums Act 1951, which was drafted "for the punishment of people who fraudulently purport to act as spiritualistic mediums or to exercise powers of telepathy, clairvoyance or other similar powers." The law states that "any person who . . . with intent to deceive purports to act as spiritualistic medium or to exercise any powers of telepathy, clairvoyance or other similar powers, or . . . in purporting to act as a spiritualistic medium or to exercise such powers as aforesaid, uses any fraudulent device, shall be guilty of an offence."

The 1951 act introduced the payment of money as the key definition of whether the action was fraudulent: "A person shall not be convicted of an offence . . . unless it is provided for that he acted for reward; and for the purposes of this section a person shall be deemed to act for reward if any money is paid, or other valuable thing given in respect of what he does, whether to him or to any other person." This part of the act does not apply "to anything done solely for the purposes of entertainment." (As an aside, it is interesting how the seventeenth- and eighteenth-century acts used the inclusive "he or she" form, compared with the 1951 act's exclusive use of "he.") The common statement that a practitioner would lose his or her powers if money passed hands may well be a response to the Fraudulent Mediums Act 1951. For example, see Theo Brown's remarks on the Devonshire charmers who refuse to take money on page 7.

The accepted conspiracy theory of the seventeenth century viewed witchcraft as part of a devilish plot to overthrow society, rather in the way that contemporary terrorists are presented in the early twenty-first century. In 1608, *A Discourse of the Damned Art of Witchcraft,* written by William Perkins, a fellow of Christ's College, was published in Cambridge. Perkins wrote, "The ministers of Satan, under the name of Wisemen and Wisewomen, are at hand, by his appointment, to resolve, direct and help ignorant and unsettled persons" (Perkins, 1608). Hence, an association with witchcraft was seen as a kind of treasonable conspiracy, deserving punishment by death, but the punishment of those convicted of witchcraft under the 1604 act must be seen in the wider context of law and punishment.

At the time the Witchcraft Act 1604 was enforced, there were many offenses that carried the death penalty, and further offenses were added over the years as the law became ever more vengeful. From Tudor times, laws to regulate human behavior became increasingly stringent, with increasing prohibitions. Sacrilege, forgery, coin clipping, fraud, letter stealing, mutiny, and arson, even being a priest of the Roman Catholic religion or a Gypsy, were among the many offenses that brought men and women to the gallows. In the case of theft, it was the value of the goods that decided whether the culprit should be put to death. In 1699 the death penalty was introduced for shoplifters who stole goods worth five shillings or more, and in 1713, stealing dwelling-house goods worth more than two pounds was a hanging offense. In 1723 numerous offenses were made capital under the Waltham Black Act, which targeted those who tried to feed their families by hunting animals on land belonging to the squires and lords. At that time there were 150 offenses for which people in England and Wales were sent to the gallows, and by 1810 the number had been increased to 222. Throughout the nineteenth century the number of capital offenses was gradually reduced. The last hanging for forgery, for example, was in 1829. Eventually only murder, piracy, high treason, and arson in Her Majesty's dockyards were deemed serious enough to warrant hanging.

World improvers, as the British philosopher John Michell called them, are always out to command and control society, and many of the capital laws originated in this drive. For example, in 1533 an Act of Parliament of King Henry VIII made sodomy (anal intercourse) with either a woman or a man a capital offense. The law only stopped hanging men for what it called "the abominable crime of buggery" in 1861, when the sentence was reduced to a minimum of ten years and a maximum of life imprisonment. This was not a sign of liberalism, however, for all sexual acts between men were made criminal offenses in 1883 (Newell 1966, 125). This repressive law was only repealed in 1967. The death penalty for certain categories of murder was formally abolished in 1969, and it was abolished completely in 1998, when hanging for high treason and piracy was removed from the statutes.

But although certain acts and practices forbidden by the law at certain times eventually become tolerated or legalized, this does not mean that every person in society accepts these new freedoms, as continuing homophobia and religious intolerance demonstrate; this runs similarly with witchcraft. Although the capital offense of witchcraft was abolished in the United Kingdom in 1735 and the legal existence of witchcraft as a working practice was thereby abolished, the force of the older British and Scottish laws continued among much of the populace. When the 1735 act was passed, the last witch trial had taken place twenty-four years earlier in Hereford, when Jane Wenham was convicted and sentenced to the gallows, but was reprieved. In some places the old fears of witchcraft surfaced occasionally, and summary unofficial violence ensued.

Persecutions of people accused of bewitchment continued well into the nineteenth century, just not with legal sanction as before, though in some cases the police turned a blind eye to the violence. In 1808 at Great Paxton in Huntingdonshire, Ann Izzard, sixty years old, was suspected of being the cause of a number of inexplicable accidents and illnesses. A mob attacked her house at night, and she was dragged from her bed, beaten, and had her arms ripped with pins. The local constable refused to assist her, and a neighbor who took her in was also persecuted and subsequently died from the abuse. A second attack on Ann Izzard took place, and she fled to live in another village. In 1809 the culprits were prosecuted and jailed, most of them for a month apiece (Saunders 1888, 156–64).

In 1865, at Sible Hedingham in Essex, an eighty-year-old disabled French fortune-teller known as Old Dummy was accused of bewitching a neighbor. He was taken by a mob who threw him into a stream, where they stoned him, from which treatment he subsequently died (Howe 1952, 23–24). The culprits were arrested, convicted of manslaughter, and imprisoned. After 1735 the claim that someone was a witch who had overlooked or cursed someone was no longer recognized as a valid excuse in law. The trial of William Bulwer at East Dereham in 1879 is a case in point, in which the authorities recognized neither that he had had the toad put on him nor that his revenge was motivated by it (see chapter 11, page 109). The last recorded accusation of bewitchment brought to the attention of the authorities in England was in 1947, again at East Dereham. Of course, it was dismissed (*News Chronicle*, January 6, 1947).

Finally, writing about the history of the witchcraft laws in his *Letters on Demonology and Witchcraft*, Sir Walter Scott observed:

It is accordingly remarkable, in different countries, how often at some past period of their history there occurred an epidemic of terror of witches, which, as fear is always cruel and credulous, glutted the public with seas of innocent blood; and how uniformly men loathed the gore after having swallowed it, and by a reaction natural to the human mind desired, in prudence, to take away or restrict those laws which had been the source of carnage, in order that their posterity might neither have the will nor the means to enter into similar excesses. (1885, 161–62)

6

Weird Plants, Root Diggers, and Witchcraft

Knowledge of the weird plants was present in the root work of traditional operative witchcraft within historic times. The fear that people who knew about the virtues of herbs and roots could use them to kill as well as cure was ever present. Medieval medicine used the same remedies and substances later found only in country medicine and witchcraft. The most important text that circulated was the *Materia Medica* of Dioscorides, written in the first century CE. It was available in Great Britain in its original Latin and English as well as Welsh and Gaelic vernacular versions, containing lists of plant-name equivalents in different languages to aid practitioners. As research into medicine continued through the Middle Ages, new works appeared. In 1498 the works of Nicholas Praepositus appeared as the *Antidotarum Parvum* and became the first official pharmacopoeia. But the most significant of these works was *The London Pharmacopoeia,* published in 1618.

Although it contained many traditional medical materials, the *Pharmacopoeia*'s publication marked the schism between "official medicine" and "folk medicine," a division that grew wider as the years passed and the scientific method was applied to official medicine. The scientific development of botanical taxonomy, chemistry, pharmacology, and physiology scarcely penetrated folk medicine, which continued to use the old methods according to traditional theories of the elements and the human body. Thus, the gap between the two medical approaches widened over time, and those trained in official medicine fought to suppress traditional practitioners, who included those now called quack doctors and doctresses, wise women, handywomen, and witches. By the nineteenth century there were campaigns to set up dispensaries in market towns so that people would not have to resort to the unlicensed practitioners who were widely thought to do more harm than good (Clabburn 1971, ii–iii).

In traditional society, before the rise of industrial medicine, there was a trade in herbs, both for culinary and medical use. This trade was carried on by men known as root diggers or wild herb men. The guild of medicinal root diggers, known as the Wild Herb Men, claimed to be working according to an old charter. It existed until 1962. Cecil Grimes of Wisbech was the last boss of the wild herb men. The charter, which gave them the right to roam and dig, was known as the Wild Herb Act, which was believed to date from Tudor times. Although they had operated throughout the country, including the counties of Essex, Suffolk, Norfolk, Cambridgeshire, and Huntingdonshire and also parts of Northamptonshire and Lincolnshire, in later years these root diggers' range had shrunk to East Anglia. They were said to possess a magical password, the Herbsman's Word, and in their traveling they dug up medicinal roots and herbs on remote patches of ground, deserted green roads and drifts, the edges of footpaths, alongside hedgerows, on canal and railway cuttings and embankments, at the margins of fruit orchards, and on cliff tops (Hennels 1972, 79). The wild herb men were very knowledgeable. Not only were they skilled herbsmen who could recognize and identify the various plants, but they also knew the places they were most likely to be found.

The digging season began in November and ended in April. The most sought-after herbs were the easily found dandelion and dock roots, used for treating blood disorders; comfrey, for treating sprains and open wounds; nettle tops, made into an extract used to treat coughs and bronchitis; and horseradish and couch-grass root, used in paper manufacture.

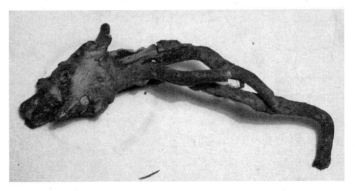

Fig. 6.1. A magical root, from Cambridgeshire

The rare orchid whose bulbs are called bull-bags, which can engender either love or hatred when used with skill, was much prized. There was also mandrake, dug in latter years for veterinary use only. Herbs were sold in towns in markets and by street sellers who had their own cries and calls, such as "Will you buy any ground-ivy?" reported from Norwich around 1742 in *Arderon's Collections* (*East Anglian Notes & Queries,* 1885–1886, 297).

The weird plants, those with dangerous qualities, were not in the remit of the Wild Herb Men, but as there was a trade in these plants too, especially for handywomen in their work as midwives and for horse doctors—as well as for the shadier realms of witchcrafters, root doctors, and the underworld men—it is likely that the journeyman herbsmen collected them as well. Many of the elixirs sold by mountebanks and quack doctors at fairs also had their origins in various roots. In former times, those collecting herbs knew the appropriate rituals for picking or digging each kind of herb so that it would be empowered and effective. A medieval rite for greater periwinkle appears on page 50.

In *The Masque of Queens,* Ben Jonson's ninth hag lists the weird plants she has brought to the witches' convent: "plants among, hemlock, henbane, adder's-tongue, night-shade, moon-wort, libbard's-bane. . . ." Like some of the wild herbs sought after by the root diggers, many of these deadly plants are not easy to find or identify. In the era before there was scientific botany with its precise taxonomy, knowledge of the weird plants was not easy to come by. Of course, the more spectacular poisonous plants like deadly nightshade and thorn apple were pointed out in childhood as things to avoid, but the identities and properties of less prominent plants were less well known. Plants containing dangerous substances may prove lethal to children, while adults may become very ill from the same dose of the same substance but not die. The main weird plants encountered in Great Britain and used in traditional medicine and also as poisons are listed on the following pages.

As plants are living organisms growing under variable conditions, there are variations in the relative toxicity of some plants from year to year and even season to season. The relative proportions of active substances in individual plants may also vary from one to another (Newman 1948a, 121). Until the end of the eighteenth century, noted Leslie Newman in 1948, little or no inquiry was made into deaths, even when the patients had been treated by local wise women, white witches, and other irregular practitioners (Newman 1948a, 125).

Fig. 6.2.
Atropa belladonna

NIGHTSHADE

Deadly nightshade (*Atropa belladonna*), or dwale, is the best-known and best-recognized weird plant, with its purple flowers and spherical black berries. Its scientific name, *belladonna,* which means "beautiful lady," comes from the Mediterranean ladies who in former times would drop the berries' juice into their eyes to dilate the pupils, thereby making them more attractive to men. The effect of the substances present in deadly nightshade, atropine and hyoscyamine, is to cause overexcitement of the subject as a prelude to death (Grieve 1931, 583–89). The roots are the most deadly part of the deadly nightshade plant, but the berry juice is not recommended as safe to use in the eyes. It has been suggested that the flying ointment supposedly used by witches contained dwale.

A Scottish instance of the use of deadly nightshade in war is recorded in George Buchanan's *The History of Scotland,* from 1582. He tells that in the time of King Duncan I, the followers of Macbeth poisoned a whole army of invading Danes during a truce by supplying them with liquor containing dwale. The Danish soldiers were either killed or disabled by the poison, and the survivors were easily slain by Macbeth's men. It was also used as an anaesthetic, as recorded by Thomas Lupton in 1585, who reported, "Dwale makes one to sleep while he is cut or burnt by cauterizing," and the herbalist Gerard, writing two years later, called it sleeping nightshade because the leaves were moistened in wine vinegar and laid on the head to induce sleep. Gerard was the first writer to use its Italian name, belladonna, rather than dwale.

Fig. 6.3.
Aconitum napellus

ACONITE / MONKSHOOD

All parts of the aconite plant (*Aconitum napellus*) are poisonous, but it is the root that is considered to be the most poisonous. The symptoms of aconite poisoning by ingestion are tingling and numbness of the tongue and the mouth, nausea, and vomiting with internal pain, irregular pulse, labored breathing, and giddiness, while the mind remains clear. In 1524 and 1526, the root was administered to criminals as an experiment, and they both died (Grieve 1931, 9). Jonson notes of this "deadly poisonous herb" that "the juice of it is like that liquor which the devil gives witches to sprinkle abroad, and do hurt, in the opinion of all magic masters" (Jonson [1609] 1816, 138). C. F. Leyel suggested that as "aconite and belladonna were said to be the ingredients of witches' 'flying ointments,' Aconite causes irregular action of the heart, and Belladonna produces delirium. These combined symptoms might give a sensation of 'flying'" (Leyel, note in Grieve 1931, 9).

Monkshood (*Aconitum napellus*) is another of the much-used poisonous plants. If ingested, monkshood produces burning sensations in the lips, numbs the mouth and throat, causes muscular spasms, convulsions, vomiting, and diarrhea, and finally paralyses the respiratory system, causing death.

Fig. 6.4.
Datura graveolens

ANGEL'S TRUMPET

Angel's trumpet (*Datura [brugmansia] graveolens*) is another striking plant, immediately recognized, and is named after its long green-and-white flowers. Like the deadly nightshade, all parts of datura are poisonous. Using it as a hallucinogen is a risky procedure as the active substance induces feelings of relaxation, followed by hallucinations and then unconsciousness that may end in death. It was a favorite herb of poisoners because the victim became drowsy and could not fight back.

Fig. 6.5.
Brugmansia stramonium

THORN APPLE

Related to the angel's trumpet is the equally lethal thorn apple (*Brugmansia stramonium*), named after its spiky fruit, which is also resorted to by foolhardy people who risk death in using it as a hallucinogen. It is also known as devil's apple or jimson weed, and its seeds have the strongest concentration of its active substances, atropine and hyoscyamine, which are not destroyed either by drying or boiling (Grieve 1931, 803–7).

MANDRAKE

Although it is not so recognizable as the previous weird plants, the mandrake (*Mandragora officinarum*) was much sought after by the root diggers, though they did not die from digging it up. Legend tells how the mandrake screams as it is torn from the earth, proving fatal to he or

Fig. 6.6.
Mandragora officinarum

she who should dig it up, for the resident demon of the mandrake is supposed to take revenge on the person who dragged it from the ground. The magical method of getting the mandrake is to go to the plant on a Friday, tie a dog to it, and then the dog will uproot it, bringing its curse on the dog and not the person who wants the root.

The root of the mandrake resembles the roots of both deadly nightshade and white bryony. It is said to be dangerous to look at the mandrake for too long, because one will go blind (Cielo 1918, 114). Because the root resembles a human being, it is considered to be an earth sprite whose magical powers can be harnessed for the magician's use. The mandrake contains the alkaloids mandragorin, hyoscyamine, and scopolomine, and it was used as an anaesthetic. It is reputed to have the powers of rejuvenation and was used as part of love potions. Hence its alternative names, the root of life or the divine root. In latter years it was procured legally by the root diggers only for horse doctoring (Grieve 1931, 510–12).

> *Then on the still night air,*
> *The bark of dog is heard,*
> *A shriek! A groan!*
> *A human cry. A trumpet sound.*
> *The Mandrake root lies captive on the ground*
> (THOMPSON 1934, 153)

Fig. 6.7.
Bryonia dioica

WHITE BRYONY

The hedgerow plant white bryony (*Bryonia dioica*) has a much dug for root that was used magically in the same way as the mandrake root, for it is similar in form. In Norfolk, white bryony is actually called mandrake. In *The Universal Herbal*, from 1832, we are told:

The roots of Bryony grow to a vast size and have been formerly by impostors brought into a human shape, carried about the country and shown from Mandrakes to the common people. The method which these knaves practised was to open the earth round a young, thriving bryony plant, being careful not to disturb the lower fibres of the root; to fix a mould, such as used by those who make plaster figures, close to the root, and then to fill the earth about the root, leaving it to grow to the shape of the mould, which is effected in one summer. (Quoted in Grieve 1931, 132)

Presented as a cut-off root without the stem or leaves, it can be mistaken for a parsnip, though when ingested it has a foul, bitter taste. Nevertheless, whole families are said to have been poisoned during times of famine by eating white bryony roots in error, believing them to be parsnips. The red berries are also poisonous, though it will take quite a few to kill even a child. But the other traditional names of white bryony show how it is regarded traditionally: death warrant, dead creepers and snakeberry. However, in appropriate quantities, it is a legitimate herbal medicine (Grieve 1931, 132–33).

BLACK BRYONY

Fig. 6.8.
Tamus communis

Black bryony (*Tamus communis*), otherwise known as blackeye root, contains a strong poison. In former times, like the mandrake, it was believed to gain its virtue by growing beneath the gallows and at a crossroads where a person who had committed suicide was buried (Trevelyan 1909, 92–93; Thompson 1934, 168–70).

Fig. 6.9.
Solanum dulcamara

WOODY NIGHTSHADE

Woody nightshade (*Solanum dulcamara*) is also a hedgerow plant. It bears purple-and-yellow flowers that resemble those of the potato plant. Woody nightshade produces red berries that contain the alkaloid solanine, which is a poison that leads to breathing difficulties and sometimes death. There was a brief craze among hippies in Cambridge in the late 1960s for smoking woody nightshade in the hope of obtaining a free and legal high. The author and publisher do not recommend this, for another traditional name for the plant is self-evident—poisonberry.

Fig. 6.10.
Hyoscyamus niger

HENBANE

Henbane (*Hyoscyamus niger*) is closely associated with operative witchcraft. It is also known as hogs' bean, Jupiter's bean, cassilago, symphonica, and deus caballinus. Containing hyoscyamine and hyoscine, henbane is a medicinal herb used in traditional medicine as a sedative and in the treatment of toothache, and it was once customary to smoke its leaves and seeds in a pipe as a remedy for neuralgia and rheumatism (Grieve 1931, 403). Henbane is said to be another of the ingredient plants of the famed witches' flying ointment, and, like mandrake, it was used in love potions. But as its name suggests, it is baneful and not a plant to play with, for it was a favorite of poisoners. Henbane root was dug for its hallucinogenic qualities, though, as with angel's trumpet and thorn apple, using it can be a one-way trip to the mole country. Not only the root is dangerous; twenty henbane seeds are a lethal dose. Even the scent of its flowers can cause disorientation (Grieve 397–404).

Fig. 6.11.
Echium vulgare

VIPER'S BUGLOSS

Viper's bugloss (*Echium vulgare*) is also known as ironweed, bluebottle, blueweed, and our savior's flannel. It is a source of the pyrrolizidine alkaloids also found in ragwort, which, if ingested, can cause moderate to severe liver damage, in the latter case leading to death in a period ranging between a fortnight and two years. Viper's bugloss seeds resemble snakes' heads, so they were used in country medicine as a remedy against snakebite and a general expellant of venom and poisons (Grieve 1931, 142). Related to viper's bugloss is hound's tongue (*Cynoglossum officinale*), traditionally used by handywomen to treat tumors and as a depressant. Scientific analysis has shown that this plant actually produces carcinogens rather than treating cancer.

Fig. 6.12.
Veratrum niger

BLACK HELLEBORE

All parts of the black hellebore plant (*Veratrum [Helleborus] niger*) are poisonous, containing the glucosides helleborin and helleborcin. Other names given to the plant are Christ herb, Christmas rose, and melampode. Even smelling the scent can damage the nasal passages. It was used in traditional medicine for its purgative and anthelmintic (deworming) properties as well as in treating hysteria and other nervous disorders. Black hellebore was used in rural magic for the blessing of cattle to keep them free of spells and the evil eye. For this, the plant must be dug up ritually, the gatherer facing toward the east. Writing in 1651, John Parkinson, King Charles I's royal botanist, stated, "A piece of the root being drawne through a hole made in the eare of a beast troubled with cough or having taken any poisonous thing cureth it, if it be taken out the next day at the same houre" (Grieve 1931, 388–89).

Fig. 6.13.
Vinca major

GREATER PERIWINKLE

The greater periwinkle (*Vinca major*), otherwise known as parwynke and sorcerer's violet, was used as an astringent and tonic to ward off all kinds of sickness, especially bleeding and cramps, and was used as an aphrodisiac. The active ingredient lowers the blood pressure, which in large doses can be extremely harmful, but country practitioners found it useful in cases of hemorrhage. Magically, it was used to ward off serious afflictions, and there was a ritual for collecting parwynke. Ritual taking of herbs was once an integral part of herbalism, but, like the rites once associated with cutting divining rods, which are now ignored by dowsers, official medicine dispensed with the rituals when the chemical-pharmaceutical worldview overtook the old magical one.

Apuleius's *Herbarium* of 1480 tells us:

This wort is good of advantage for many purposes, that is to say, first against devil sickness and demoniacal possessions and against snakes and wild beasts and against poisons and for various wishes and for envy and for terror and that thou mayst have grace, and if thou hast the wort with thee thou shalt be prosperous and ever acceptable. This wort shalt though pluck thus, saying, "I pray thee vinca pervinca, thee that art to be had for many useful qualities, that though come to me glad blossoming with they mainfulness, that thou outfit me so that I be shielded and ever prosperous and undamaged by poisons and by water"; when thou shalt pluck this wort, though shalt be clean of any uncleanness, and thou shalt pick it when the moon is nine nights old and eleven nights and thirteen nights and thirty nights and when it is one night old.

Fig. 6.14.
Senecio jacobaea

RAGWORT

One of the very dangerous weird plants is the ragwort (*Senecio jacobaea*), a pretty little flower that contains the alkaloid pyrrolizidine, the active substance also found in viper's bugloss, which, if ingested, can cause irreversible liver damage. Ragwort was prized for this because it keeps its properties even when dried.

Fig. 6.15.
Actaea spicata

TOADROOT

Toadroot (*Actaea spicata*), otherwise known as bugbane, black baneberry, and herb Christopher, is a rare plant found growing only on limestone in northern England. Toads are attracted by its smell, but its scent appears to be offensive to humans, and it was also used to drive away bugs, fleas, and lice. The black, many-seeded, egg-shaped berries are very poisonous. Its American relative (*Actaea alba,* white cohosh) is known as one of the "rattlesnake herbs," its white berries being used as a remedy against snakebite.

Fig. 6.16.
Linaria vulgaris

TOADFLAX

Toadflax (*Linaria vulgaris*) is unrelated to toadroot. It goes by numerous names, including snapdragon, larkspur, lion's mouth, devil's head, dragon bushes, ramstead, churnstaff, gallwort, ribbon, and monkey flower. Like toadroot, it has an offensive smell, which is caused by the presence of an acrid oil that is reputed to be toxic. Boiled in milk, toadflax was used as a fly poison.

Fig. 6.17.
Aristolochia longa

BIRTHWORT

Birthwort (*Aristolochia longa*) is a root used by handywomen for removing obstructions after childbirth. It was also used as a means of procuring miscarriage in early pregnancy. The active substance is aristolochine, or aristolic acid, which causes severe digestive problems and can even lead to total failure of the kidneys.

Fig. 6.18.
Vitex agnus-castus

MONKS' PEPPER

Medieval monks were fed "monks' pepper," made from the berries of the chaste tree (*Vitex agnus-castus*), which look like peppercorns, because the active substances (flavonoids, agnuside, and p-hydroxybenzoic acid) in them alters the hormonal balance in the body, thereby suppressing the libido. But in large doses, it has the effect of producing formication, the sensation of ants crawling all over the body beneath the skin.

Fig. 6.19.
Conium maculatum

HEMLOCK

Hemlock (*Conium maculatum*), otherwise known as herb bennet, poison parsley, kecksies, spotted corobane, and musquash root, is a member of the family of plants that includes carrots, parsley, fennel, and parsnips. When ingested, hemlock is a sedative and antispasmodic, but larger doses produce violent vomiting and convulsions. If the dose is large enough, these symptoms are followed by paralysis of the central and peripheral nervous systems, leading to death through respiratory failure. The poisonous qualities of hemlock are destroyed by cooking. Hemlock mixed with betony (*Stachys betonica,* also called bishop's wort) and fennel seed (*Foeniculum vulgare*) was considered a cure for the bite of a mad dog (Grieve 1931, 393).

Fig. 6.20.
Arum maculatum

ADDER'S ROOT

Adder's root (*Arum maculatum*) is a very poisonous plant. Like most indigenous wild plants, it goes by myriad local names; Newman noted that *Arum maculatum* has more than 250 local names in the Eastern Counties alone, including adder's tongue, cuckoo pint, lords and ladies, dead man's finger, Jack in the pulpit, and bloody man's finger (Newman 1948a, 130). All parts of it are equally dangerous, causing swelling of the mouth and tongue when ingested and an agonizing death. It is one of the herbs brought to the witches' convent by the ninth hag in Jonson's *The Masque of Queens.*

Fig. 6.21.
Artemisia absinthium

WORMWOOD

Wormwood (*Artemisia absinthium*), otherwise known as green ginger or wormseed, is a source of the glucoside absinthin, used to flavor absinthe, "the green fairy," a drink much favored by artists and writers.

In his *July's Husbandry,* Thomas Tusser wrote:

While Wormwood hath seed to get a handful or twaine
To save against March, to make flea to refraine;
Where chamber is sweeped and Wormwood is strowne,
No flea for his life dare abide to be known.
What saver the better (if Physick be true)

For places infected than Wormwood and Rue?
It is a comfort for hart and the braine
And therefore to have it.

The active component of wormwood, absinthin, is an emetic hallucinogen. Habitual use of absinthe affects one's visual color perception, emphasizing yellow, which often predominates in the work of artists who favor the drink. It was very popular among artists and writers in the Symbolist period toward the end of the nineteenth century. In its use to drive away fleas, it is associated with Foe-ing Out Day, March 1, the traditional day of spring cleaning, when patterns are chalked on the threshold to ward off vermin and evil sprites. Wormwood was said to counteract the effects of poisoning by toadstools or hemlock and being bitten by a sea dragon (Grieve 1931, 858). It was also used on Saint Luke's Day as a love charm in combination with marigold, marjoram, and thyme.

Fig. 6.22.
Ruta graveolens

RUE

Rue, or herby grass (*Ruta graveolens*), the herb of grace, is immediately recognizable by its blue-green leaves. The medieval church used to sprinkle holy water mixed with the herb to purify a church before saying mass, so it has a function of warding off harm. The herbalist Gerard noted, "If a man be anointed with the juice of rue, the poison of wolf's bane, mushrooms, or todestooles, the biting of serpents, stinging of scorpions, spiders, bees, hornets and wasps will not hurt him." Like wormwood, rue was used in houses to drive away fleas. It was customary for judges to have sprigs of rue placed on the bench of the dock to ward off contagious diseases brought by the accused from prison. Rue is an ingredient of the magical concoction called the vinegar of the four thieves.

Fig. 6.23.
Lolium temulentum

DARNEL

The grass called darnel (*Lolium temulentum*) sometimes grew among wheat or rye fields. If darnel grains were present in the milling process, then the bread contained the active substance of ergot alkaloids that produces vertigo, violent tremors of the limbs, loss of strength, and visual impairment that makes everything appear green. Darnel is a plant that takes one to the green otherworld, though it is extremely dangerous to use it in this way.

Fig. 6.24.
Cannabis sativa

HEMP

Hemp (*Cannabis sativa*) was grown widely for fiber production in former times, and in some places parcels of land called hempshires recall the places where it was cultivated before it was made illegal in the United Kingdom on September 28, 1928, and was extirpated.

In Fenland, hemp tea was prescribed by handywomen as a remedy against the ague, the endemic illness of the mosquito-infested fens of Lincolnshire and Cambridgeshire. The cultivation of hemp for medicinal purposes was never quite eliminated in the fens.

Fig. 6.25.
Nepeta cataria

CATMINT

Catmint (*Nepeta cataria*), also known as catnip or catnip tea, was prepared as an infusion for drinking in the era before the importation of tea began, and it was known as "quite as pleasant and a good deal more wholesome." It should be infused; boiling will drive off its volatile active components. "The root when chewed is said to make the most gentle person quarrelsome, and there is a legend of a certain hangman who could never screw up his courage to the point of hanging anybody till he had partaken of it" (Bardswell, *The Herb Garden,* quoted in Grieve 1931, 174).

Fig. 6.26.
Papaver somniferum

OPIUM

The opium poppy (*Papaver somniferum*) was grown in England before it was made illegal in 1909, and until then, opic (opium) pills were sold by peddlers who went from pub to pub in the Fens, selling them to regulars who would take one along with a beer chaser. Laudanum, a tincture of opium (opium dissolved in alcohol), was available everywhere until the early twentieth century, and as it was a component of many patent medicines, patients became addicted and kept coming back for more. Opium was the active ingredient of various medicines, including paregoric and mithridatium.

Fig. 6.27.
Ferula foetida

ASAFOETIDA

Asafoetida, also called devil's dung and food of the gods, is an oleogum resin obtained from the roots of the plant whose scientific name is *Ferula foetida*. This is not a native plant, coming originally from Iran and Afghanistan with a related species growing in Tibet. It was used as a volatile oil to treat respiratory ailments and also was burned surreptitiously to produce a smoke that brings unconsciousness, being used by magically inclined thieves to enter occupied houses unopposed. It plays a significant role in West Indian Obeah.

✳

When someone's food or drink had a substance added surreptitiously, it was said to have been "doctored." "Sea witches," who plied their trade in ports, among other things selling the wind to sailors on knotted ropes, also sold concoctions called "Mickey Finns" to seamen who used them to shanghai others. The seaman to be shanghaied would be given a doctored drink from which he would pass out. Then he was taken aboard a ship about to sail, where he would be forced to work. Because of the ready availability of many poisonous plants growing wild, it may appear to have been an easy thing to use them to kill. But in addition to the problem mentioned above of the natural and often unpredictable variability in toxicity of wild plants, putting aside the ethical considerations, there were practical concerns as well. The problem, as Newman defined it, was "to prepare a tasteless draught or powder in which the active principle would be present in excess of the lower limit of the lethal doses but within the possibility of illicit administration" (Newman 1948, 122). Large doses often led to vomiting, eliminating the poison from the body of the intended victim, so to become an effective poisoner was no simple matter. In the past, forensic analysis was absent or too poorly developed to detect many natural poisons in a corpse. But in the twenty-first century, even minute traces of the active substances that cause death can be detected, let alone the larger doses necessary to kill.

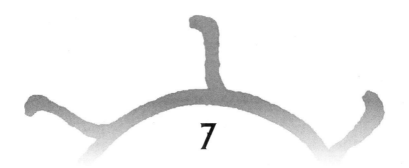

7

Spells, Incantations, and Charms

Whenever you do it
Whatever you should
Just do your best
And do it good.

How historical witches learned their trade is largely unrecorded. There are a number of known oral transmissions, but the overlap between what was transmitted in each case is not very large, and there is little to indicate a connected movement at any time. Because they are customarily portrayed as poverty-stricken old women living in ramshackle hovels, it is assumed that women who practiced magic were always illiterate and thus not in possession of any books. But, as today, when unique old manuscripts exist in the possession of individuals, there have always been books circulating outside the remit of institutions such as universities or, later, learned societies. In Scotland and Wales these books were in the vernacular languages, Gaelach and Cymraeg (Gaelic and Welsh). Those that lasted longest were those considered the most valuable. They were medical textbooks of techniques and remedies that contained material that now would be considered magical.

In Wales the position of the "mediciner" of the household was enshrined in law by the Welsh king Howel Dda about the year 930. In Scotland the households of Gaelic-speaking lords and clan chiefs had various hereditary functionaries, including bards and physicians. Medical kindreds existed in Celtic society as part of the clan system. The medical text belonging to the MacBeth/Beaton family called *The Red Book of Appin* is the most celebrated of these works. It had an amuletic power; it was held in such awe that its very presence was considered healing. Such a book was called *iuchair gach uile eòlais*—the "key to knowledge." The members of the family MacBeth/Beaton were hereditary physicians in the household of the Lords of the Isles, and they possessed a considerable library of medical and other valuable manuscripts written in Gaelic.

Writing in the seventeenth century, Martin Martin noted, "Fergus Beaton hath the following ancient Irish manuscripts in the Irish characters, to whit: Avicenna, Averroes, Joannes de Vigo, Bernardus Gordonius, and several works of Hippocrates" (Cheape 1993, 119). The corpus of European medicine was preserved not only in the editions in Greek, Arabic, and Latin but also those in Gaelic. Because the Gaelic tradition was driven down, the tradition was all but extirpated and the place of Celtic culture in maintaining learning is scarcely recognized. Learned but poor people, especially those in remote parts of Great Britain, did not have the wherewithal or access to printing these hereditary works. They were transmitted as handwritten copies and so were always very few in number.

From the six indigenous languages in Great Britain in the sixteenth century—English, Welsh, Gaelic, Cumbrian, Cornish, and Romani—successive British governments had the policy of reducing it to one. The persecution of the Gaelic language by Crown and Parliament for more than three hundred years was a deliberate attempt to make the Highlands of Scotland exclusively English-speaking and Protestant. Socially this was a clash between the traditional Celtic custom of open-handed charity endorsed by the Catholic religion, with the holding of lands in common for the common good, and the government's

Protestant social order, which stood for enclosure of the common land and its transfer to private ownership and the selective distribution of charity to "the deserving poor." The imposition of English was accomplished through the children. The Scottish Education Act of 1872, which made schooling compulsory, stipulated English to be the only language used and taught in Scottish schools. This sectarian social engineering was part of the deliberate, and largely successful, government program to extirpate both the Gaelic and Welsh languages from Great Britain, the other two Celtic languages having faded away.

With the creation of an official government culture inculcated in children through the schools, traditional culture was denigrated and extirpated. The nine rural arts of ancient Welsh culture were among them, as was the traditional worldview of the English rural magicians. Once official culture penetrated throughout society, many ancient books were then considered worthless. Most were disposed of or wantonly destroyed, some by people terrified of the supposedly evil contents. Priceless pages were torn out and cut down by tailors for sewing patterns. Others fueled the fires. Not all of the Welsh manuscripts that transmitted the three pillars of knowledge were destroyed, for they remained valued as part of Welsh culture, even when the Cymraeg language was undergoing persecution by the agents of Crown and Parliament. Many of these manuscripts were preserved by the restored orders of druids and bards and published in print, though most remain untranslated into English and other languages.

In England there are recorded references to magical books in manuscript, which might have been grimoires in the classical sense, in the possession of individuals such as witches, cunning men, blacksmiths, and millers. In Huntingdonshire the book once concealed in the Great Gransden windmill was called the miller's *Infidel's Bible*. Nothing is known about it. As recorded by Catherine Parsons in her remarkable memoirs of witchcraft in Horseheath (Parsons 1915; 1952), Daddy Witch, who was a woman despite her name, "gained much of her knowledge from a book called *The Devil's Plantation*" (Parsons 1915, 39). A magical text called *The Secret Granary* is known to have existed in eastern England, but its contents have never appeared in print, if any copies still exist at all.

From the late eighteenth century, printed occult material was widely available, and there were schools that taught occult lore. In 1797, *The Conjuror's Magazine* published material on ceremonial magic, astrology, and alchemy. The grimoire *Cyprianus* was printed for the first time in 1797, and in 1801, Francis Barrett, who ran a school of occultism in Marylebone, London, published *The Magus, or Celestial Intelligencer,* a compendium of magical lore based on the writings of Heinrich Cornelius Agrippa and others. Early in the nineteenth century, magical, divinatory, and astrological books continued to appear, including *The Philosophical Merlin, Napoléon's Book of Fate, Raphael's Witch, The Straggling Astrologer, The 6th and 7th Books of Moses,* and *A Book of the Laws of Pluto.* As well as material from earlier works, it is these and other contemporarily published British and American works that were employed by the witches and cunning men whose spells and arts found their way into the county folklore books of the nineteenth and twentieth centuries.

SPELLCRAFT

Because elements of pre-Christian magic and lore have been detected in recorded witchcraft practices and spells, it is often assumed wrongly that the entire corpus of practice in historical British witchcraft is pagan. Recorded evidence shows that spells of healing especially drew strongly from Christian sources, sometimes the mainstream Bible and occasionally from apocryphal sources (Davies 1996, 29). In medieval times, Catholic priests would, as a matter of course in medical cases, perform benedictions over water to heal a man's eyes and bless an ointment or medicinal draught before it was administered. There were graces before meals and a benediction over ale. Priests said benedictions over weapons about to be used in warfare, blessed the plough, and said a benediction over a hunter's nets for catching wild animals. They prepared holy water to disperse fiends (Wordsworth 1903, 391). This ecclesiastical custom is not finished, for in the winter of 2010–2011, the bishop of Lincoln blessed the Lincolnshire gritting machines and snowplows at their depot. In Gaelic-speaking Scotland, charms known as An Soisgeul (the Gospel) were sewn into clothing as protectants long after Protestantism was in the ascendancy. They consisted of a verse of scripture, a hymn, or words of benediction written by a priest (Cheape 1993, 117). Many of these benedictions ceased when the Protestant sect became dominant, but among vernacular culture all over Great Britain, they continued, mostly unobserved by the authorities. So the tradition of saying benedictions, prayers, or spells, frequently empowered by "the three holy names," the epithets of the God of the Christian trinity—the Father, the Son and the Holy Ghost—remained embedded in traditional culture.

There are several published accounts of magical texts and other magical items being found on the bodies of people after their death, including clergymen. In 1709 a silk bag was found hanging around the neck of the recently deceased Reverend Robert Forbes at Rougham in Norfolk. In it was a manuscript with a cryptic text that read:

Eywn uydlab ase byw udgaa eyud gwr yu esa Lbib bL tw udcab x Lwe byw lwca Sazwr yln sdb by ac ys xdshr qd ysab byge sm spew Lwaca astr Lsn mgb sxdshr mgd yscw mgb sm spew eyg maq wewd esda bywaw eqdra asii mwcwd tw bcdoicwrt el by sm spew snwm snwm acwwb Lwaca

It was believed to be for the prevention of the ague (Dowson 1932, 233–38).

In 1879 a different charm against the ague was found around the neck of another dead man at Hurstpierpoint in Sussex. It read:

When Jesus Christ came upon the cross, for the redemption of mankind, He shook, and his Rood trembles. The Cheaf Priest said unto him, "Art thou afraid, or hast though an ague?" He said unto them, "I am not afraid, neither have I an ague, and whosoever Believeth in these words shall not be troubled with any Fever or ague. So be it unto you." (Henderson 1866, 169)

A Welsh healing spell preserved in the ancient writings of the physicians of Myddfai tells us:

For all sorts of agues, write in three apples, on three separate days. In the first apple + *o nagla pater*. In the second apple + *o nagla filius*. In the third apple + *o nagla spiritus sanctus*. And on the third day he will recover. (Williams 1861, 51)

Alternatively, instead of charms, some practitioners provided amulets. For example, a West Country amulet against ague uses a wooden chip taken from a gallows.

These chips must be sewn into silken bags and worn near the heart. (Hewett 1900, 74)

Other charms using Christian names of power or stories about Jesus appear in a manuscript that belonged to an eighteenth-century blacksmith-farrier at Clun in Shropshire. One, a remedy against burns, says:

Mary mild has burnt her child by the sparkling of the fire; out fire, in frost, in the name of the Father Son and Holeygost Amen Amen Amen—to be said nine times and the Lords Praier before and after. (Morgan 1895a, 204).

Another of his charms, to draw out a thorn from the body, goes:

To drive out a thorn—then came Jesus forth wearing the crown of thorns and the purpel robs and pilat said write to them behold the man Amen Amen Amen—to be said nine times and the Lords Praier before and hafter hold your midl finger on the place and go round it each time and mark it thus +. (Morgan 1895a, 203)

A charm against worms from Bridgend, Glamorgan, in Wales, was recorded in 1909.

God the Father down did ride
Quick and fast the fork he tried
He lifted worms that were out of sight—
One was black, the other was white;
One was mottled, one was red;
Soon the worms were killed and dead;
Heal, O Lord, as soon as said!

(TREVELYAN 1909, 226)

A charm from nineteenth-century Shropshire to stop bleeding says:

Through the blood of Adam's son
Was taken the blood of Christ.
By the same blood I do thee charge
That the blood of [name of person]
      run no more at large.

(BURNE AND JACKSON 1883, 183)

A Devonian bruise charm invokes the sun and the moon as well as the three holy names.

To charm a bruise—
Holy chica! Holy chica!
This bruise will get well bye-and-bye,
Up sun high! Down moon low!
This bruise will be quite well very soon!
In the name of the Father, Son and Holy Ghost,
Amen.

(HEWETT 1900, 68)

Another of the Shropshire blacksmith-farrier's charms, also for a sprain or bruise, uses words ascribed to Jesus as well as the three holy names.

Our Saviour Jesus Crist roate on a marbel stone Senow Joint to Joint
Bone to Bone he rote these words every one. In the Name of the
Father Sone and Holey Gost Amen Sweet Jesus Amen Sweet Jesus
Amen. Going round the afflicted place each time with your hand
and the Lords Praier each time and marck it thus + three times or if
very bad nine times. (Morgan 1895a, 203)

It is not surprising that the Lord's Prayer appears so many times
in recorded instances of British vernacular magic. The church has
always used it in this way, and in 1972 the bishop of Exeter's obscure
but important report on exorcism, titled *Exorcism,* reinforced its
use in this way. *Exorcism* is a manual of principles and rituals for
the use of the Anglican clergy, the published opinion of a commission convened by the Church of England's bishop of Exeter, Robert
Mortimer, chaired by the noted Anglican Benedictine exorcist Dom
Robert Petitpierre, and ecumenically including a Roman Catholic
expert. "The Lord's prayer is a form of exorcism," the report tells us. It
begins with an invocation of the holy name and ends with a petition
for deliverance from the devil. It is said to be very suitable for that
use by the laity, either in times of personal temptation or in a group
involved in a tense or potentially evil situation (Mortimer 1972, 20).
Its magical function is implicit; the commission concluded that exorcism has been and can be performed by any Christian, and even by
non-Christians, in the name of Christ (Mortimer 1972, 21). The
latter statement, backed up by biblical authority, reveals the magical
function of the prayer as used historically by witches, cunning men,
and others in their practices.

Numbers are important in magic and the rites of rural and trade
fraternities. The numbers 3, 7, and 9 occur frequently. Some incantations use magical words whose meaning is not apparent along with
sequences of numbers. Those with diminishing series of numbers have
the intention of diminishing the temperature of the body or the power
of venom. A charm against adder bite published in 1871 goes:

"Bradgty, Bradgty, Bradgty, under a shining leaf." To be repeated three times and strike your hand with the growing of the hare. "Bradgty, Bradgty, Bradgty" to be repeated three times before eight, eight before seven, and seven before six, and six before five, and five before four, and four before three, and three before two, and two before one, and one before every one, three times for the bite of an adder. (Couch 1871, 148)

A book that belonged to a nineteenth-century West Country conjurer contained the following spell to remove bewitchment from cattle.

A Receipt for Ill Wishing. Take a handful of white salt in your right hand and strewe it over the Backs of all your cattle: begin at the head of the near side and go to the Tail, and from the Tail to the head up the off side, and as you let it out of your hand say thee words: "As Thy servant Elisha healed the waters of Jericho by casting salt therein, so I hope to heal this my Beast: In the Name of God the Father, God the Son, and God the Holy Ghost. Amen."

Another spell from the same conjurer recommended the following:

If any Cattle is bad, do thus. Cut a bit of hair from between the Ears, a bit from behind each shoulder, and a bit from the stump of the Tail, a little Blood, a Teaspoonful of Gunpowder, and put the whole into a small Bladder, and tie the top of it; then get some Green Ashen wood, and make a fire, and set it on the brand *irons,* and take the Bladder into your right hand, and say these words: "I confine all Evil, and all Enemies of mine and my cattle into the fire for ever, never to hurt me or mine any more for ever: in the Name of God the Father, God the Son, and God the Holy Ghost. Amen." Then drop it into the fire, and let it burn out. Read the first thirteen verses of the 28th Chapter of the book of Deuteronomy and no more every morning before you go to see your Cattle. (Elworthy 1895, 394–95)

In her book *Nummits and Crummits: Devonshire Customs,* published in 1900, Sarah Hewett gives a number of magical formulae from Devonian witchcraft, including the following two.

- Charm for Obtaining Love and for Success in all Undertakings: Whoever wears this charm, written on virgin parchment, and sewn up in a small *round* silken bag continuously over the heart, will obtain all the love he or she may deserve and will be successful in every undertaking.
- Charm for Protection from Enemies: This talisman should be made from pure cast iron and engraven at the time of the new moon. Before suspending it round the neck fumigate it with the smoke of burnt spirits of Mars (a mixture of red saunders, frankincense, and red pepper), or a ring of pure gold might be made, with the characters engraven on the inside. The size and form of the talisman is immaterial so long as the proper time for making it is observed and the prescribed incense is used before it is worn. In any form it will protect one from enemies, and counteract the power of the evil eye! (73–74)

The talisman bears the Christian sigil Chi-Rho, the lower arm of which is in the form of an anchor. Around it is written *vince in hoc*—"conquer in this [sign]"—and the sigil of Mars. This is another instance of Christian sigils used in witchcraft in England, a direct parallel with folk-magic traditions in mainland Europe and the hoodoo practitioners in the United States.

Some spells had Christian elements together with an inversion of religious practice. A woman who believed she had been overlooked and was being plagued by "strange little black objects sitting on the boxes at night" went to a wise man at Wells in Somerset to have the spell removed. The wise man told her the name of the witch who was causing the problem and said he could break the charm and take away the power of the witch, but it would take a lot of prayer and work. About the hour of midnight, the woman and her husband were to sit in front of their fireplace and burn salt, and for one hour no words were to be spoken, except the words of the following spell.

> *This is not the thing I wish to burn.*
> *But Mrs. ____'s heart of ____ Somerset to turn,*
> *Wishing thee neither to eat, drink, sleep or rest*
> *Until thou dost come to me and do my request;*
> *Or else the wrath of God may fall on thee*
> *And cause thee to be consumed in a moment. Amen.*

This accomplished, they were to retire backward to the foot of the stairs, climb the stairs still backward, repeating at the same time the Lord's Prayer also backward, and then not to speak a word to one another until they were in bed; in this way they would break the spell. The man and his wife tried this with implicit faith that the enchantment would be broken, or the evil eye averted (*Dorset Notes & Queries* December 1894, quoted by Elworthy 1895, 432–33).

Spells involving any materials are empowered and activated by words and actions, specific materials, and compass directions. For example, in his notes to *The Masque of Queens,* Ben Jonson states, "Throwing of ashes and sand, with the flint-stone, cross-sticks, and burying of sage, etc., are all used (and believed by them) to the raising of storm and tempest," and his theatrical hags perform the action as directed by their dame.

Fig. 7.1. Wooden box in the shape of a heart, circa 1860

> *Cast them up: and the flint-stone*
> *Over the left shoulder bone;*
> *Into the west.*
>
> (JONSON [1609] 1816, VII, 136)

And one of Robert Herrick's charms in rhyme specifies:

> *If ye feare to be affrighted*
> *When ye are (by chance) benighted:*
> *In your pocket for a trust*
> *Carrie nothing but a Crust:*
> *For that holy piece of Bread*
> *Charmes the danger, and the dread.*
>
> (HERRICK [1648] 1902, 298)

Tradition values "keeping up the day," because certain days of the year are special for various reasons—equinoxes and solstices, the stations of the sun during the year, festal days, and those dedicated to heroes, saints, and gods. Many love-charm rituals must be performed on certain days, like New Year's Eve, Saint Mark's Eve, and Saint Luke's or Saint Thomas's Day, such as the following one, which uses herbs as the operative materia magica.

> On Saint Luke's Day, take marigold flowers, a sprig of marjoram, thyme, and a little wormwood; dry them before a fire, rub them to powder; then sift it through a fine piece of lawn, and simmer it over a slow fire, adding a small quantity of virgin honey and vinegar. Anoint yourself with this when you go to bed, saying the following lines three times, and you will dream of your partner "that is to be":

> *Saint Luke, Saint Luke, be kind to me,*
> *In dreams let me my true-love see.*
>
> (GRIEVE 1931, 858–59)

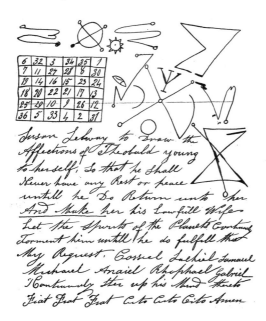

Fig. 7.2. Love charm to draw the affections of Theobald Young, with an invocation of spirits and angels, from the nineteenth century

"Keeping up the day" relates also to the gathering of herbs for specific purposes. They each have a best time of year when their active ingredients are at their most potent, and some are connected with certain saints and their days. For example, the herbs of Saint John, most effective on Saint John's Day near the summer solstice, are mistletoe (*Viscum album*), Saint John's wort (*Hypericum* spp.), hawkweed (*Hieracium pilosella*), vervain (*Verbena officinalis*), orpine (*Sedum telephium*), mullein (*Verbascum* spp.), and wormwood (*Artemisia* spp.) (Newman 1948a, 130). The names of herbs appear in some spells, usually formulaic, such as swearing by "parsley, sage, rosemary, and thyme" or "by yarrow and rue." The names of powerful herbs have become names of power.

The formula *Abracadabra* is the most widely known and immediately recognizable magical word. It is the staple of a certain type of stage magician of the old school. But it is properly a talisman against fevers and related maladies. A prescription for its use is said to have come from the third-century CE Roman physician Q. Serenus Ammoniacus, who directed it to be written in the form of an inverted

```
A B R A C A D A B R A
A B R A C A D A B R
A B R A C A D A B
A B R A C A D A
A B R A C A D
A B R A C A
A B R A C
A B R A
A B R
A B
A
```

triangle, each line losing the final letter until there is but a single *A* (Elworthy 1895, 399).

Hewett recounts how this talisman of *Abracadabra* was given by a white witch to a person who desired to possess a talisman against the dominion of a gray witch, pixies, evil spirits, and the powers of darkness. It was written on parchment and enclosed in a black silk bag one-inch square. The owner was told that if it should ever touch the ground, it would lose its power (Hewett 1900, 73).

Magic squares are an ancient form of talisman that were used in traditional British witchcraft. Frederick Thomas Elworthy records a use for the famous SATOR formula, a magic square that is known from Roman Imperial times onward. "For the bite of a mad dog the following words are to be written upon the crust of a loaf which . . . is to be applied there several times. The performer is to repeat the Lord's Prayer five times for the five wounds of Christ, etc." (Elworthy 1895, 400–401).

```
S A T O R
A R E P O
T E N E T
O P E R A
R O T A S
```

Another written magic-square charm from Wales recorded by Marie Trevelyan is a formula against vermin: "To drive away rats, write the following magic square on parchment and put in the mouth of the King of the Rats. This will drive all rats away" (Trevelyan 1909).

R A T S
A R S T
T S R A
S T A R

A numerical magic square adds to 72, taken each way, in each line.

28 35 2 7
6 3 32 31
34 29 8 1
4 5 30 33

This, according to Elworthy, is "a veritable amulet, and if your enemy's name be written underneath it, and you wear this as a charm, his envy will be baffled and his eye will be powerless against you" (Elworthy 1895, 402–3).

Fig. 7.3. Written charm, circa 1800, with sigil *Abracadabra*, and so forth

Hewett records procedures used by white witches to counter the powers of black witches, using objects from the repertoire of iron magic and toadmanry.

> To Destroy the Power of a Witch. Take three small-necked stone jars: place in each the liver of a frog stuck full of new pins and the heart of a toad stuck full of thorns from the holy thorn bush. Cork and seal each jar. Bury in three different churchyard paths seven inches from the surface and seven feet from the porch. While in the act of burying each jar recite the Lord's Prayer backward. As the hearts and livers decay so will the witch's power vanish. After performing the ceremony no witch can have any power over the operator. (1900, 74)

Special magical nails made by blacksmiths for the purpose were used to nail horseshoes to beams, doorposts, and beds to bind spirits. Writing in 1892, Camilla Gurdon noted a story from a Suffolk informant, "Mrs. H.," who told of a horseshoe used for what she called "exorcising spirits."

> I once lived in a curious old house—The Barley House, out Debenham way—and that were haunted. There were a great horseshoe nailed into the ceiling on one of the beams and they say that were to nail in a spirit so as he couldn't get out—a lot of clergymen done it. (559)

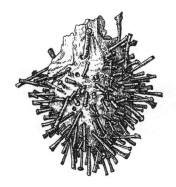

Fig. 7.4. Heart stuck with pins, from Devon, nineteenth century

Jonathan Hardy told H. Colley March a story he had heard when collecting folklore in Dorset in 1897.

> A woman was sure that she was in the power of a witch. Her soap would not lather at the washing. She was advised to nail up a horseshoe (there were special nails for this) and to lay a besom across the threshold, for when the witch came she could not pass over it, and must ask for it to be removed, and so would be detected. Also evil spirits could be kept from coming down a chimney by hanging a bag in it containing salt. The bag must be hung on one of these special nails. (March 1899, 480)

In 1900, Hewett noted a spell used by a white witch "To Frustrate the Power of the Black Witch."

> Take a cast horseshoe, nail it over the front door, chant in monotone the following:

> *So as the fire do melt the wax*
> *And wind blows smoke away*
> *So in the presence of the Lord*
> *The wicked shall decay*
> *Amen.*
>
> (HEWETT 1900, 68)

A cast horseshoe is one that has fallen off a horse, not one made by casting metal. In these cases, it is the nailing that is the operative act, the hammering in of a doctored nail with a ritual that empowers the shoe and the nail to carry out their specified function. The horseshoe must be nailed up with its horns pointing upward, because then bad luck or a witch cannot pass the threshold (Glyde 1872, 50). To set it the other way would result in one's luck running out (Villiers 1923, 92). Here, it is seen as a container or receptacle of luck that operates according to gravity. Roy Palmer notes that in Herefordshire and Worcestershire, when the horseshoe has its points upward, it is connected with the moon, and with its points downward, with the Greek character *omega,* the final letter of that alphabet (Palmer 1992, 109). In 1894, George Day saw a horseshoe nailed to the door of a cow house in Ilford, Essex, and asked the lad there the reason for it. He was told, "To keep the wild horse away" (Day 1894, 77). The belief in the power of the nailed horseshoe remains to this day.

> The famed Lincolnshire wise woman Mary Atkin was the wife of "a most respectable farm bailiff, who did not hold with her goings on, although he dared not check them." A report about her from the late 1850s tells how she nailed horseshoes to a bed as a remedy for the ague. Atkin was offered quinine as a remedy, but after having been given one bottle and using it, she refused a second bottle, saying she "knawed on a soight better cure then yon mucky bitter stuff" [standard English: knew of a much better cure than that mucky bitter stuff]. And with that she took me into his room and to the foot of the old four poster on which he lay. There, in the centre of the foot-board, were nailed three horseshoes, points upward, with a hammer fixed cross-wise upon them. "Thear lad," she said, "when the Old 'Un comes to shaake 'im yon ull fix 'im as fast as t' chu'ch steeaple, he weant nivver pars yon." And when I showed signs of incredulity she added, "Nay, but it's a chawm. Oi teks the mell i'my left hand, and Oi taps they shoes an' Oi saays,
>
> > *'Feyther, Son and Holy Ghoast,*
> > *Naale the divil to this poast.*
> > *Throice I smoites with Holy Crok,*
> > *With this mell Oi throice dew knock,*
> > *One for God*
> > *An' one for Wod,*
> > *An' one for Lok.'"*

Mary Atkin took a mell (hammer) in her left hand and tapped the shoes' nails, at the same time incanting the charm, which invokes "the three holy names," Father, Son and Holy Ghost, to nail the Devil to the post, binding "The Old 'Un" who is deemed responsible for giving the shakes to the ague patient. (Gutch and Peacock 1908, 125)

The devil was pinned down, not to rise. Elworthy records that the saying "That the horseshoe may never be pulled from your threshold!" was one of the good wishes or sentiments" of the eighteenth century (Elworthy 1895, 218).

An account from Knowle Hill, Somerset, in 1894, tells how a young woman was behaving strangely.

Her brother visited a man "who was a real witch" who told him that she had been overlooked by the evil eye of a neighbour. He told the brother to go to a blacksmith and buy a new nail, and not to let the nail out of his hand until he saw the neighbour "make a track"; then he was to get the nail and hammer it into his footprint to "nail down his track." He did so, and the man then developed a limp, and the sister went back to normal. When the man died, a mark was found on the sole of his foot where the track had been nailed. (Elworthy 1895, 84–85)

Perhaps as a countermeasure against this magical practice, boot makers made protective patterns of hobnails on the soles of boots. The most common patterns were the heart, the cross, the quincunx, and the tau cross. It was traditional to display sample hobnail boots in boot makers' shops with these patterns made in polished brass nails (Lambert and Marx 1989, 13).

Blacksmiths and nail makers were the manufacturers of nails in the days before machine factories took over. All over Europe there are ancient traditions connecting blacksmiths with magic. The eighteenth-century blacksmith-farrier at Clun mentioned earlier in this chapter, on page 63, had his book of healing spells for humans. In the early twentieth century, George Kirk was a blacksmith whose forge was at Bourn in Cambridgeshire. He said that his power came from his frog bone. As well as nails and horseshoes bringing protection and luck, "the water used by a blacksmith for cooling his hot iron was believed to be a good cure for many ills. The idea being that the water absorbed strength from the metal" (Parsons 1952, 40). A rite recorded in Derbyshire in the early twentieth century advised giving a spoonful of water in which a hot iron had been cooled to babies shortly after birth. And "blacksmith water" was known to have cured a "bad leg" at Scotter in Lincolnshire (Peacock, Carson, and Burne 1901, 472).

Smithing is one of the crafts that relies on fire—its kindling, feeding, and tending. The mystery of fire is at the heart of making things; various crafts require different fireplaces, ovens, kilns, fuels, and temperatures. Fire is a very important element in the pagan tradition, and the four fire festivals of the year are celebrated to this day. Magical and ritual purity are necessary when lighting one. One of Herrick's charms reminds us of this.

> *Wash your hands, or else the fire*
> *Will not teend to your desire;*
> *Unwasht hands, ye Maidens, know,*
> *Dead the fire, though ye blow.*
>   (HERRICK [1648] 1902, 250)

In practical terms, if we do things in the wrong way, we will not get results.

Fig. 7.5. Cross as basis of blacksmith-made door handle, at Hereford

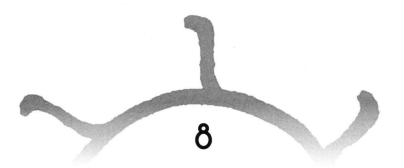

8

Witchcraft, Amulets, and Mascots

Amulets properly should be empowered by magic, so they are an integral part of operative witchcraft. The ceremonies for making or taking amulets, along with their ritual empowerment, are the subject of many writings. The distinction between a magical amulet and a lucky charm is not easy to determine, and the manufacture of such items on an industrial scale from the nineteenth century further blurs the distinction. In 1908, it was written:

Amongst the educated classes, while protection from the evil eye and from witchcraft is now rarely sought, "pocket pieces" have persisted "for luck" and for the prevention and cure of rheumatism and certain other aliments, and these classes have also been the principal field for the huge sale of rheumatism rings, "electropathic" belts, and other objects, which appeal to the charm instinct, while professing to have a scientific reason for their success. The revival and survival of amulets have been, however, mainly among bridge-players, actors, sportsmen, motorists, gamblers, burglars, and others engaged in risky occupations. (Wright and Lovett 1908, 288)

Fig. 8.1. Charles Pennick's skull gambling mascot

The words *mascot* and *lucky charm* were interchangeable in the early part of the twentieth century. The use of lucky mascots on cars, such as the Rolls Royce "Spirit of Ecstacy," led to mascots being associated with commercial emblems and logos, thereby largely losing their lucky or magical connotations. Mascots still exist in sports, however, where they retain some of the earlier meaning. Numerous mascots or lucky charms called "pocket pieces" were manufactured for these specialist markets. For example, in the United States in 1918, it was reported that among commercial travelers, "A lucky pocket-piece twirled in the left hand is supposed to insure [*sic*] an order where the customer is undecided" (Cielo 1918, 140). The present author possesses a small ivory skull wearing a top hat that belonged to his paternal grandfather, who was a professional musician and gambler.

In 1851 the Northamptonshire folklorist Thomas Sternberg wrote:

Certain charms and amulets were (and still are) resorted to in order to procure immunity from the arts of the witch. Among the most common of these was the "lucky bone." . . . The *lucky-bone*, as its name indicates, is worn about the person to produce good-luck; and it is also reckoned an excellent protection against witchcraft. It is a bone taken from the head of a sheep, and its form, which is that of the T cross, may have, perhaps, originated the peculiar sanctity in which it is held. (150, 154)

This T cross, or tau cross, which is in the shape of the character *T* when used in writing, is named after the Greek name for that letter. An alternative name for this glyph is the gibbet cross (Whittick 1971, 224). It is associated with Saint Anthony of Egypt, who is depicted with a tau cross as a staff, along with his sacred pig and bell. Saint Anthony lived in ancient tombs and conjured up the ancient Egyptian gods to conduct a spiritual struggle with them, the theme of the "Temptation of Saint Anthony" in various works of art. Thus, the tau cross is a magical protection against powerful hostile spiritual forces that one has called up.

SIGILS ASSOCIATED WITH WITCHCRAFT

From the late Middle Ages, various magical books circulated among literate magicians, cunning men, and witches. These included the classical grimoires, lost or undiscovered English books like *The Devil's Plantation* and *The Secret Granary*. There are also those from German-speaking lands, such as *Jerauchia* and *Stamphoras* (Bächtold-Stäubli, 1942, vol. VI, 1001) and the widely circulated *Romanus-Büchlein*, which, in the United States was reworked by Georg Hohmann and eventually translated into English as *The Long Hidden Friend*. In addition to incantations, medical recipes, and magical formulae, these published works contained sigils and signs that undoubtedly were part of the repertoire of craftspeople. Pattern books too were a means of transmission. From these may be derived the warding signs that were scratched onto surfaces and chalked onto doors and window frames, such as the Ipswich warding sign, Old Scratch's gate, and the apotropaic *X* with four dots.

Fig. 8.2. Ipswich warding sign

Fig. 8.3. Apotropaic *X* with four dots

Fig. 8.4. Double cross sigil on a nineteenth-century
horse-drawn wagon, from Wales

The pentagram, used by many today as an emblem of paganism, has often been associated with historical witchcraft, both as a sigil drawn by witches in their rituals and as an apotropaic sign against them. Since the emergence into the public of pagan witchcraft, it has become a prime symbol of the religion. The first public witchcraft organization, the Witchcraft Research Association, founded in 1964, called its newsletter *Pentagram*. This sigil has many names: pentacle, pantacle, pentangle, pentagramma, Solomon's seal, the flaming star, the rempham, and the druid's foot (German *Drudenfuss*).

The five-pointed star drawn by a single line is important in sacred geometry because the fivefold division of the circle is the starting point for the geometric proposition known as the golden section or golden cut. This is a proportion that exists between two measurable quantities of any sort when the ratio between the larger one and smaller one is equal to the ratio between the sum of the two and the larger one. Geometrically it is the ratio in the pentagram between the side of the inner pentagon and its extension into the pentagram, a ratio of 1:1.618, mathematically symbolized by the Greek glyph Φ. In any increasing progression or series of terms with Φ as the ratio between two successive terms, each term is equal to the sum of the two preceding ones. Because of its unique properties, which include displaying the geometric

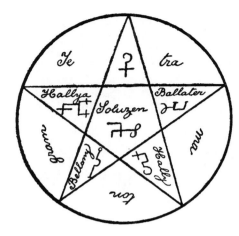

Fig. 8.5. Operative witchcraft pentagram talisman

principle underlying the growth of living things, it is a sigil of life and the power of unlimited extension (Pennick 1980, 25–28; 2005b, 64–65). In his exhaustive compilation of ancient glyphs and sigils, *Decorative Patterns of the Ancient World,* Sir Flinders Petrie illustrated ancient pentagrams from Cappadocia, Lombardy, and Cuma, dated before the year 700 CE (Petrie [1930] 1990, XLVIII, B9, B23, B44). Medieval and later folk magic ascribed to the pentagram a protective power. In English folk tradition, it appears as a threshold glyph in the traditional English counting song called "The Twelve Apostles."

> *Four for the Gospel makers,*
> *Five for the symbol at your door.*
> *Six for the six proud walkers . . .*

In 1893 the pioneer folk song collectors Lucy Broadwood and J. A. Fuller Maitland explained that this "five for the symbol" signifies the pentagram (Broadwood and Maitland 1893, 154–59). Historically it was a banishing sign. For example, in his tale of Dr. Faustus, *Faust,* Goethe tells how the evil spirit Mephistopheles could enter Faust's place despite the "druid's foot" traced on the threshold. Mephistopheles gains entry because the Drudenfuss at the entrance has not been drawn properly: the lines are not as perfect as they ought to be; the outer angle is incomplete. Only by making a perfect pentagram, a continuous line, was it deemed effective. Various rituals of the pentagram derived from the teachings of the Hermetic Order of the Golden Dawn and the early writings of Rudolf Steiner (Steiner, unpublished typescript in the Alexander von Bernus library). In his *Magick in Theory and Practice,* Aleister Crowley describes the lesser and greater rituals of the pentagram (Crowley 1991, 379–82).

The six-pointed star, now associated almost exclusively with Judaism, did not assume that narrow meaning until the late nineteenth century, when Zionism arose as a Jewish political movement. Jews or those suspected of being Jews were forced to wear the sigil by the German National Socialists, and after the defeat of Nazi Germany, in 1947 it was adopted as the emblem of the state of Israel. But before that, the hexagram had a long history in pagan, Christian, Masonic, and magical contexts. The hexagram is composed of two overlapping equilateral triangles. Symbolically, it signifies the union of the four elements: fire, air, water, earth. The upright triangle also signifies the male energy and the

Fig. 8.6. English talismans, from the Nigel Pennick collection

downward-pointing triangle, the female. Combined, the hexagram is the unity of opposites, which is a symbol of the cosmos or God, unifying the world above and the world below. The Hebrew name for this sign is Magen David, meaning the Shield of King David, which indicates its apotropaic and magical uses in warding off harmful influences. Like the pentagram, it has ritual ways of using it, as described by Crowley in the lesser and greater rituals of the hexagram (Crowley 1991, 382–87).

In antiquity the cross was largely identified with the sun until it was adopted widely as a Christian emblem. Because Jesus of Nazareth was crucified, it became the central emblem of the religion, though the connection between a wooden cross as a form of execution and the solar cross is fortuitous. The incorporation of a large body of pagan solar lore into Christian symbology meant that the previous solar uses and meanings of the cross were also appropriated. But during a long period, the cross did not have the preeminence that it later attained as an almost exclusively Christian glyph. That happened from the ninth century onward (Whittick 1971, 224–25). Before that, the swastika, a stylized fish, the grapevine, the sixfold Chi-Rho, and the Greek letters *alpha* and *omega* were all emblematic of the Christian faith and its doctrines. The Chi-Rho, a monogram composed of the Greek characters *chi* ($X = Ch/K$) and the Roman equivalent *rho* ($P = R$), was a major contender as the primal Christian glyph before the cross gained universal acceptance.

Because crosses can be drawn with equal or unequal arms, the two main sects of Christianity, Eastern Greek Orthodox and Western Roman Catholicism, have two different-shaped crosses associated with

Fig. 8.7. Hexagram on a demonic talisman, from the early nineteenth century

them. The Orthodox cross is equilateral and is called the Greek Cross because of its ecclesiastical use. The cross with one long arm is called the Latin Cross. The Protestant churches took over the latter form from their Catholic antecedents. The Greek cross, however, is the one always used to empower prayers and talismans.

In brewing and baking, the sigil known as "two hearts and a criss-cross" was traditionally used to protect the mash or dough. It is composed of two hearts with a cross between them. In 1895, Frederick Thomas Elworthy noted that an old man in Somerset had told him that in brewing, before the mash was covered up to ferment, the sigil was drawn to ward off the pixies (Elworthy 1895, 287). Robert Herrick, in his *Hesperides,* alludes to this in a *charme.*

> *This I'll tell ye by the way,*
> *Maidens, when ye leavens lay,*
> *Crosse your dow [dough], and your dispatch*
> *Will be better for your batch.*
>
> ([1648] 1902, 298)

In addition to invoking the intrinsic magical powers of the cross and the hearts, bakers used a pin to prick the emblem into biscuits, the "pricking" mentioned in the nursery rhyme "Pat-a-Cake, Pat-a-Cake, Baker's Man."

Fig. 8.8. Apotropaic sigil on a witch post, seventeenth century, in Rydale, Yorkshire

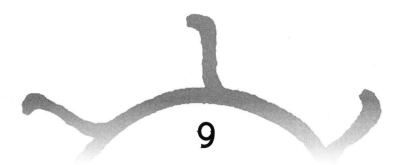

9

Binding Magic and the Art of Fascination, or the Evil Eye

To bind the dogs that they cannot bark
To bind the birds that they cannot fly.
To bind the ground, so that nothing shall bring forth fruit,
   nor flourish in it,
Also that nothing can be built upon it, rendering it gast.

One of the most feared powers of the witch was the "evil eye," a magical and occult binding. Binding magic is one of the classical forms of magic. It was prevalent in the Northern Tradition, being one of the arts of the rune-master. In later times, once the elder faith had been driven down, magicians and witches were said to practice binding magic on merchants, so they could not buy or sell; ships, so they could not sail; mills, so they would not work; wells and reservoirs, so that water could not be drawn from them; and the ground, so that nothing could grow and be fruitful there and neither could any building be erected there. Clearly, blaming witches for binding people, things, and places was an easy way of finding a reason why something did not work. It is more difficult to analyze a problem and find a solution to it. But the concept of things going wrong randomly was not within the remit of traditional thinking.

Fig. 9.1. Proprietary lucky charm sold by Gamages in London in 1908

The mathematical concept of randomness and Heisenberg's uncertainty principle had not yet been discovered and disseminated. Even bad luck was seen as emanating from the activities of evil spirits.

In any case, witches and magicians have always attempted to alter and shape the way things are, whether they be envisaged as the "Web of Wyrd" or the uncertainty principle. In his influential magical book of 1801, *The Magus, or Celestial Intelligencer,* Francis Barrett wrote, "Now how is it that these kinds of bindings are made and brought to pass, we must know. They are thus done: by sorceries, collyries, unguents, potions, binding to and hanging up of talismans, by charms, incantations, strong imaginations, affections, passions, images, characters, enchantments, imprecations, lights, and by sounds, numbers, words, names, invocations, swearings, conjurations, consecrations, and the like" (Barrett [1801] 2007, 50).

A person magically bound to do something (as in the expression "she is bound to die") is said to be spellbound. The magical binding of someone's spirit into a bottle or another sealed container, thereby stealing their soul, makes them dispirited. We say that someone has "lost his spirit" or that someone "drove his or her spirit away." Conjurations of living peoples' spirits and trapping them are a universal theme in European witchcraft, American hoodoo, and West Indian Obeah. The bottle is the most common instrument of this art in all three traditions. In Cambridgeshire cunning men bound the spirits of witches into bottles in that way. Similarly, in the West Indies, Myal men attempted to prevent Obeah men from catching the shadows of the deceased at funerals and trapping them in bottles (Banbury 1895, 151; Emerick 1916b, 39). Some love magic is couched in binding spells, and most recorded ones are for men over women. The probable reason for this is the greater likelihood of men being literate in the past and the strong tradition of male magicians in the classical-styled current milieu. A seventeenth-century charm book has three alternative charms for binding women.

1. "How to make a woman follow thee" tells the practitioner to "write your name and the name of the maid in anny leafe with the blood of a white henn and touch her with it and shee shall follow thee."

2. Another way: take the blood of a bat and write in thy hand with it g: h; b; m + 2: b : d: and then touch her therewith. The cross shown here is the banishing sign of a cross with four dots, one in each angle of the cross.

3. Write in an apple these three names: AATNELL: LOLIELL: CLOTIELL and after say, "I conjure thee apple by these three names that what woman so ever eats of thee she may soe Remaine in my love that she take no rest + Donec voluntatem me aservile." (Gaster 1910, 376)

Of the toad-bone ritual (see "The Toad-Bone Ritual," page 113), which is usually associated with horsemanry, the Lincolnshire folklorist Mabel Peacock noted that "the commonest motive for the use of such a charm is, as might be expected, the desire to secure an illegitimate hold on the affections of a woman against her inclinations" (Peacock 1901a, 169).

The functioning of the evil eye clearly fascinated those who feared witchcraft. The witch hunters' bible, *Malleus Malificarum,* states that "there are witches who can bewitch their judges by a mere look or glance from their eyes" (Kramer and Sprenger 1971, 139). The idea that a person wishing ill of someone through envy or spite can cast an evil glance that affects the object of the glance is well known from ancient Hebrew mythology, and Christian writers used biblical precedence for their attacks on magic. The intimately connected theory of fascination and hypnosis, confused in witchcraft as also belonging to the evil eye, has a long history. It appears in the English edition of Heinrich Cornelius Agrippa's *Three Books of Occult Philosophy,* from 1651. In chapter L, titled, "Of Fascination, and the Art Thereof," Agrippa writes:

The instrument of fascination is the spirit, namely, a certain pure, lucid, subtle vapour, generated of the purer blood, by the heat of the heart. This does always send forth through the eyes, rays like unto itself; those rays being sent forth, do carry with them a spiritual vapour, and that vapour a blood, as it appears in bleary, and red eyes, whose rays being sent forth to the eyes of him that is opposite, and looks upon them, carries the vapour of the corrupt blood, together with itself, by contagion of which, it does infect the eyes of the beholder with like disease. So the eye being opened, and intent upon anyone with a strong imagination, does dart its beams, which are the vehicle of the spirit into the eyes of him that is opposite to him, which tender spirit strikes the eyes of him that is bewitched, being stirred up from the heart of him that strikes, and possesses the breast of him that is stricken, wounds his heart, and infects his spirit. Whence *Apuleius* saith, your eyes sliding down through my eyes, into my inward breast, stirs up the most vehement burning in my marrow.

Know therefore that men are then most bewitched, when with often beholding they direct the edge of their sight to the edge of their sight of those that bewitch them, and when their eyes are reciprocally intent one on the other, and when rays are joined to rays, and lights to lights, for then the spirit of the one is joined with the spirit of the other, and fixes its sparks: so are strong ligations made, and so most vehement loves are inflamed with only the rays of the eyes, even with a sudden looking on, as if it were with a dart, or stroke penetrating the whole body, whence the spirit, and amorous blood being thus wounded, are carried forth upon the lover, and enchanter, no otherwise than the blood, and spirit of the vengeance of him that is slain, are upon him that slays him. . . . So great is the power of fascination, especially when the vapours of the eyes are subservient to the affection. Therefore witches use collyries, ointments, alligations, and such like, to affect, and corroborate the spirit this or that manner. To procure love, they use venereal collyries, as hyppomenes, the blood of doves, or sparrows, and such like. To induce fear, they use martial collyries, as of the eyes of wolves, the civet cat, and the like. To procure misery or sickness, they use Saturnine, and so of the rest [spelling modernized].

In *The Magus, or Celestial Intelligencer,* Barrett also wrote a section titled "On the Art of Fascination, or Binding by the Look or Sight," clearly derived from the writings of Agrippa.

We call fascination a binding, because it is effected by a look, glance, or observation, in which we take possession of the spirit, and overpower the same, of those we mean to fascinate or suspend; for it comes through the eyes, and the instrument by which we fascinate or bind is a certain, pure, lucid, subtle spirit, generated out of the ferment of the purer blood by the heat of the heart, and the firm, determined, and ardent will of the soul which directs it to the object previously disposed to be fascinated. This doth always send forth by the eyes rays or beams, carrying with them a pure subtil

spirit or vapour into the eye or blood of him or her that is opposite. So the eye, being opened and intent upon any one with a strong
imagination doth dart its beams, which are the vehicle of the spirit,
into whatever will affect or bind, which spirit striking the eye of
them that are fascinated, being stirred up in the heart and soul of
him that sends them forth, and possessing the breast of them who
are struck, wounds their hearts, infects their spirits, and overpowers
them. Know, likewise, that in witches, those are most bewitched,
who, with often looking, direct the edge of the sight to the edge of
the sight of those who bewitch or fascinate them; whence arose the
saying of "Evil eyes, &c. . . ." ([1801] 2007, 53–54)

The direct employment of the power of compulsion through fascination is now called by another name—hypnosis. The ability to hyp-
notize was used by some cunning men to compel others. This power
is remembered in two words in current usage. When compulsion was
used to stop someone from talking, they were *tongue-tied;* when it was
used to stop them from thinking clearly, they were *spellbound.* The
power of compulsion is told of Master Fidkin of Arley, Herefordshire,
who put people under a spell that made them wander the village all
night (Palmer 1992, 154). Old Winter of Ipswich was another cunning man who compelled. Once he caught a man stealing wood from
a woodpile and compelled him to carry the load on his back, walking
in circles with it until he collapsed. Similarly, the wizard Dr. Coates
of Hereford had the power of compulsion; it was said, "Once when a
man got into his garden to steal the cabbages, he made him sit upon
a cabbage till morning; I know it was a cold night" ("Nonagenarian,"
Hereford Times, April 15, 1876). The power of compulsion, using
the evil eye, is a direct application of the power that is demonstrable.
"Overlooking" by the evil eye associated with witches was an indirect
claim that someone must have cursed the person or animal in this
way. The person or animal was said to be "overlooked" or "blinked"
by "eye-biting witches," and it was then necessary to take remedial
action against the action.

Fig. 9.2. The "wizard's eye," a Victorian image of the evil eye

In his monograph on the subject, *The Evil Eye,* Frederick Thomas Elworthy wrote:

> Here in Somerset, the pig is taken ill and dies—"he was overlooked."
> A murrain afflicts a farmer's cattle; he goes off secretly to the "white
> witch," that is the old witch-finder, to ascertain who has "overlooked
> his things" and to learn the best antidote, "cause they there farri-
> ers can't do no good." A child is ill and pining away; the mother
> loses all heart; she is sure the child is overlooked and "is safe to die."
> Often she gives up not only hope but all effort to save the child; the
> consequent neglect of course hastens the expected result, and then
> it is: "Oh! I know'd very well he would'n never get no better." "Tidn
> no good vor to strive vor to go agin it." This is no fancy, or isolated
> case, but here in the last decade of the nineteenth century one of the
> commonest of everyday facts. (1895, 3–4)

Elworthy also wrote, "Domestic animals, such as horses, camels, cows, have always been thought in special danger. In the Scotch Highlands if a stranger looks admiringly on a cow the people still believe she will waste away from the evil eye, and they offer him some of her milk to drink, in the belief that by so doing the spell will be broken and the consequences averted" (Elworthy 9, quoting *Notes & Queries*, I, vi, 409). Elworthy notes that in England of all animals it is the pig most often overlooked (Elworthy 1895, 11). It was customary in some places to keep a goat among horses and cows to keep them safe. There are recorded examples from the nineteenth and twentieth centuries from mews and livery stables in London, horse tram (streetcar) stables in Sheffield, and farms in Berkshire. One explanation is that goats keep calm in fire and can be used to lead the horses from a burning stable; another is that the goat wards off the evil eye from the other livestock (Foster 1917, 451; Gardner 1933, 218).

Fig. 9.3. Mummified cat found in a barn at Newport, Essex, used as an apotropaic charm against fire

In the latter part of the nineteenth century, artists and craftsmen of the Aesthetic movement adopted the peacock and the sunflower as favorite subjects for decorative art. In the 1990s, a visitor to my house recoiled in horror when he saw a peacock feather in an Arts and Crafts vase standing on a shelf. He tried to explain why I ought not to have it but was loath to admit that his terror came from an old superstition concerning the evil eye. It appeared that he felt the eye of the peacock feather bewitching him and attempted to get it removed. I have not been able to find any documented instances of witches using peacock feathers. Elworthy noted in 1895, at the time when peacock feathers were fashionable in artistic circles, that although in Roman paganism the peacock had been considered protective against evil because it was the sacred bird of the goddess Juno, in the nineteenth century the eyed feather was considered abominable (Elworthy 1895, 119–20). As a correspondent to *Notes & Queries* in 1893 recounted, "Some eight or ten years ago a gentleman well known to me went to call on an intimate friend of his. Unfortunately for him, he had the eye of a peacock's

Fig. 9.4. Peacock patterning to ward off the evil eye,
on pargetting at Dunmow, Essex

feather in his hat. When the lady of the house saw it, she snatched it from him and threw it out of the hall-door, rating him as if he had been guilty of some great moral offence" (*Notes & Queries* s8, iv, 521, December 1893).

Because the toad is deemed to be an evil animal connected with black witchcraft, unbewitching techniques include killing toads cruelly. In 1920s Jersey, a butcher who suffered illnesses and difficulties with his business and clearly put it down to overlooking was told how "to set things right again." He imprisoned a toad in a tin box in the house and allowed it to starve to death (Marett and Carey 1927, 180). Another means of unbewitching is to kill a toad, cut out its breastbone, and throw the remains of the toad into water. Then the breastbone is burned (Bales 1939, 70). In 1801, Barrett wrote, "If a nail, dart, knife or sword, or any other iron instrument be thrust into the heart of a horse, it will bind and withhold the spirit of a witch, and conjoin it with the mummial spirit of the horse, whereby they may be burnt in the fire together, and by that the witch is tormented, as by a string or burning" (Barrett [1801] 2007, 177). This principle was used in practice, as hearts stuck with pins or nails have been and are found concealed in chimneys of old houses. There were recognized remedies against the evil eye. Many amulets and talismans are accorded to power of warding it off. These have been detailed in the previous chapter.

In *The Evil Eye,* Elworthy recorded an incident recounted to him in a letter from Mr. J. L. W. Page on October 20, 1890: "The other day I was at the Court House, East Quantoxhead, and was shown in the chimney of a now disused kitchen—suspended—a sheep's heart stuck full of pins. I think Captain L. told me that this was done by persons who thought themselves 'overlooked' or 'ill wished'; also to prevent the descent of witches down the chimney" (Elworthy 1895, 55). Elworthy cites another case in Devon in which a woman moved out of her house "and a neighbour, searching about the house found, in the chimney as usual, onions stuck thickly with pins." There was also an image of a penis into which was stuck a large number of pins. He added, "The people who crowded to see these things had no doubt whatsoever as to their being intended for a certain man who kept a little shop near, and had been known as a visitor to this woman, who thus vented her spite upon him" (Elworthy 1895, 55, n. 80).

In 1900, Sarah Hewett recorded a talismanic "Charm for Protection from Enemies" that employed the power of iron and Mars to counteract the power of the evil eye (Hewett 1900, 73–74). Another remedy for being overlooked was to use silver water. Edward Lovett records the remedy used by a Scottish wise man or wizard for cattle that were not thriving and said to have been blinked. Water was brought from a brook or creek over which living and dead had passed—one that crossed a road leading to a churchyard. Then silver was put in the water, a special coin carried by the wise man. It was then ladled out over the sick cow. The cow got the rest of the water to drink, and the wizard was given whiskey (Lovett, Barry, Frazer, and Webb 1905, 335).

Anything reflective, especially something made from silver or quicksilver, is a means of warding off the evil eye. Witch balls are lustrous glass spheres, usually blue or green, but occasionally made from clear greenish glass, in which case they are sometimes called "fishing floats." Proper witch balls were made by silvering the inside of a blown-glass sphere with a chemical mixture containing quicksilver. A witch ball should be hung in a window, and people who live in Victorian or Edwardian houses without leaded glass above the front door sometimes hang one there.

Fig. 9.5. A witch ball

Since the 1980s, with a renewed interest in Chinese feng shui, octagonal *bagua* geomantic mirrors have in some cases taken the place of witch balls, with the identical function of warding off energies harmful to the inhabitants of the house on which the mirror is placed (Lip 1979, 112). The advantage of a witch ball over a bagua mirror is that the witch ball, being spherical, deflects harmful influences coming from any angle, whereas a bagua mirror, being flat or only slightly dished, deflects only that which is directly in front of it.

The expression "eat your heart out" is linked to the heart–evil eye complex. In his 1888 *Glossary of Words Used in the Neighbourhood of Sheffield,* Sidney Oldall Addy wrote, "When a man has deeply coveted but failed to obtain an animal, such as a cow or a horse, he is sometimes said to have 'heart-eaten' it. A heart-eaten being, it is said, will not prosper. A farmer near Bradfield wished to purchase a cow from a neighbor, but did not succeed in doing so. Shortly afterward the owner of the cow told him that she had 'picked' her calf. 'Well I didn't heart-eat her,' the farmer said" (Addy 1888, xxii).

Another aspect of compulsion, of which fear of the consequences plays a large part, is the custom of only speaking of some event after the death of the subject of the story. This applies especially in the case of magical acts and performances. A story that typifies the tradition comes from Longstanton in the Hundred of Northstow in Cambridgeshire. Toward the end of the nineteenth century at Longstanton, Bet Cross was the local woman reputed to be a witch. She was said to have played tricks on people, including stopping horses that were going past her garden. After she died, someone suddenly recalled seeing her flying on a hardle (hurdle). The person who told the tale claimed that the airborne Cross had seen him and warned him, "You can tell on it when you think on it." This gave rise to a Longstanton adage, "You can tell on it when you think on it, and you know when that'll be" (M.G.C.H. 1936, 507; Porter 1969, 172).

10

The Powers of Operative Witchcraft

The animals gather together
Or else are put to flight
By certain fumes the horses stop
And day turns into night

THE HORSE WITCH

Accounts of witches in England in the nineteenth and early twentieth centuries tell of their stopping horses and carts at a distance and refusing to let them move until rewarded in some way. At Longstanton in Cambridgeshire, the reputed witch Bet Cross is said to have stopped horses outside her garden, and horses were stopped by witches in the witchcraft centers of Horseheath Histon and Wisbech (M.G.C.H. 1936, 507; Parsons 1915, 41; Porter 1969, 57). A Herefordshire account of horse stopping was told to the Herefordshire folklorist Ella Mary Leather by an inmate of the workhouse at Ross who remembered "going over Whitney bridge . . . when behind the cart he was driving came a waggoner with three horses, and had no money to pay toll. He defied the old woman at the toll house, and would have driven past her, but she witched the horses so that they would not move" (Leather 1912, 55).

Another typical example of how a horse could be stopped comes from a story from Upwood, Huntingdonshire, related in 1927. A man was bringing home a load of wheat and his wagon stopped unexpectedly, and the horses refused to move any farther. After a while, an old woman came from her cottage nearby, picked up a straw from the road, and then the horses proceeded without difficulty (Tebbutt 1984, 84–85). It is clear that the straw was doused in a jading substance perhaps as an experiment. Clearly, it appeared to be a form of magic to anyone not in the know; hence, the story that the woman was a witch. The suddenness with which horses could be made to stop was described by the horsewoman Ida Sadler as stopped "as if they were shot" (Sadler 1962, 15).

An ability to make a horse stop and stand motionless until bidden to go again was an essential skill in a society that relied on real horsepower. A drinking toast from the Horseman's Grip and Word society in Scotland praises this ability.

> *Here's to the yoke that our forefathers broke,*
> *And here's to the plough that was hidden.*
> *Here's to the horse that can pull*
> *And stand like a stone when bidden.*
> (RENNIE ET AL. 2009, 121)

This ability was not usually connected with the evil eye, for it was a practical ability of men who worked with horses who had been taught it as part of their membership in the Society of the Horseman's Word, the Whisper, or the Confraternity of the Plough. Horses, having evolved as grazing animals with no defense against predators except speed, are extremely sensitive animals. They have senses of hearing and smell far superior to that of humans and a high level of awareness and sensitivity to their surroundings. These hypersensitive characteristics were used by those in the know to control horses. This is why "horses are thought to be peculiarly susceptible to witchcraft" (Leather 1912, 23).

The materia magica for drawing (calling) horses to one, or for taming unruly or vicious horses, are various oils that play on a horse's refined sense of smell. Aromatic oils that attract horses are known as drawing oils. One concoction favored in East Anglia is a particular mixture of the oils of cinnamon, fennel, oregano, and rosemary. The user dabs some drawing oil on his or her forehead and stands upwind of the horse to attract it. Aniseed and crushed hemp seed also draw horses to the person carrying them. Those who control horses in this way carry a walking stick that has a notch or small cavity just above the ferrule, where drawing oil is hidden on a piece of cotton wool (Evans 1971, 210). A woman who can attract horses in this way or control other animals and people by similar methods is an old biddie, for it is she who bids them to do her will.

Animals that comply are always rewarded with a stroke, a kind word, and a "sweetener," something sweet, such as sugar, gingerbread, and other sweet-scented cakes. These treats are given at the same time as other actions are performed—gestures and movements and sounds—that condition the horse to behave in a particular way. This is the principle of all animal training, long before Pavlov's experiments on salivating dogs gave it a scientific name, the conditioned reflex. The connection between the horse and the horseman is very close. "It was at one time the custom to tell cart horses of the death of their master," Leather noted in Herefordshire in 1912 (Leather 1912, 23).

Stopping horses also uses substances with a certain kind of strong smell—evil-smelling substances called jading materials. Put in front of a horse, these substances will make it stop and refuse to move until they are taken away. One recipe for horse stopping is to use the dried and powdered liver of a rabbit or stoat mixed with dragon's blood, a natural resin (Evans 1971, 208). Another is to use a pounded mixture of rue, feverfew, and hemlock, rubbed on the horse's nose. An ointment made by boiling cuckoo flowers and bay leaves, smeared on the stable door, keeps the horses in (Porter 1969, 93–94).

Another important material in the materia magica of horsemanry is the pad of fibrous material that lies beneath the tongue of the fetal foal. It is taken out at birth and can be combined with drawing substances

(Evans 1971, 214). This pad is known as the meld in Cambridgeshire; in Norfolk and Suffolk, it is called the milt, milch, or melt.

An oil is prepared from the meld, which is steamed to extract an oil that is mixed with oil of rhodium and attar of roses, and then kept in a bottle. The horseman puts drops of this oil on his glove when feeding or handling stallions to keep them docile (John Thorn, personal communication; Evans 1971, 214–15; Bayliss 1997, 13). The meld is also dried in an oven until it hardens, then it is pounded to powder, mixed with olive oil, and baked. The resulting material is put in a muslin bag and kept under the horseman's right armpit. There, it absorbs sweat with the horseman's personal odor, which is used to teach the horse the horseman's individual smell. In the past, there are records of people identifying other people by their smell, as recorded in the *Sturbridge Initiation* at the fair once held at Barnwell near Cambridge.

> *Over thy head I ring this bell,*
> *Because thou art an infidel.*
> *And I know thee by thy smell.*
> (HONE 1828, VOL. 2, 1,548)

Newmarket has been a major center of horse racing for centuries. The lore and techniques of horsemanry have, of course, always been strong there. One magical technique recorded from the grooms at Newmarket involves a frog-bone ritual: "Grooms catch a frog and keep it in a bottle or tin until nothing but the bones remain. At New Moon they draw these up stream in running water; one of the bones which floats is kept as a charm in the pocket or hung round the neck. This gives the man the power to control any horse, however vicious it may be" (Burn 1914, 363–64). The V-shaped piece of hornlike material on the underside of a horse's hoof is also called the frog. The "full brace" of horn buttons of the traditional Suffolk horseman's suit have this V facing downward, with seven colored points above it to signify the seven nails of the horseshoe. They also signify the seven stars, the constellation known as the Plough, referred to in the horseman's toast on page 99, "the plough that was hidden" (Tony Harvey, personal communication).

Men and women who worked with horses and knew the tricks of the trade trained their horses to perform certain actions that were not strictly necessary for their work. During the era when witchcraft was a punishable offense, people who showed off their skills with horses ran the risk of prosecution and capital punishment. In 1664 in Renfrewshire, a lad was arrested on a charge of witchcraft because "for a halfpenny he would make a horse stand still in the plough, at the word of command by turning himself widdershins or contrary to the course of the sun" (Davidson 1956, 71). We can recognize this effect of the word and a particular action on horses as a conditioned reflex that the horses had been trained to do. To those who were not in on the secret, this was supernatural, a performance that only someone in league with the devil could possibly attempt.

An example of this was recorded by Arthur Randall in his book *Sixty Years a Fenman*. When he was working on a farm near King's Lynn, Norfolk, in 1911, a horseman once asked him, "Have you ever seen the Devil, bor?" Shocked, Randall answered that he had not and hoped he never would. Then the horseman said, "Well I have, many a time, and what's more, I'll show you something." Then he demonstrated his power. He thrust a two-pronged fork into a dunghill, and the horse was harnessed up to it. The horse was told to pull, but however hard it pulled, it was unable to pull the fork out of the dunghill. Then the horseman released it, and it could. After demonstrating his powers, the horseman warned the young Randall, "Don't you tell nobody what you've just seen, bor" (Randall 1966, 109–10).

The secret knowledge of horse training was kept among those who were members of the rural fraternities and those who had found out how to do it by other means. There was no theory, only the practice of horsemanry, so in all probability even those who could control horses could not explain how it was done, even if they were not bound under oath and pain of death never to reveal the secret to an outsider. In 1962, Sadler wrote a short memoir on her fifty years working with horses with two anecdotes that show this training in action. Sadler tells how her grandfather, who was a "great horseman," was in a Suffolk pub and a man there bet him a gallon of beer that he could not get his horses out of the stable with their halters off and drive them around in front of the pub. "He had four Suffolk horses—called them out of the stable—put two in the double-breasted waggon shafts and two on the tree (that's in front of the other two). He got in the waggon and drove them to the front of the pub and had the gallon of beer" (Sadler 1962, 15). Also, she once had a young mare on a set of harrows and was leading her as it was a windy day. "Suddenly, she [the horse] gave a jump and somehow the snop on the lead came undone, and away she went full gallop around a seven-acre field, back to me, turned a circle, and stopped right beside her" (Sadler 1962, 15).

FAMILIAR SPIRITS

She said she had a spirit in the likeness of a yellow dun cat.
(WITCH'S "CONFESSION," GIFFORD 1607)

The laws against witches and conjuration state, "These witches have ordinarily a familiar or spirit, which appeareth to them: sometime in one shape, sometime in another, as in the shape of a man, woman, boy, dogge, catte, foale, fowl, hare, rat, toad, etc." (Ashton 1896, 159). One of the duties ascribed to the familiar by the witchfinders was to act as a messenger between the devil and the witch, keeping her informed of the place of the next convent of the witches with their master. The time was already known: after midnight on Friday was the Sabbat. Women were sometimes accused by witchfinders during the witch hunts of transmogrifying into animals themselves, confusing the issue about familiars. The belief in witch transmogrification continued long after the moral panic about witchcraft, into the twentieth century. In 1901, Mabel Peacock wrote of Lincolnshire "people suspected of 'knowing more than they should,'" stating that "one of these students of unholy lore could, according to belief, assume the shape of a dog or toad at will, when bent on injuring his neighbour's cattle. As a dog he was supposed to worry oxen and sheep, while under the form of a toad, he poisoned the feeding-trough of the pigs" (Peacock 1901a, 172; 1901b, 510).

Familiar or pet names were often brought out as evidence at trials of those accused of witchcraft. Although household animals, and many farm animals, were given their own names, the witch hunters saw in certain of them, especially the more unusual ones, some nefarious intentions. The recorded ones have a notable variety, for they contain some names documented nowhere else, also the names of spirits and deities: Elimanzer, Tom Twit, Vinegar Tom, Thomas a Fearie, Makeshift, Hob, Holt, Hell-Blaw, Bonnie, Brauny, Great Browning, Little Browning, Jarmara, Jesus, Jupiter, Venus, Rutterkin, Robin Goodfellow, Lunch, Newes, Little Rodin, Griezzell Greedigut, Sackin, Sacke-and-Sugar, Spirit, Son of Art, Piggin, Peck in the Crown, Pyewackett, Lierd, Lightfoot, Pluck, Puppet, Blue Cap, Red Cap, Ball, Bid, Tib, Jill, Will, Willet, William, and Walliman (Rosen 1991, 382; Wilby 2000, 288, 296; Palmer 2004, 147).

In 1607, George Gifford reported that a woman accused of witchcraft had confessed that she had three spirits: one, called Lightfoot, was like a cat, another, called Lunch, like a toad, and the third, like a weasel, she called Makeshift. Lunch, the toad, "would plague men in their bodies" (Gifford 1607; Hutchinson 1966, 226). During the English Civil War, Parliamentarians asserted that Boy, the white poodle dog belonging to Prince Rupert, was not a real dog but rather a familiar spirit. The German dog accompanied him everywhere, even under fire on the battlefield, and seemed to be invulnerable. Only at Marston Moor, the site of the Royalists' decisive defeat, was the dog hit by a bullet, from which it died. Later in 1644, a Parliament supporter in London published a pamphlet about the event, where the dead dog was given a voice and said he was not really a German dog but came from Lapland or Finland "where there none but Divells and Sorcerers live." The pamphlet said that Boy was shot at the Battle of Marston Moor with a silver bullet fired "by a valiant souldier, who had skill in Necromancy." There was a mock invitation that read, "Sad Cavaliers, Rupert invites

Fig. 10.1. Prince Rupert and his dog Boy, with the city of Birmingham burning behind them

you all, that doe survive, to his Dog's Funeral. Close mourners are the Witch, Pope and Devill that much lament yo'r late befallen evil." This political text shows how close the connection was at that time between sectarianism, factionalism, and the labeling of one's enemies as practitioners of diabolical witchcraft (Ashton 1896, 162–63).

Just as people were sometimes accused of witchcraft for controlling horses in an unnatural and spectacular way, so were people who trained dogs, cats, and other animals. Long after it could prove fatal to own animals that looked or behaved unusually, people still played on the fears of gullible neighbors with trained animals. At Willingham, north of Cambridge, Jabez Few, who died in the late 1920s, was a practical joker who called his trained white rats "imps" (Porter 1969, 175–76). Neighbors were terrified of them.

The name Old Mother Redcap has been carried by several women believed to be witches. The most famous Old Mother Redcap was an alewife in medieval London whose given name was Elinor Rummynge, and the connection between brewing and the concoction of medicines and other substances is direct. The name Red Cap also appears among the Horseheath imps, which were supposed to be kept in a box somewhere in the village. According to Catherine Parsons, these imps were named Bonnie, Blue Cap, Red Cap, Jupiter, and Venus. Unlike their keepers, they were immortal and had to be handed on. In 1915, Parsons announced that they were then in the keeping of a woman from Castle Camps (Parsons 1915). A newspaper report of 1928 recounts that a black man called at a house in Horseheath and asked the woman there to sign a receipt book. If she did, she was told that she would be the mistress of five imps. Shortly afterward, the woman was seen accompanied by a cat, a rat, a ferret, a mouse, and a toad. After that, her neighbors believed her to be a witch, and many people visited her to obtain cures (Robbins 1963, 556).

Fig. 10.2. Crosses over the door and windows
in a Victorian terraced house in Cambridge

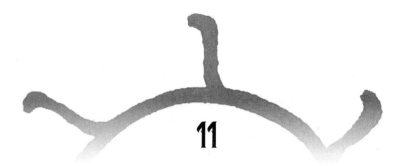

11

Witchcraft and the Power of the Toad

I'm going out to Shippea Hill
If I can't find it there
Then I never will.

Toads are reputedly venomous beasts, too dangerous even to touch, for they are said to absorb poison from the earth, which accumulates in their bodies. Parents always warned their children that toads are highly poisonous and should never be touched. There are accounts of people dealing with toads they wanted to remove from their houses. The toads were never handled, but people used tongs to pick them up, keeping the toads beyond arms' length. An account from the 1920s in Scotland tells how "a servant-woman of the writer from the neighboring Isle of Lewis was terrified beyond speech when a toad came near her" (MacCulloch 1923, 91).

Among the animals into which witches were reputed to transform themselves was the toad. Eric Maple recounts an Essex tale of a Canewdon witch who would do just that. Then other witches, also in the shape of toads, visited her to renew their power (Maple 1960, 246). East Anglian countrymen, who were known by the nickname Tuddy, were always treated with respect, for they were believed to be toadmen (see "The Toad-Bone Ritual, page 113). In Cambridgeshire dialect a person who is killed has been *totalled*.

A Cambridgeshire dialect word for spellbinding a person, an animal, or a place is *tudding*, the source of this power being that of the toad. This word has also been recorded in East Anglia. "The toad plays a prominent part in gypsy (as in other) witchcraft," wrote Charles Leland in 1891, "since in most Romany dialects there is the same word [*beng*] for a toad or frog, and the devil. . . . I have been informed by gypsies that toads do really form unaccountable predilections for persons and place" (Leland 1891, 255–56). Walter Henry Barrett wrote a story, based on personal reminiscences, in which Crazy Moll, a horse-stopping witch, affected an animal so badly that people encountering it said, "That animal's tudded." The threat of having the toad put on one is a frightening prospect. In another story set at Halloween, Barrett and his friends encounter witches and are afraid that some of them would be tudded before morning (Barrett 1963, 121, 135).

In East Anglian tradition, a person who has been bewitched says that someone has "put the toad on him" (Bales 1939, 66–75). I have been told of the same expression existing in Sheffield. Putting the toad on someone involves burying a toad at a specific place on a path near

Fig. 11.1. A common, garden-variety toad

the victim's dwelling. It is interesting that in Cockney rhyming slang "frog and toad" means road. Sarah Hewett's Devonshire formula for nullifying the power of a black witch with toads' hearts and frogs' livers was recounted in chapter 7. A way to prevent a house from being struck by lightning, recorded in Suffolk, is to bury hedge toads in the garden (Jobson 1966, 112).

In 1879, at East Dereham in Suffolk, William Bulwer was accused in a legal case that involved a toad being buried to put the toad on him. Tried at the Petty Sessions there, he was charged with assaulting a sixteen-year-old woman, Christiana Martins, at Etling Green because he believed her mother had put the toad on him: "Mrs. Martins is an old witch, gentlemen, that is what she is, and she charmed me. I got no sleep for three nights, and, one night, at half-past eleven o'clock, I got up because I could not sleep, and went out and found a 'walking toad' under a clod that had been dug up with a three-pronged fork . . . she put this toad there to charm me." He picked up the toad in a cloth and took it upstairs to show his mother, then he threw it out of the window into the pit in the garden. Later, he saw the woman's daughter and attacked her. Bulwer was found guilty of assault and fined one shilling with twelve shillings and sixpence costs (reported in *The Rock*, April 25, 1879; *The Folk-Lore Record*, 2, 1879, 207; Newman 1946, 33).

The place the toad was buried and the use of a three-pronged fork to do the burying bore all the signs of someone putting the toad on the inhabitants of that house, but, of course, the legal authorities by then had no recognition of magical cursing, and his account was received with incredulity as the delusions of a rustic. Sixty years later, in 1939, E. G. Bales recounted how a man who was experiencing difficulties, having been reported to the police, suspected someone "had put the toad on him." So he caught a toad and put it in a saucepan and boiled it to death. As the toad was dying, the man who had tudded him came to the door and begged to apologize for reporting him to the police (Bales 1939, 70).

In 1648, Robert Herrick published "A Charme, or an Allay for Love," a separation spell that involved a toad.

If so a Toad be laid
In a Sheeps-skin newly flaid,
And that ty'd to a man 'twil sever
Him and his affections ever.
(HERRICK [1648] 1902, 203)

The more mundane gray witches, who did not claim to transmogrify into toads, used the toad for healing as well as cursing. Their recorded techniques are the same as those used by the mountebank doctors and cunning men who plied their trade at fairs and markets, like the mid-nineteenth-century practitioner Doctor Buckland, who lived and practiced in the neighborhood of Stalbridge in Dorset. Buckland held an event each May. "This gathering was called the Toad Fair," and patients "who came from far and near" were treated for disorders such as the king's evil and the effects of the evil eye using legs torn from live toads or frogs (reported by "A Guardian" in *The Standard,* September 22, 1880; *Dorset Superstitions,* 1880, 288). In 1897, Robert Young of Sturminster Newton recalled Buckland's methods: "He used to amputate the limb of a living frog, and the daughters, with all speed, put the leg into a muslin bag and suspended it around the neck of the patient, inside the clothing, allowing it to rest on the chest." A folklorist who investigated Buckland was told by Thomas Hardy that "a toad-bag" was "even now a common expression" (March 1899, 479; Dacombe ca. 1935, 117).

Ella Mary Leather recounts how Thomas Whittington, a Walford farm laborer, was cured by the same charm of a long-lasting abscess in his arm. A toad's leg was the cure, a Gypsy woman told him. So when he was cutting a hedge, Whittington found a toad and cut one of its legs off. Then he dug a turf out under the hedge and buried the toad alive there. Then he put the severed leg in a silk bag made from his best silk handkerchief and wore it around his neck. The Gypsy woman told him to look the next morning to see if the toad had gone, and it had. He was healed in three weeks (Leather 1912, 77–78).

Another toad-bag cure uses a whole toad. Charlotte Latham, writing in 1878, tells how a person at North Chapel in Sussex who suffered from a scrofulous complaint "was recommended to wear a live toad round his neck until it was dead; he has done so and felt better for the inhuman remedy" (Latham 1878, 45). In 1952, Catherine Parsons wrote that at Horseheath in Cambridgeshire, whooping cough was treated by rubbing the sufferer's palm with a live frog. Immediately afterward, the frog was buried alive, and as it rotted away, so the cough diminished (Parsons 1952, 40–41). Toads are covered in bumps that resemble warts, and so there are charms that use a toad to remove warts: "Catch a live toad and hang it up somewhere where you will pass every day" is a remedy recorded in Lincolnshire (Hadow and Anderson 1924, 357).

Swallowing live frogs was recommended as a cure for weakness and consumption (*County Folk-Lore* 1899, 179), while a cure for whooping cough involves holding the head of a toad for a few minutes inside the mouth of the affected person (*Bye-Gones* 1873, 253). In Hungerford in Berkshire in the nineteenth century, a "cancer doctress" was practicing. She claimed to be "curing cancers by means of toads" (Read 1911, 305). Barrett also recorded a Fenland treatment for breast cancer in use in the first half of the twentieth century. A handywoman would fetch a toad out from under the water butt and rub its back until its warts expanded

Fig. 11.2. A mummified toad in an unwrapped bundle, from Suffolk

and it began to exude liquid venom. Then the toad was rubbed on the tumor until it ceased to give out its fluid. The toad was then put back in its place under the water butt, and a plaster of houseleek was applied to the tumor (Barrett 1974, 75).

Those who knew that British toads are not lethally poisonous used their knowledge for their own ends. In a letter written by Gilbert White, he noted how a quack doctor at Selborne "ate a toad to make the country-people stare" (Read 1911, 305). But the toad eaters who accompanied the mountebanks were there to demonstrate the efficacy of the elixirs that the quacks were selling (Allen 1995, 155–60). A toad would be shown to the spectators, who were shocked to see someone even handling such a dangerous venomous beast. Then the toad eater would eat the toad and, suitably convulsing, fall down, apparently dead. The doctor, as in a mummers' play, would then give a spiel about his elixir, give the apparently dead man a drop, and miraculously bring him back to life again. The lethal power of the toad actually appears in a mummer's play from Bassingham in Lincolnshire, whose text from a performance at Christmas of 1823 was, unusually, written down. It is known as *The Bassingham Men's Play,* and the character called the Valiant Hero, equivalent to the fool in many mummers' plays, threatens Dame Jane by telling in the usual overexaggerated manner of mumming how he

> *Slew ten men with a seed of mustard.*
> *Ten thousand with an old crushed toad.*
> *What do you think to that, Jane*
> *If you don't be off, I'll serve you the same.*
> (BASKERVILL 1924, 242)

The rare limestone plant toadroot (*Actaea spicata*) has an odor that is attractive to toads but offensive to humans. It bears extremely poisonous black berries. Toadflax (*Linaria vulgaris*) also has an offensive smell. In former times it was boiled in milk to create a fly poison. In *Nature's Paradise,* William Coles wrote that the plant was called toadflax "because Toads will sometimes shelter themselves among the branches of it" (Coles 1650). However, others claim that the name comes from the supposed resemblance of the flower to the mouth of a toad (Grieve 1931, 815–16).

THE TOAD-BONE RITUAL

There is a wondrous crooked road
That leads us to the truth.

Possession of the toad bone, gained through a specific ritual, is what makes someone a toadman, toadwoman, or toadwitch. To find the bone, one must bury a dead toad (some say a frog can also be used) in an ants' nest and leave it until the flesh has decayed, leaving behind only the bones. These bones must then be taken to a stream that runs north–south, where they are floated in the running water to separate them. The bone that appears to turn against the current is *the bone*. The rest are left in the water. This rite was described by the Norfolk horseman Albert Love as the Water of the Moon, a title frequently given it today, but that name is unknown from any other source. According to Love, the toad was specified as a hopping toad, interpreted as a natterjack (*Bufo calamita*), and the rite has to be performed at the full moon or, alternatively, Saint Mark's Eve. In the fens of Cambridgeshire and Lincolnshire, the natterjack toad is not specified. A contemporary toadman, for the tradition continues, will never show his bone to another person. Someone who says he or she has "been to the river" is a toadman or toadwoman.

In West Norfolk the toad bone is called the witch-bone (Bales 1939, 69). Some statements by self-confessed toadmen and toadwomen explicitly speak of the devil in connection with the toad-bone ritual, for a toadman was accounted as a kind of witch (Evans 1965, 246). However, the Huntingdonshire folklorist C. F. Tebbutt characterized it as "one form of witchcraft with no menace to others" (Tebbutt 1984, 85). Tebbutt tells how "an informant" was told in 1908 by

Fig. 11.3. "The bone," a toadman's toad bone

George Kirk, a blacksmith working at Bourn in Cambridgeshire, how the smith had conducted this ritual to gain power over horses. But here it was a frog whose bone was used: "Keep this bone, and you can then give yourself to the devil and have the power I have got," Kirk told his assistant (Tebbutt 1984, 86).

The Cambridgeshire folklorist Enid Porter recalls an account from 1949 from a man at March, Cambridgeshire, who said that the toadman had to carry the bone at midnight to the stables on three consecutive nights for the final initiation. The toadman typically has power over not only horses but also pigs and women, and the toad-woman has power over horses, pigs, and men. The toad bone can be used as an empowerment to the substances used in jading and drawing horses. In the region of Stowmarket, the toad bone is the operative agent in wart charming. It also gives the toadman the power to see in the dark and the ability to drive a vehicle easily across a muddy field in which any other would get stuck. Charles Roper reported in 1893 of "a rustic living in the neighbourhood of the Fen" who told him that a team man living by Poppy Lot "could allus do what he wanted. He'd go straight across the ground with his horses and a load where any other man would ha' stuck fast, if he'd been fool enough to try it, even with an empty wagon; and then at night, no matter how dark the stable way, he had light enough o' his side to see what he wanted" (Roper 1893, 795).

In 1901 an American fortune-telling book, *The Zingara Fortune Teller,* was published in Philadelphia; it was written by "A Gypsy Queen," whose provenance appears to be in the Spanish Gypsy tradition. Described in it is the Frog Charm, instantly recognizable from the English toad-bone rite.

> Take a healthy well-grown frog. Place it in a box which has been pierced all over with a stout darning needle or gimlet. Then carry it in the evening twilight to a large ant-heap, place it in the midst of the heap, taking care to observe perfect silence. After the lapse of a week, repair to the ant-heap, take out the box and open it, when in place of the frog you will find nothing but a skeleton. Take this apart very carefully, and you will find among the delicate bones a scale shaped like that of a fish and a hook. You will need them both. The hook you must contrive to fasten in some way or other into the clothes of the person whose affections you wish to obtain, and if he or she has worn it, if it is only for a quarter of a minute, he will be constrained to love you, and will continue to do so until you give him a fillip with the scale. (Gypsy Queen 1901)

The toad and frog are in some ways interchangeable magically, as in the recorded accounts from Cambridgeshire blacksmiths and grooms. The distinction is blurred in American references, for in parts of the American South, a term sometimes used for a toad has been *toad-frog.* This complicates the transmission of magical remedies through written or printed accounts. Writers on hoodoo, where toad magic is a significant element, always use the expression *toad-frog* for a toad. In John Lee

Fig. 11.4. A toad bone in a locket, from Cambridgeshire, circa 1850

Hooker's blues song "Groundhog Blues," which refers to the American hoodoo practice, "toad-frogs' hips" are the materia magica used to "kill that dirty groundhog." The toad proper is the most used in British folk magic compared with the frog, and the toad bones the author has seen could well be described as hips.

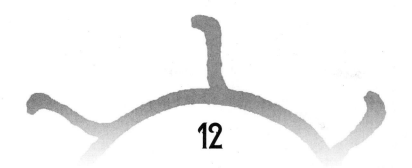

12

The Paraphernalia of Witchcraft

THE WITCH'S BROOMSTICK

The stock illustration of a witch is an old woman straddling a besom, the traditional broomstick used before it was largely ousted by factory-made brooms. Besoms are traditionally made from three woods. The stale or handle is made from ash, the broom part from twigs of birch, hazel, or rowan. Willow withies are used to bind the twigs to the stale. It is unlucky to make or purchase a new broom during the twelve days of Christmas or during May: "Buy a broom in May / Sweep one of the house away" (Crossing, 1911, 136). The broom can be used to sweep bad luck away. One witch's recipe uses flour and sugar dusted over the floors. That is then swept to the middle of the house, where it is all picked up, then taken to running water and thrown in. It is bad luck to leave one's old broom behind when one moves to a new house. One must bang the dust off it and take it to the new house, though in the rite of entering a new house one requires a new broom, a new loaf, and a box of salt.

The Broom Man is part of the traditional molly dance set, and in certain mummers' plays a character called Little Devil Doubt carries a broom with which he mock-menaces the audience and demands

Fig. 12.1. The late Cyril Papworth doing the broom dance on Plough Monday 1997 in Cambridge

money. In the late twentieth century Cyril Papworth, the doyen of Cambridgeshire broom dancing, had a movement in his Comberton broom dance where he straddled the broom in the same way that witches are portrayed. Elly Mary Leather wrote, "It was said that a witch had no power over anyone riding a broomstick" (Leather 1912, 53). The traditional tunes for dancing the broomstick are "Pop Goes the Weasel," "Cock o' the North," "The Keel Row," and "The Cross-Hand Polka" (Leather 1912, 133; Palmer 1974, 24; Cyril Papworth, personal communication and unpublished typescript).

A tradition recorded in Yorkshire and Lancashire has a person guising as Little Devil Doubt and sweeping devils out of the house on New Year's Eve between ten and midnight. The guiser, who appears in blackface and does not speak, sweeps the house dust into the fireplace and then collects his fee. In several mummers' plays the character Little Devil Doubt, who, of course, carries a broom, says:

I'm Little Devil Doubt.
I'll sweep you all out.
Money I want,
And money I crave.
If you don't give me money,
I'll sweep you all to your grave!

In many performances, Little Devil Doubt sweeps over the feet of the spectators, and this is also a means of sweeping unwanted people from one's house. Another magical method of sweeping unwanted people out of the house as they leave is sweeping behind them all the way to the door, then along the garden path to the gate, if the house door does not open directly onto the street. Sidney Oldall Addy records that at Eyam in Derbyshire the doorsteps must be swept on March 1 each year, "and they say that unless you do this you will have fleas all the year" (Addy 1907, 36). The same tradition exists in Cambridge, where it is called Foe-ing Out Day, and the swept steps are then chalked with the Cambridge Box threshold pattern. Addy notes that in the East Riding of Yorkshire, one must sweep the dust up "for luck" (Addy 1907, 37). A broom laid across the threshold keeps out unwanted people, and a witch who wishes the inhabitant ill cannot cross it, nor can a rent collector (e.g., Eddrup 1885, 333), and "when an animal was led away to market the besom was thrown on it to ward off all harm from witches" (Gregor 1881).

An enigmatic old rhyme used by some morris dance sides tells of a weird old woman who carries a broom while traveling in the air.

There was an old woman tossed up in a blanket
Ninety-nine miles beyond the moon.
Where she had gone, I couldn't but ask it,
For in her hand she carried a broom.

> *"Old woman, old woman, old woman," quoth I.*
> *"Whither so, whither so whither so high?"*
> *"I've gone to sweep cobwebs off of the sky."*
> *"Can I come with you?"*
> *"Yes, by and by."*

A Lincolnshire mummers' play has a character called Old Esem Esquesem, who carries a broom. Unusually, it is he, not an old woman, who is killed and brought to life (Chambers 1933, 210). Edmund Kerchever Chambers writes, "At Leigh the performance is begun by Little Devil Doubt, who enters with his broom and sweeps a 'room' or 'hall' for the actors, just as in the sword-dances a preliminary circle is made with a sword upon the ground" (Chambers 1933, 217). The Northstow Mummers, of which this author is Lord of Misrule, performs as its main performance the play of the Old Tup, a version derived from Sheffield, which also has the character Little Devil Doubt, who drives the action along by his answers and questions.

In former times, the means of sealing a common-law marriage was for the bride and groom to jump over a broomstick together. This tradition continues today at pagan handfastings. Liminal places such as boundaries, gateways, and bridges are places outside normal jurisdiction. One such place is the bridge that links the counties of York and Durham at Barnard Castle. In the early nineteenth century, couples underwent unauthorized marriage ceremonies there, conducted by Cuthbert Hylton, the son of a clergyman, who chanted the rhyme:

> *My blessing on your pots*
> *Your groat's in my purse*
> *You are never the better*
> *And I am never the worse.*

And then the couple jumped over a broomstick to solemnize the union. This was an interesting choice of incantation, for it was a version of this ancient rhyme used by witches for the cure of certain diseases.

Fig. 12.2. Kitty-Witches' Row, a medieval alley
in Great Yarmouth, Norfolk

Your loaf is in my lap
And your penny in my purse,
You are never better
And I am never worse.

(DENHAM 1892, I, 82)

Jumping over a broomstick is a symbolic and lucky act, but if one accidentally should step over a broom, it will bring bad luck unless one resteps over it backward to undo the harm.

THE TIMES OF DAY, ASTROLOGY, AND THE WITCHES' DIAL

The esoteric tradition reminds us that the time of day that one performs any act either empowers or nullifies its effectiveness. This is ignored or forgotten in modernity except by those with an interest in astrology. Since early times, the horoscope of the instant of foundation has been deemed indicative of the future of an enterprise (Pennick 1999a, 248–71). The art of electional astrology seeks to find the most auspicious configuration of the heavens to determine the precise time (the punctual time) to conduct a ceremony or begin any activity, such as laying the first stone of a building. A horoscope is drawn up in advance, and the action is performed at the precise moment indicated. This performance is the instant of birth of the project, equivalent to the time of birth in human natal astrology. In post-Reformation England, astrology was used officially as well as by merchants, witches, and magicians. Electional astrology was used in the foundation of colleges, institutions, and churches. Unusual and precise times of stone laying, known as the "punctual time," attest to elections, as with some London churches built after the Great Fire and certain Cambridge colleges (Pennick 2005b, 34–35).

Accurate computational astrology emerged in England under Cromwell's republic and continued at the Restoration with the work of several almanac makers who were also astrological commentators (Kelly 1977, 240–41). Influential English astrological works of the period include *Merlinus Anglicus* and *Christian Astrology* by William Lilly (1644 and 1647); Jeremy Shakerley's *Tabulae Britannicae* (1653); *Genethlialogica: or, the Doctrine of Nativities* and *Collectio Geniturarum* by John Gadbury (1658 and 1662); Thomas Streete's *Astronomia Carolina* (1661); and almanacs by Vincent Wing as well as anonymous or pseudonymous authors. In the following centuries there has been an unbroken succession of almanacs and books concerning astrology. These have always been available to literate witches.

As a rule of thumb, punctual times were not always calculated; instead a less rigid schedule was adopted. So in England, the day of twenty-four hours was formerly divided customarily into thirteen parts (Lawrence 1898, 339).

1. After midnight
2. Cock crow
3. Between the first cock crow and daybreak
4. The dawn
5. Morning

6. Noon
7. Afternoon
8. Sunset
9. Twilight
10. Evening
11. Candle time
12. Bedtime
13. Dead of night

This "thirteen times of day and night" is a rule-of-thumb way of telling time, practical enough for a life not ruled by the clock. In the days before mechanical time telling was readily available, the hours of the day and night (and there were several kinds) were told by the sun by day and by the stars at night. The hand sundial is the simplest way of doing this; effectively, the human hand becomes a sundial. One's hand is held out; palm upward at head height from the body, and a small straight stick is held in the crook of the thumb at the angle of the latitude that gives a visible shadow. This acts as a shadow-casting gnomon. Before noon, the stick is held in the left hand, orientated toward the west; after noon, it is in the right hand, pointed to the east. The shadow cast by the stick shows the time by the position of its shadow against the joints of the fingers and the fingertips.

Fig. 12.3. Diagram of a hand sundial,
from Germany, circa 1500

Until the early part of the twentieth century, turf dials, otherwise called witches' dials or shepherds' dials, were made in the rural parts of southern England. Although in former years they had been universal, by the twentieth century only shepherds in the counties of Kent, Surrey, Sussex, and Essex were known to make them. They seem to have gone out of use during World War I. It was customary for the shepherds to use the dials to determine the time to begin the drive from the pasture back to reach the sheepfold before sunset. The simplest form of the shepherd's dial is made by cutting a circle about eighteen inches in diameter in the turf and thrusting a straight stick about a foot long into the ground "plumpendicular" (vertically) at its center. Then a stick with notches that mark the hours is laid east–west inside the circle to the north of the central stick, each end touching the circle at right angles to a meridional (north–south) line.

As with the hand sundial, the meridional line comes from one's local knowledge of the landscape, using a "farthest beacon," a distant landmark. The center stick serves as the gnomon, and the time can be told from where the shadow touches the notches. In the absence of a notched stick, small ridges can be made in the earth as markers. An alternative version makes an identical circle, but a shorter stick is put into the center. Then another stick, about a foot long, is put in the ground on the circle, due south of the center stick. Other sticks are placed on the circumference at appropriate distances for the hours or tides to either side of the meridional one. It is customary to use seven sticks, which all serve as gnomons. The shorter one at the center becomes the marker of the hours, a reversal of the principle of the other type of witches' or shepherds' dial (Gossett, 1909, *passim*).

These traditional methods of reckoning solar time were used in northern Europe until the arrival of cheap clocks and watches and the imposition of standardized time in time zones, first by the railway companies, then by acts of Parliament. This created the concept of legal time, where the official mean time or daylight savings time determined by the central government became the everyday reality, with people being forced to use it rather than the natural real time told from the

Fig. 12.4. A sundial built by Herbert Ibberson
in Hunstanton, Norfolk, from 1908

sun, which, thereafter, was deemed wrong and ignored. After that, ancient, traditional methods continued to be used by only a very few people, such as traditional astrologers, magical talisman makers, and country people who refused to be "druv." Now real time, almost everywhere on Earth, is out of kilter with official clock time.

PINS, NAILS, AND THORNS

Pins, nails, and thorns are used magically for both attack and defense. In the Northern Tradition the rune called *thorn* has this magical function. This dual defensive and attacking nature of the thorn, or its human-made versions, pins and nails, is present in traditional magical lore. Finding a pin in the street is considered lucky, but only if it is picked up, as the following two rhymes tell.

See a pin and pick it up
All the day you'll have good luck:
See a pin and let it lie
In the evening, you will cry.

See a pin and pick it up
All the day you'll have good luck:
See a pin and let it lay
You will have bad luck all day.
(RUDKIN 1936, 16–17)

There is a custom, which I have encountered personally, that if one wants a pin from another, one must take it oneself, not be given it. In 1866, William Henderson noted, "Many north country people would not, on any account, lend another a pin. They will say, 'You may take one, but mind, I do not give it'" (Henderson 1866, 88). Similarly, Thomas Firminger Thistleton Dyer writes that one must never give a pin but instead offer one to be taken (Dyer 1889, 98). The possibility is that a pin given by another may be doctored, and by taking the offered pin, one will put oneself into that person's power. Taking one from a packet or a pincushion reduces the chance that the pin has been doctored.

Pincushions traditionally have the pins pushed into them to make patterns. The patterns made by pins in fabric, or laid at specific places for magical purposes, have meaning. Doctored pins are pushed into the top of the lapels of a man's jacket as a form of magical protection against bewitchment. The cross and the heart are common pincushion patterns, and the patterns made by pins in other contexts are significant in pin magic. The simplest of these is the cross, where two pins are laid on a surface, one pointing north and the other east. The Criss Cross Row is made by pushing two pins though fabric at right angles to one another, or four pins crossed to make a square, with each pin pointing in a different direction. The Double Cross uses three pins, two crossing a third at right angles, with their points in opposite directions. Elsewhere in folk tradition, there is a notable similarity between the magical pin patterns and the lock or nut of traditional sword dancing, where swords are locked together and held up as the culmination of episodes of the dance (e.g., Sharp, n.d., 52). Practitioners of the nameless art in East Anglia teach that in taking magical possession of a room, one puts a pin in each corner and hammers a fifth into the floor at the center. This nails down harmful sprites and prevents unwanted people from entering or, if they do, from remaining there long. An attack spell using pins is the Spokeless Wheel. This charm employs three pins, arranged like the spokes of a wheel, put over a door where the intended victim will go.

Pins are the essential tools of dressmakers and tailors, and they too have a magical dimension. Pins taken from the wedding dress of a bride are lucky, and they have the power to bring on another wedding. Charlotte Latham noted in 1878 that "a bride, on her return from church, is often robbed of all the pins about her dress by the single women present, from the belief that whoever possesses one of them will be married in the course of a year" (Latham 1878, 32). Pins from a wedding dress are also prized as indicators to be used in picking out the winners of horse races. Pins stuck in the edge of the lapel of a man's jacket are apotropaic against the evil eye and other bewitchments. To ward off harm in baking, pins are also used to prick protective patterns into biscuits and bread.

Sticking objects full of pins is a magical act that needs conscious deliberation. Objects can be stuck as a form of binding, attacking, or warding off harm. In 1871 a correspondent to *Derbyshire Notes & Queries* noted, "On St Thomas's Eve there used to be a custom among girls to procure a large red onion, into which, after peeling, they would stick nine pins, and say,

"Good St Thomas do me right
Send me my true love this night
In his clothes and in his array
Which he weareth every day.'"

Eight pins were stuck around one in the center, to which was given the name of the swain—the "true love." The onion was placed under the pillow upon going to bed, and the girl was certain to dream of or see in her sleep the desired person (*Derbyshire Notes & Queries* 4s: 8, 1871, 506). Saint Thomas's Eve is December 20, after nightfall. But onions stuck with pins were not only used in love magic; they could also be used in binding magic against enemies. Frederick Thomas Elworthy records an incident when an onion stuck with pins was found in a chimney. On the paper that the pins pinned to the onion was the name of a "well-known and highly respected gentleman, a large employer of labour" (Elworthy 1895, 55). Writing in 1896, Peter Hampson Ditchfield noted, "Another custom when a lover is faithless, is to prick the 'wedding' finger, and with the blood write upon paper her own name, and that of the favoured swain, afterward to form three rings (still with the blood) joined underneath the writing, dig a hole in the ground, and bury the paper, keeping the whole matter a secret from every one. This is believed to be an unfailing charm" (Ditchfield 1896, 198). Three circles chalked on a hearth form a charm to prevent witches from coming down the chimney, and related to this is a sigil of the bindings of love, the jimmal, a ring in treble form—that is, three circles—which is referred to in Robert Herrick's poem "The Jimmal Ring, or True-Love-Knot."

Thou sent to me a True-love-knot; but I
Return'd a Ring of Jimmals, to imply
Thy love had one knot, mine a triple tye.
(HERRICK [1648] 1902, 107)

Elworthy recorded an incident that took place in Somerset in 1885.

Only ten years ago an old woman died here in the Workhouse, who was always a noted witch. She was the terror of her native village (in the Wellington Union). As it was fully believed she could "work harm" to her neighbours. Her daughter also, and others of the family, enjoyed the like reputation. Virago-like she knew and practised on the fears of the other inmates of the House. On one occasion she muttered a threat to the matron that she would "put a pin in for her." The other women heard it, and cautioned the matron not to cross her, as she had vowed to put a pin in for her, and she would do it. When the woman died there was found fastened to her stays a heart-shaped pad stuck with pins; and also fastened to her stays were four little bags in which were dried toad's feet. All these things rested on her chest over her heart, when the stays were worn. (1895, 54, n. 80)

In 1900, Sarah Hewett recorded the use by Devon white witches of frog's livers stuck full of new pins and toad hearts stuck full of thorns in a rite to destroy the power of black witches (Hewett 1900, 74). (See also the account of an onion stuck with pins found in a chimney, chapter 9, page 128).

Writing in the 1820s in Scotland, Sir Walter Scott in his *Letters on Demonology and Witchcraft* tells of a feeding house for cattle, where "there was found below the threshold-stone the withered heart of some animal stuck full of many scores of pins—a counter-charm, according to tradition, against the operation of witchcraft on the cattle which are kept within" (Scott 1885, 273). In 1875 at Worle, near Weston-super-Mare, some pigs died and the owner sent for a wise man from Taunton, who determined that the deaths had been caused by four wives of the village. To counter with witchcraft and punish the perpetrators, the wise man took a heart from one of the pigs, stuck it with pins, and threw it into the fire. The pigs' owner and his wife then waited for the woman to come and ask why they were hurting her. Some time later, the suspected woman was killed when she fell into her own fire (Elworthy 1895, 55–56).

In 1892 a bottle was discovered in a chimney at Shutes Hill Farm at Chipstable in Somerset. When the contents were examined, they were found to be a bullock's heart pierced with nails and "an object, said to be a toad, also stuck with thorns" (Ettinger 1943, 246). Leather noted in 1912:

> A farmer at Peterchurch [Herefordshire] refused to give anything to two gypsies who begged from him. That very week two colts died, worth about £60. Fearing further losses, he sent to a wise man in Llandovery . . . the remedy prescribed was the burning of a bullock's heart, previously stuck all over with pins. Those that caused the trouble, said the wise man, would be obliged to come and "pother" it out of the grate as it burned. And they did! (51)

A spell from Mendip in Somerset was given by a white witch to a woman who believed her sick pig had been overlooked. She was told to stick a sheep's heart full of pins and roast it in front of a fire, occasionally sprinkling salt into the flames. The people who came to witness the rite were told to chant:

> *It is not this heart I mean to burn,*
> *But the person's heart I wish to turn,*
> *Wishing them neither rest nor peace*
> *Till they are dead and gone.*
>   (Elworthy 1895, 56)

In 1933 the Lincolnshire folklorist Ethel Rudkin described a similar charm from Willoughby, its function being to regain a lover. The person wishing to get his or her lover back should capture a frog or toad and imprison it in a jar. Paper should be tied across the jar's mouth and pins pushed through it. Then the spell is said:

> *It's not this frog (toad) I wish to prick*
> *But my lover's heart I want to prick.*

Then the jar is turned over, and the animal falls onto the pins and is impaled. This has to be done nine nights in succession (Rudkin 1933, 199). A wart-removal remedy from Lincolnshire is similar, spiking a toad to perform the magic, but with the use of an intermediary: "Take a toad and rub it on the warts, then pass the toad to someone else, who must take and hang the toad on a thorn bush—as the toad dies and withers, so will the warts" (Rudkin 1933, 201).

These are historical magical procedures that involved serious cruelty to animals. Of course, neither the present author nor the publisher condones these in any way. They were clearly considered transgressive and shocking at the time they were performed and written down, despite the everyday cruelty to animals that went on routinely then in other contexts. They are presented here to give a full picture of the types of activities performed by witches and other rural practitioners of magic.

Invultuation (also invultation) is the practice of making images or effigies of people and animals. In 1603, King James I of Great Britain wrote:

> To some others, at these times he [the Devil] teacheth how to make pictures of wax or clay: that by the roasting thereof, the persons that they beare the name of, may be continually melted or dried away by continuall sicknesse . . . they can bewitch and take away the life of man or woman, by roasting the pictures. (Stuart 1603, ii, v)

Invultuation remains to this day with the burning of someone in effigy, as in the custom of Guy Fawkes' Night or during political demonstrations (e.g., *Notes & Queries* 8s, 11, 1897, 107, 236, 314, 395). The second verse of "Remember, Remember the Fifth of November," a song of sectarian rage rarely sung for many years, alludes to this.

> *A rope, a rope to hang the Pope*
> *A piece of cheese to choke him.*
> *A barrel of beer to drink his "health,"*
> *And a damn good fire to roast him.*

Roasting and burning an effigy of the pope on a Bonfire Night bonfire is a sectarian magical act of invultuation. The most notorious action ascribed to witches by witch hunters is invultuation for magical purposes. Images of humans, often called poppets or puppets, are commonly stuck with pins, the act of "putting a pin in for someone." The modern name frequently given by the press to these pin-stuck figurines when they are discovered in old buildings is voodoo dolls, but in the British context they have nothing to do with the voodoo practices of French-speaking Haiti and Louisiana, for they predate the colonization of the Americas. For example, Jacques Duèze, when he had become Pope John XXII (reign 1316–1334), believed that people were making wax images of him and were sticking them with pins. He also received a ring as a present and believed a devil had been enclosed in it (Seymour 1913, 44). In Thomas Middleton's play *The Witch: A Tragi-Comedie*, Heccat asks, "Is the heart of wax stuck full of magique needles?" And Stadlin answers, "'Tis done, Heccat" (quoted by Ashton 1896, 176).

Pins were part of the materia magica put in witch bottles made to counter bewitchments. In his *Saducismus Triumphatus, or Full and Plain Evidence Concerning Witches and Apparitions,* Joseph Glanvil described the use of witch bottles with pins. Glanvil tells us the story of how William Brearly, a clergyman fellow of Christ's College in Cambridge, took lodgings in a village in Suffolk. The landlady appeared to have suffered for some time from ill health, which was ascribed to a phantom "thing in the shape of a bird." The haunting was reported to "an old man who traveled up and down the country," who recommended that her husband should "take a bottle, and put his wife's urine into it, together with pins and needles and nails, and cork them up, and set the bottle to the fire, but be sure the cork be fast in it, and that it not fly out." The man followed the prescription, but the cork blew out. A second attempt followed, and "his wife began to mend sensibly, and in competent time was well recovered. But there came a woman from a town some miles off to their house with a lamentable outcry, that they had killed her husband. . . . At last they understood that her husband was a Wizard and had bewitched this man's wife, and that this counterpractice prescribed by the Old Man, which saved the man's wife from languishment, was the death of the Wizard who had bewitched her" (Glanvil 1681).

In the nineteenth century this ritual was conducted by the Essex cunning man Cunning Murrell. He used an iron bottle that he filled with parings of horses' hoofs, pins, and chemicals. It was then welded shut by a blacksmith and put on a fire until it exploded, thereby eliminating the ill-doer (Howe 1958, 139). In 1908 a witch bottle and the theory behind it were reported by folklorists from Lincolnshire.

A few years ago, in pulling down an old house in a neighbouring village [probably Messingham], a wide-mouthed bottle was found under the foundation, containing the heart of some small animal (it was conjectured a hare), pierced as closely as possible with pins. The elders said it had been put there to "withstand witching." Sometime after, a man digging in his garden in the village of Yaddlethorpe came upon the skeleton of a horse or ox, buried about three feet beneath the surface, and near to it two bottles containing pins, needles, human hair, and a stinking fluid, probably urine. The bottles, pins, etc., came into my possession.

Fig. 12.5. Magical bottles, from Cambridgeshire

There was nothing to indicate the date of their interment except one of the bottles, which was of the kind employed to contain Daffy's elixir, a once popular patent medicine. The other bottle was an ordinary wine pint. At the time when these things were found, I mentioned the circumstance to many persons among our peasantry; they all said that it had "summut to do with witching"; and many of them had long stories to tell, setting forth how pins and needles are a protection against the malice of the servants of Satan. (Gutch and Peacock 1908, 96)

Ancient witch bottles containing the materials described by Glanvil have been discovered in many places in southern England. Those whose contents have been scientifically analyzed show that they contained pins or nails and urine in addition to other organic materials (e.g., Bunn 1982, 5; Massey 1999, 34–36). One found in Ipswich contained a heart-shaped piece of felt stuck with pins, and another excavated from the hearth at Bridge Cottage in Wetheringsett, Suffolk, contained thorns as well as remains of the customary nails and urine.

Fig. 12.6. Ceramic model of a church found in a chimney at Histon, Cambridgeshire, probably put there to ward off witchcraft

Pins were also used by witchfinders in the era of the witch hunts. Then official torturers thrust pins into their victims "on the pretence of discovering the devil's stigma, or mark, which was said to be inflicted by him upon all his vassals, and to be insensible to pain. This species of search, the practice of the infamous Hopkins, was in Scotland reduced to a trade" (Scott 1885, 240). As Scott mentions, in eastern England in the seventeenth century, Matthew Hopkins, the "Witchfinder General," used pins as his chief method of torture under the pretext that he was looking for devil's marks. Hopkins wrote, "They are most commonly insensible, and feele neither pin, needle, aule, &c. thrust through them" (Hopkins 1647). In Scotland there were officials known as "the common prickers" who were employed to thrust three-inch pins into those accused of witchcraft until they could not feel one, at which point the pricker proclaimed that he had found "the devil's stigma," which proved the tortured person to be a witch who could then be put to death. As late as 1808, long after the end of witch hunting, women were being ripped with pins as witches, as with the case of Ann Izzard at Great Paxton (see chapter 6, page 38) (Saunders 1888, 156–64). Of course, these persecutions were just a pretext for unimaginable cruelty on helpless victims in the name of the law, perpetrated by men who gloried in brutality and who, in the days of witch hunting, were well paid for it. There were no human rights in those days and few even in the nineteenth century, and we should remember that torture of prisoners is not unknown in the twenty-first century. As the words of John Lilburne, the seventeenth-century Leveller, remind us, "What may be done to one may be done to anyone."

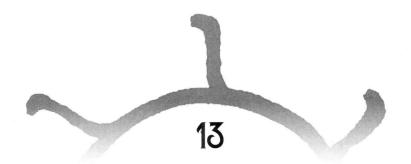

13

The Power of Magical Places

FOUR-LANE ENDS, FOUR-WENTZ WAYS— THE MAGIC OF THE CROSSROADS

I started school one morning
I threw my books away
I left a note for teacher
I'm at the crossroads today.

Crossroads are places of transition, where the axis linking the underworld with the upperworld intersects this world on which we walk. As with all liminal places, they are places of physical and spiritual dangers. There, the distinction between the physical and nonmaterial worlds appears less certain, and the chance of encountering something supernatural is more likely. The term *crossroads* generally refers in folklore to a meeting of two or more roads or the branching of one into two or more, at whatever angle. The folklorists Theo Brown and Martin Puhvel note the fallacy of trying to see Christian veneration of the cross at the core of the crossroads mystique, even if it appears to be present (Brown 1966, 126; Puhvel 1976, 174, n. 1). Junctions of roads, whether a trifinium, or trivium, where three roads meet or a crossroads where four do, are places where the wayfarer is confronted with a choice of which way to go. That is why the word *crossroads* appears as a metaphor, such as "we are at a crossroads in history" and so forth. The names of some crossroads in England, four-lane ends and four-wentz ways, look at them not as places where two roads cross but as the end of four roads, roads that lead to a central point from the four corners of the world. Through the crossroads is the cosmic axis, leading below to the underworld and above to the upperworld. Thus a crossroads, especially when the roads are oriented toward the four cardinal directions, is a central place that links the four corners of the world with other spiritual dimensions, a place where one may access the domains of gods, spirits, and the dead.

Burials at liminal points such as crossroads, roadsides, and parish boundaries are notable in English tradition. Bob Trubshaw observed that in southern England many pagan burials of the Anglo-Saxon period are found near parish boundaries, which may postdate the burials (Trubshaw 1995, 4–5). Five hundred years after the downfall of Anglo-Saxon England, the executed dead who had been convicted of particularly horrendous crimes were sometimes gibbeted at crossroads. People who were gibbeted received no burial at all; their corpses were dipped in tar and then were hung in chains as a grisly warning to others. Ephraim Chambers's 1727 *Cyclopædia* describes the gibbet as "a machine in manner of a gallows, whereon notorious criminals after execution are hung in irons, or chains, as spectacles, *in terrorem*." Those executed at crossroads gallows and not left to hang as a warning to others were buried close by, often under the road itself, "out of the sanctuary," not in consecrated ground (Glyde 1872, 28–29). The practice of gibbeting continued until 1834 (Pringle 1951, 68).

Until 1823, under Church of England laws, suicides, nonconformists, Jews, Gypsies, outlaws, and executed criminals were not to be given burial in consecrated ground. Jewish communities and nonconformist chapels owned their own burial grounds, but Gypsies, witches, and those assumed to have killed themselves sometimes ended up under the edge of the road or even beneath the road surface itself. In Suffolk, at a former crossroads on the Bury St. Edmunds–to–Kentford road, is the

Gypsy's Grave, otherwise known as the Boy's Grave, a flower-bedecked plot reputed to be the burial place of a shepherd boy who hanged himself after being accused of stealing sheep (*Lantern* 10, 1975, 3; Burgess 1978, 6). Here, the Gypsy and the suicide are the same person. Another kind of outcast was the witch. Catherine Parsons recounted that when the famous Cambridgeshire witch known as Daddy Witch died, her body was buried in the middle of the road from Horseheath to Horseheath Green, opposite the "hut by the sheep-pond at Garret's Close," where she had lived. The site of her grave was said to be discernable from the dryness of the road at that place, reputed to be caused by the heat from her body (Parsons 1915, 39). The Horseheath *Women's Institute Scrapbook* for 1935 states that one must nod one's head nine times for good luck before passing over Daddy Witch's grave (Porter 1969, 163). At nearby Bartlow was a bump at a crossroads where a witch was said to be buried (Porter 1969, 161).

People who committed suicide or were conveniently labeled as suicides were buried at the crossroads or by the roadside. It was customary to bury them at a crossroads, especially on the parish boundary, though there are instances of roadside burial too. John Galsworthy's short story "The Apple Tree" tells of a suicide's grave at a crossroads. The records of such burials go back to the sixteenth century; a parish record from Pleasley in Derbyshire from 1573 tells how a man found hanging was buried at midnight at the highest crossroads with a stake in him (Roud 2003, 443). Another in the parish register at Palgrave, near Diss in Norfolk, dated December 30, 1587, records a man named John Bungey being buried in the road (Burgess 1978, 7). As with the Pleasley man, a stake was sometimes driven through the body of a suicide buried on a roadside, in the road, or at a crossroads. In 1814 "an unknown man found dying of poison, self-administered, in Godmanchester, Huntingdonshire, was buried at the crossroads leading to Offord" (*Peterborough Weekly Gazette,* July 30, 1814). Hangman's Lane in Norwich was another such place of a suicide's burial, recalled by correspondent "R. M. L.," who told in 1896 how his father remembered "seeing a suicide carried past his house at twelve at night, to be buried at the cross roads at Hangman's Lane. An immense crowd followed, to see the stake driven though the body" (*Norfolk and Norwich Notes & Queries*, August 15, 1896).

Certain trees are reputed to have grown from the stakes hammered through the bodies buried by the roadside. At Redenhall, Norfolk, was one, a willow tree called Lush's Bush that marked the grave of a woman who poisoned herself in 1813 after being suspected of infanticide; she had a stake hammered through her heart (*Lantern* 12, 1976, 9; *Spellthorn* 3, 1979, 2). Another tree with an unlucky reputation, Cruel Tree at Buckden, which was finally cut down in 1865 during roadwork, was believed to have grown from a stake driven through the body of a murderer who suffered burial at the crossroads of the Great North Road and Mere Lane on the parish boundary of Brampton and Buckden, Huntingdonshire (Tebbutt 1984, 18).

There are many further examples of the practice recorded from other parts of England (Russett 1978, 16). In 1886 the Tyneside folklorist William Brockie wrote:

In the Mile End Road, South Shields, just at the corner of a garden wall . . . lies the body of a suicide, with a stake driven through it. It is, I believe, that of a poor baker, who put an end to his existence sixty or seventy years ago, and who was buried in this frightful manner, at midnight, in unconsecrated ground. The top of the stake used to rise a foot or two above the ground within the last thirty years, and boys used to amuse themselves by standing with one foot upon it. (151–52)

Some crossroads bear the name of the person buried there; for example, Chunk Harvey's Grave at Thetford in Norfolk and Alecock's Grave at Stanton, Suffolk. Dobb's Grave, at the junction of the parishes of Brightwell, Foxhall, Kersgrave, and Martlesham, is reputed to be the grave of another shepherd who hanged himself (*East Anglian Miscellany* 2, 1910, 692). Bond's Corner, a crossroads near Grundisburgh, Suffolk, is explicitly said to be the grave of a suicide

(Burgess 1978, 7). Clibborn's Post at Tewin, near Hertford, marks the grave of the highwayman Walter Clibborn, buried in 1782 with a stake through his body (Lucas 1990, 103).

In 1823 burial on the roadside or at crossroads was prohibited by law in an Act of Parliament that made it unlawful for any coroner who had reached a suicide verdict at an inquest to order the body to be buried in any public highway. The tradition of ramming a stake through the body was also prohibited. From then on, suicides were to be interred in churchyards or other burial grounds, at night between nine and midnight, without religious rites and ceremonies. The stipulation of night burial and riteless interment was abolished in 1882 (Roud 2003, 444).

Suicides were thought to become earthbound spirits that were dangerous to living people (Tebbutt 1984, 17). Thomas Sternberg records how in Northantson on Christmas Eve, "rustics, also, carefully avoid cross-roads on this eventful night, as the ghosts of unfortunate people buried there have particular license to wander about and wreak their evil designs upon defenceless humanity" (Sternberg 1851, 186). More generally, Marie Trevelyan noted a belief that in Wales the dead appear at crossroads at Halloween (Trevelyan 1909, 254). A tradition from the highlands of Scotland tells us not to shun the junctions of roads on Halloween, but if one sits on a three-legged stool at the meeting of three roads then, one will hear the names of those doomed to die in the coming year. Also, one may see the spirits of the dead if one stands at a crossroads with one's chin resting on a forked stick. First will be seen passing the shades of the good, then the shades of those who have been murdered, then the damned. In Wales on *teir nos ysbrydion,* a three-spirit night, one can also go to the crossroads and listen to what the wind has to say. One may thereby learn all the most important things that concern him or her during the forthcoming year (Puhvel 1976, 169–70). Girls wishing to identify their future lover would scatter hemp seeds for nine nights at a crossroads, chanting:

> *Hemp seed, hemp seed, hemp seed I sow*
> *Hoping my true love will come here to mow.*

Afterward, they would look at men traveling the road to see which one it would be (Trevelyan 1909, 236).

Another Welsh belief asserts that on May Eve, witches dance at crossroads with the devil (Trevelyan 1909, 152). Writers on the famous German magician Doctor Faustus tell us that he went to a crossroads in a forest near Wittenberg to raise the devil: "Toward evening, at a crossroads in the these woods, he drew certain circles with his staff; thus in the night between nine and ten o'clock he did conjure the Devil." It was traditional in Wales for the pallbearers at a funeral, when carrying the coffin, to set it down at each crossroads and pray (Trevelyan 1909, 275). The rite is recorded in Ella Mary Leather's *The Folk-Lore of Herefordshire*: "On the Welsh side of the county, in the Golden Valley, in the Kington district, two curious funeral customs prevailed within living memory. The coffin was taken on a roundabout way to the church, and it was put down for a few moments at every cross road, the mourners standing still" (Leather 1912, 122).

The crossroads is a "favourite place to divest oneself of diseases or other evil influences" (Crooke 1909, 88). It is customary for used materia magica to be disposed of at a crossroads. Also, the crossroads is the conductor of the baneful energy emanating from the evil eye, dispersing it to the four quarters of the world and thus preventing it from injuring the person or object of its focus. Folklore tells us that warts and other diseases can be got rid of at crossroads. A tradition recorded in Shropshire is that a person suffering from warts must rub an ear of wheat against each wart, wrap the wheat ears in a piece of paper, and then throw it away at a crossroads. The warts would disappear, transferred to whoever found the piece of paper and picked it up (Burne and Jackson 1883, 200).

A ritual recorded by Evelyne Gurdon in Suffolk in 1893 tells: "You must go by night alone to a crossroads, and just as the clock strikes the midnight hour, you must turn about thrice and drive a tenpenny nail up to the head in the ground, then walk away backward from the spot before the clock ends striking twelve, and you will miss the ague; but the next person who goes over the nail will catch the malady in your stead" (Gurdon 1893, 14).

Alice Kyteler, tried as a witch at Kilkenny in Ireland in 1324, was said to have killed animals, dismembered them, and flung parts at cross-roads "as an offering or sacrifice to a devil of very low degree" (Wood-Martin 1902, vol. 2, 174). The devil appearing at the crossroads is a theme in both European and American tradition. In German-speaking lands, he appears as a black man who will ask questions. One must answer his seven questions correctly without replying *ja* or *nein*. If one passes the test, one is rewarded with treasure (Drechsler 1903, 108; Peuckert 1961, 47 and 1963, 190). In American magical tradition, the fork of the road is where all devils meet. Great things can happen there (Hyatt 1974, vol. 3, 2286). Classified among hoodoo practices is the claim that one can go to a crossroads to become a competent musician, dancer, or "slick person" (successful gambler). This can be accomplished by means of going to the crossroads alone, where one stands at the center of the crossroads, then walks up all four "forks" in succession, after which "you can play anything" (Hyatt 1978, vol. 5, 4008, #10524). One may go to the crossroads at midnight for nine successive nights (Hyatt 1978, vol. 5, 4008, #10534) or nine Sunday mornings before daybreak (Hyatt 1978, vol. 5, #10535), from whence we get Leroy Carr's blues song, "Blues before Sunrise." Other versions of the going-to-the-crossroads-alone motif tell how one must go there on nine mornings in succession (Hyatt 1978, vol. 5, 4009, #10530, 10532–3), facing the eastern quarter where the sun rises, "the house of the rising sun." Hoodoo "hands"* for specific purposes are made facing the rising sun. Here, *house* has its meaning as a division of the horizon.

The commonest tradition is that one meets a black man identified as the devil who will give one the ability to play the banjo or guitar. According to one source from Brunswick, Georgia, one must go to the "three-forked" road on Sunday at midnight or 4:00 p.m. and stand with a banjo or guitar "to attract the Devil," and if you can stand what you see by yourself, you will be a worldly success (Hyatt 1978, 5, 4006, #10508).

---

*A "hand" is a bag containing various magical items, appropriate to the desired function of the "hand."

Sometimes the black man/devil will tune the instrument, after which the initiate can play well; that is, the "Devil learn you all the tricks they is going" (Hyatt 1978, 5, 4006, #10538). Like similar European rituals, one can go to the crossroads and, by cursing the Trinity, become an "underworld man" (Hyatt 1978, 5, 4004, #10497); alternatively, one can curse God and sell one's soul to the devil (Hyatt 1978, 5, 4004, #10498) with the words "Devil take me, I sell my soul to you" (Hyatt 1978, 5, 4004, #10500). The rite is said to be alluded to in Robert Johnson's song "Cross Road Blues," recorded in San Antonio, Texas, on November 27, 1936, in the nonmagical key of B (Charters 1973, 50–51). Unsuccessful at the time, this song has since the 1960s spawned an industry centered on the crossing point of Highway 49 and Highway 61 at Clarksville, Mississippi.

The black man who taught the guitar at the crossroads, perhaps personating the devil like the president of the initiations in the Horsemen's Hall in Scotland and England, was a transmitter of secret knowledge to musicians, such as the proper tuning of the instrument to play the blues (Hyatt 1978, 5, 4010–11). The blues are played in many different tunings, not the standard one, which is generally taught to those who wish to learn the guitar. Variously called Sebastopol tuning, cross tuning, cross Spanish, slack tuning, Bentonia tuning, Piedmont tuning, and so on, these often minor key tunings are generally unknown to the beginner, who struggles in vain to reproduce the sounds of established musicians playing in them. In both European traditional music and the blues, tunes concerned with the world of spirits and the dead are played in minor keys; for example, the Irish tune "The King of the Fairies" and the blues songs "St. James Infirmary" and "Devil Got My Woman."

CHURCHYARDS AND GRAVEYARDS

Churchyards and graveyards are places set aside for the dead. They are places of dread because we all know that one day we will die and end up in one. They are also feared because perhaps the spirits of the dead reside there, and they might affect us in some unfavorable way should

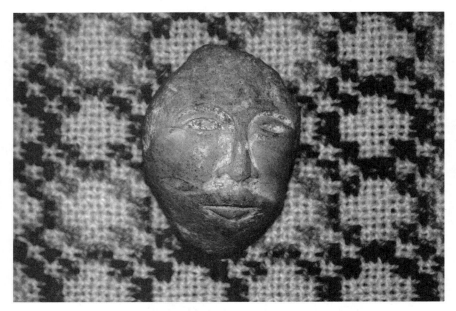

Fig. 13.1. Carved head, about two inches long,
found in a churchyard in Hertfordshire

we go there at night or on the wrong day of the year. Graves and tombs contain the remains of individuals who led particular lives. The graves of famous and infamous people are noted features of graveyards and places resorted to by pilgrims, tourists, the curious, and practitioners of magic who intend to contact the spirits or use bones, graveyard earth, and fragments of coffin as materia magica. The materials of the churchyard are deemed to possess magical and physical qualities; for example, coffin dust is said to be toxic (Newman 1948a, 127).

Because the spirit was once present in the body, the tomb is not just a nondescript place to deposit the corpse but rather a symbolic location that becomes associated with the individual buried there. Traditionally, the tomb or grave is the dwelling place of the shade or ghost of the individual. It must be kept clean and adorned with flowers and other offerings so that the memory of the deceased will be kept up and also that the shade might not wander from the grave and do mischief. Malevolent spirits that manifest as the vicious bar guest or bogeyman are held to be those who are not honored as worthy ancestors but are instead ignored or vilified. One belief about the bar guest, black ghost, or bogeyman is that he is the ghost of a suicide or murderer, of an unjust oppressive landlord, or of a murder victim who is thus denied rest in the proper place for spirits and instead must wander the Earth aimlessly and do mischief, for many are the tales of strange appearances suddenly seen perched on the top of a gate or fence, whence they sometimes leaped upon the shoulders of the scared passenger.

There are apotropaic ritual devices to ward off evil spirits from a place or to pin them down so they will not wander. A cross on a grave, apart from being a marker that someone is buried there, also serves to prevent spirits from manifesting. In many religions there are special days on which family and ancestral graves or tombs are swept, cleaned, and tended, thereby maintaining the protective power. All Souls' Day is the customary one in the Catholic tradition, held on November 1, at the time of Samhain; it is observed in some countries as the Day of the Dead.

But graveyards are also places where the materia magica needed for certain purposes can be obtained. The necromantic conjuration of spirits of the dead in graveyards and the use of bones in magic by witches or bonesmen was always an argument for cremation, though it was illegal in Great Britain until the nineteenth century. As Sir Thomas Browne wrote in *Hydriotaphia* in the mid-seventeenth century, "To be gnawed out of our graves, to have our skulls made drinking-bowls, and our bones turned in to pipes, to delight and sport our enemies, are tragical abominations escaped in burning burials" (Browne 1658, 152). Clearly people did take human bones from churchyards and use them. Writing in 1851 about the T-shaped "lucky bone" carried in Northamptonshire, Sternberg also noted that the kneecap of a sheep or lamb, worn as an amulet, was a remedy to ward off cramps. But he also mentions one instance he found of someone who possessed a human kneecap for the same purpose (Sternberg 1851, 24–25), which parallels the human knucklebones used in American hoodoo and carried by British bonesmen. Digging in graveyards for human bones for magical purposes is, of course, forbidden.

Fig. 13.2. Graveyard at Bury St. Edmunds, Suffolk, England

In 1895, William Blyth Gerish published an East Anglian church-yard charm taught by the Chedgrave Witch to a Loddon girl at the beginning of the nineteenth century. The rhyme or charm gives a grave-yard rite for a woman to gain a husband.

> *To gain a husband, name known or unknown,*
> *Make your choice on a graveyard stone.*
> *Quarter-Day's night if there fare a moon,*
> *Pass through the church gate right alone;*
> *Twist three crosses from graveyard bits,*
> *Place them straight in your finger slits,*
> *Over the grave hold a steady hand*
> *And learn the way the side crosses stand.*
> *One is yourself and your husband one,*
> *And the middle to be named of none.*
> *If they both on the middle cross have crossed,*
> *His name you win, and a year you've lost;*

For he who lies in the namesake mould
His soul has sold—or he would have sold,
And you give a year which the dead may use
Your last year on earth-life that you lose.
(GERISH 1895, 200)

As amply demonstrated in previous chapters, the toad is popularly considered to be an evil animal, sometimes a transmogrified witch, a demon, or the devil, and the graveyard is a place where one might expect a toad to appear. Rites transgressive of the church using churchyard toads were recommended by witches to women who wished to entrap men who would be "compelled to accept the yoke of wedlock." According to Mabel Peacock, the woman who wanted to marry a particular man had to go to church and take the eight o'clock holy communion. She should take the communion bread but not swallow it. "After you come out of the church, you will see a toad in the churchyard." Then she had to spit the bread out so that the toad would eat it. After that, her man would be compelled to marry her (Peacock 1901a, 168).

In 1902 a similar but more complex rite was described from Devon. The writer was informed by an old woman whose mother as a girl had been taught by a Gypsy witch how to gain power over people. Like the previous rite, it also involved taking the sacrament and keeping it in the mouth until the end of the service. But then, upon coming out of church, the woman had to walk around the churchyard three times "saying the Belief and the Lord's Prayer backward. Then you will see a great black toad, which is Old Satan. Give it the bread to eat, and after that you can do anything you wish to people" (Salmon 1902, 427).

MAGICAL ENCLOSURES

It is traditional to believe that the devil can be called up by making a circle on the ground while chanting a particular form of words. The

Fig. 13.3. A magical circle keeps the devil out when he is called up.

circle can be marked using various materials: flour, chalk, soot, salt, or sand. People who discover such a circle often call it a "witch's circle." It is an ancient practice, and it is always much feared and worrisome to those who discover one. If such a circle is near a house, it may indicate that an on lay has been created there to bewitch the inhabitants. Circles were the focus of some witch trials; for example, at Haddenham in Cambridgeshire in 1615 when Dorothy Pitman was tried for witchcraft. One question she was asked was "whether she had at any time made any circle, or did she know of the making of any circle by 'charmer, or enchantment,' to do any mischief?" (*Depositions and Informations,* F.10, Ely, 1615, cited by Parsons 1915, 38, 45).

The circle, of course, is part of classic magic, protecting the magician inside from those dangerous entities she or he may have evoked. The chalked circle was known and feared by country people. Leather recounts a story about Jenkins, the son of a famous cunning man in nineteenth-century Herefordshire. He demonstrated the irrational and erratic behavior associated with witches and cunning men. One inexplicable event involved chalk circles.

> Once he went to a hop-picking ball; he was the fiddler, but all at once he put down his fiddle and drew a hen and chickens on the floor in a circle with chalk. Thinking it was black magic and some evil spell might fall upon them none would step within it, and the dancing was stopped. The fiddler went on with his drawing; he drew a sow and pigs, then a flock of geese. There was no more dancing that night, for by the time he had done they had all gone out of fear. (Leather 1912, 59)

Parsons, in her account of witchcraft at Horseheath, tells that "a circle is drawn on the ground, with perhaps a piece of chalk . . . the Lord's Prayer is said backward, and the devil suddenly appears within the circle, perhaps in the form of a cockerel, but all kinds of things are said to suddenly spring out of the ground" (Parsons 1915, 37). She notes that "the devil usually appeared . . . in the form of an animal, such as a rat, mouse, or toad" (Parsons 1915, 32). "And if the person standing within the circle becomes so frightened that he steps out of the circle, we are told the devil would fly away with him" (Parsons 1915, 37). Another means of raising the devil, recorded in Herefordshire, was to put one's hat on crossed sticks stuck in the ground and walk nine times around them, repeating the Lord's Prayer backward. To lay him again, it was necessary to reverse the proceedings (Leather 1912, 40).

In the West Country, such circles are known as gallitraps. As magical circles, gallitraps are traditionally created by a conjuring parson to entrap criminals. In his West Country researches, Brown saw the gallitrap in terms of an artificial entrance to the underworld (Brown 1966, 125). The word *gallitrap* is also used in the West Country to describe "a waste piece of land." Gallitraps are uncultivated, usually triangular pieces of ground, such as the no-man's-lands at trifinia of roads, which are also called variously in Scotland the Gudeman's Croft, the

Old Guidman's Ground, the Halyman's Rig, the Halieman's Ley, the Black Faulie, or Clootie's Croft, and the Devil's Holt and the Devil's Plantation in eastern England.

Sir Walter Scott wrote:

> In many parts of Scotland there was suffered to exist a certain portion of land, called the gudeman's croft, which was never ploughed or cultivated, but suffered to remain waste, like the Temenos of a pagan temple. Though it was not expressly avowed, no one doubted that "the goodman's croft" was set apart for some evil being; in fact, that it was the portion of the arch-fiend himself . . . this was so general a custom that the Church published an ordinance against it as an impious and blasphemous usage. Within our own memory, many such places, sanctified to barrenness by some favourite popular superstition, existed, both in Wales and Ireland, as well as in Scotland. (1885, 78–79)

This fenced-off sacred place that is left to itself is redolent of the *stafgarðr*, "fenced enclosures," recorded in Scandinavia of heathen times, which clearly also existed in the British Isles (Olsen 1966, 280).

A 1955 article in the *Agricultural History Review* told about "the Halieman's Ley or Guidman's Croft, which was a small plot of land unploughed and dedicated to the devil, in Ireland they were dedicated to the fairies" (quoted by Davidson 1956, 72). In Lincolnshire, "in the neighbourhood of Frieston, triangular corners of fields are filled with trees, and the groups are known as 'Devil's Holts.' The belief is still current that these were left for the devil to play in, otherwise he would play in the fields and spoil the crops" (C. B. Sibsey, quoted by Rudkin 1934, 250). The trifinium, or trivium, the junction of three roads, sometimes contains a piece of uncultivated ground, commonly called a no-man's-land or a cocked hat after the three-cornered hat popular in the eighteenth century (Brown 1966, 124). The expression "I knocked him into a cocked hat" talks of easily knocking someone off the road at a junction.

The custom concerning these special tracts of ground is for the farmer to promise never to till the earth there (McNeill 1957, vol. 1, 62; Pennick 2004, *passim*). Sir Walter Scott noted that it was not so much the hostility of the clergy that caused these tracts to be ploughed up, but economics: "The high price of agricultural produce during the late war render it doubtful if a veneration for greybeard superstition has suffered any one of them to remain undesecrated" (Scott 1885, 79). But not all were destroyed. In England the tradition existed through the twentieth century, and there are still gallitraps, devil's holts, and devil's plantations existing in the twenty-first. One can see stands of trees in circular enclosures or small mounds within arable fields that are uncultivated and go by the same name. These enclosures were also noted by Scott: "For the same reason [as the gudeman's crofts] the mounts called *Sith Bhruaith* were respected, and it was deemed unlawful and dangerous to cut wood, dig earth and stones, or otherwise disturb them" (Scott 1885, 79).

Related to these special tracts of ground are the clumps of pine trees that stand isolated from other trees in many places in England and

Fig. 13.4. A devil's plantation near Rugby, England

Wales. These are always Scots pines (*Pinus sylvestris*), which grow closely together—dark, tall, and visible from afar. These groups of pines were planted as markers on trackways and roads connected with the ancient craft of droving. Sheep and cattle have been herded across the British countryside for thousands of years, and by the medieval period flourishing businesses existed to drive herds of animals long distances. By the seventeenth century there were established routes from Wales into southeastern England and from Scotland to East Anglia and London. When the drove stopped for the night, the animals needed to graze, and there were stances where this could happen. Along the routes where the herds passed were farms where the drovers could pasture animals overnight to feed, for a payment to the farmer. These stopping places or stances were marked by clumps of Scots pine trees, planted to be visible from considerable distances in the open country across which the drovers brought their herds. Many remain today untouched in the manner of devil's plantations.

14

West Indian Obeah and Its Common Features with British Witchcraft

The British Acts of Parliament against witchcraft did not only affect Great Britain, for the British monarch also ruled an expanding empire, and there too people practiced forms of magic that were labeled as witchcraft and dealing with the devil. The copious traditions of magic among slaves and their descendants in the West Indies and the United States contain elements of both African and European magic, and the approach to the magical tradition called Obeah conducted by slaves in the West Indian colonies followed the pattern of antiwitchcraft laws and witch hunts in the United Kingdom. In the West Indies the colonial authorities made many attempts to stamp out the practice of Obeah among the slaves and, when slavery ended, among their descendants. In 1760 the slaves in Jamaica rose up in what was called the Tacky Slave Rebellion. Practitioners of Obeah were prominent leaders of the rebellion, and after the rebellion was crushed, new laws were introduced by the colonial authorities to suppress the practice (Newall 1978, 29). The laws against Obeah were couched in the terms of the Witchcraft Act of 1735, which supposed witchcraft to be a fraud and imposition.

The Laws of Jamaica of 1684 contained the Act for the Better

Ordering of Slaves, which instructed that "every master or overseer of a family in this island shall cause all slaves' houses to be diligently and effectively searched every fourteen days, for clubs, wooden swords, and mischievous weapons, and, finding any, shall take them away and cause them to be burnt." The searching of slaves' dwellings also extended to items deemed to be of magic, "the instruments of obeah." In practice, it appears that "the instruments of obeah" could mean almost anything the masters wanted them to. In the nineteenth century, a woman was even prosecuted for telling fortunes with playing cards on the grounds that cards were classified under "the instruments of obeah." Clause XIII of another law, passed in 1696, attempted to stamp out the use of poisons among the slaves, as they were associated with Obeah: "Divers slaves have of late attempted to destroy several people, as well white as black, by poison." The law made the use of poison a capital offense "treated as murder," and those convicted were "condemned to suffer death, by hanging, burning, or any other way or means as to the said justices and freeholders shall seem most convenient" (Williams 1932, 160). In 1717, An Act for the More Effective Punishing of Crimes Committed by Slaves prohibited assemblies of more than five slaves together (Williams 1932, 161).

In 1760, after the rebellion, a new act read:

And in order to prevent the many mischiefs that may hereafter arise from the wicked art of the Negroes, going under the appellation of Obeah Man or Woman pretending to have communication with the Devil and other evil spirits, whereby the weak and superstitious are deluded into a belief of their having full power to exempt them, when under their power, from any evils that might otherwise happen: Be it therefore enacted . . . that from and after the first day of June [1760] any Negro or Slave, who shall pretend to any supernatural Power, and be detected in making use of any Blood, Feathers, Parrot Beaks, Dogs Teeth, Alligator Teeth, broken bottles, Grave Dirt, Rum, Egg-Shells, or any other Materials relative to the Practice of Obeah and Witchcraft, in order to delude and impose upon the minds of others, shall upon conviction thereof, before

two Magistrates and three Freeholders, suffer death or transportation [relocation to a remote, undesirable place]. (Williams 1932)

The law was not given the Royal Assent, but the persecution of
Obeah was carried out with the full force of the law. Similarly, another
act was passed in 1781 "in order to prevent many mischiefs that may
hereafter arise from the wicked art of Negroes going under the appellation of Obeah Men and Women, pretending to have communion with
the Devil" (Williams 1932, 163).

The fortnightly search for weapons and the instruments of Obeah
was not without reason. In Jamaica slaves rose up against their masters
in 1742, 1760, 1765, 1766, 1791, 1795, 1808, and 1815, and their descendants rebelled in 1865. In Dominica there were rebellions and civil wars
in 1785–1791, 1795, and 1810–1814, while in Barbados there was a
slave uprising in 1816. Practitioners of Obeah were blamed for foment-
ing resistance every time. It is clear that Obeah was viewed as a symbol of resistance by both the slaves and their captors. In the 1780s, the
famous Jamaican outlaw Jack Mansong, "Three-Fingered Jack," carried
an Obeah bag given to him by the celebrated Obeah man Amalkir as
protection. Amalkir lived in a remote cave, and robbers and runaways
came to him for protective spells (Burdett 1800, 34). The obi* found by
the fugitive slave, one of the Maroons, who killed Jack was "a goat's horn,
filled with a compound of grave dirt, ashes, the blood of a black cat,
and human fat, all mixed into a kind of paste. A cat's foot, a dried toad,
a pig's tail, a slip of virginal parchment, of kid's skin, with characters
marked in blood on it were also in his obeah bag" (Burdett 1800, 34).

Another British government investigation, in 1789, asked expert witnesses specific questions about the practice of Obeah, such as "whether
Negroes called Obeah Men, or under any other denomination, practising Witchcraft, exist in the Isle of Jamaica?" The answer, of course, was

---

*Maroons were escaped slaves living in self-sufficient communities in remote places and
largely unmolested by the authorities. Obi is equivalent to the "instruments of Obeah",
or a horn containing items that might be in a "Hoodoo hand," "Nation Sack," or "Mojo"
in American parlance.

yes (Williams 1932, 109). In 1793, Bryan Edwards's *The History, Civil and Commercial, of the British Colonies in the West Indies* stated, "The term obeah is now become the general term to denote those Africans who in that island practise witchcraft or sorcery" (Williams 1932, 209). In 1808 and again in 1816, further acts to control the slaves and to suppress Obeah defined "the instruments of obeah" yet again: the 1816 act stated, "If there shall be found in the possession of slaves any poisonous drugs, pounded glass, parrots' beaks, dogs' teeth, alligator teeth, or other materials notoriously used in the profession of obeah or witchcraft, such slave upon conviction shall be liable to suffer transportation from this island, or such other punishment, not extending to life, as the court shall think proper to direct" (Williams 1932, 165).

After the abolition of slavery in the British Empire in 1833, the authorities were aware of the constant threat of rebellion, and another law for the suppression of Obeah was passed in 1845 (Robinson and Walhouse 1893, 210). Former slaves and their descendants rose up again in rebellion in Jamaica in 1865. Evidence was given to a royal commission convened in Jamaica after that uprising and the subsequent trial and execution of George William Gordon. One of the expert witnesses, Beckford Davis, was questioned on the prevalence and influence of Obeah. As with other investigations by the authorities, the minutiae of the instruments of Obeah were dwelt on. Davis stated, "Obeah men are acquainted with the venomous plants of the country . . . imposing on the Negroes by means of charms and things of that kind, such as dried fowl's head, a lizard's bones, old eggshells, tufts of hair, cats' claws, ducks' skulls; things of that kind. I have seen a good deal of it." Davis continued that the Obeah men "have no fixed residence; they wander the country wherever they can pick up dupes." One Obeah man arrested and sent to Port Antonio for trial, Davis noted, had a chest and "a book full of strange characters." The questioner asked Davis, "Did you ever see an Obeah Stick?" to which he answered, "Oh yes, plenty of them." Questioner: "With twisted serpents round them?" Davis: "Yes, some, and some with the likeness of a man's head, only of a very distorted cast" (Report 1866, II, 521).

A nineteenth-century report on Obeah by a British commissioner at Tortuga told its readers:

Obeah men officiate for a primitive people in a threefold capacity of priests, magicians and medicine men. The necromantic function is most prominent and many of them do little but practise sorcery, closely resembling the witches of the seventeenth and eighteenth centuries in Great Britain and the New England states, the definite personal contact with the Evil One being much less prominent. The obeah man catches "jumbies"—i.e. the spirits of the dead. He bottles them with secure corks; he finds them permanent employment by staking them on the see-shore, instructing the unhappy spirit not to leave his post until he has bailed the sea dry; or he sets the jumby on some other person. He gives charms to be taken into court to influence the magistrates' decision, or to obeah his adversary's tongue, so that he will be unable to speak properly, thus losing the case. He keeps wives faithful and gives seduction powders; he protects gardens and fruit-trees with some vile stinking stuff in a bottle; he makes shops profitable; he prevents boats from being wrecked; he cures diseases; he kills your enemy or his stock, or sends him away crazy; he compels the unwilling shopkeeper to give credit, and makes him unable to press for settlement of his account; he professes to be able to find treasure; he counteracts or takes off the obeahs of a professional brother; all with equal indifference, provided he receives his fee, which is usually large, frequently ending in his stripping his unhappy client of everything he possesses. His power may be summed up by saying that he knows how to propitiate or deceive strong spirits, and by his own secret knowledge and experience is able to make weak ones do his bidding. He also by certain rites and magical arts professes to have control over persons and things, so that he is able to bring about what he wishes or engages to do. (Udal 1915, 280–81)

Twentieth-century trials of Obeah men by the British Imperial authority in the West Indies recalled the witch trials of earlier times

Fig. 14.1. An instrument of Obeah. This was a carved figure confiscated from an Obeah man, embodying magical items and with feathers supposed to have special powers.

in Britain. In 1904 an act was passed by the Legislative Council of the Leeward Islands forbidding the possession of "the instruments of obeah." Those found in possession of these items were prosecuted for "practising obeah," but by then conviction no longer brought the practitioner to the gallows. Charles Dolly, of Plymouth, Montserrat, was found guilty of practicing Obeah in August 1904 (Udal 1915, 270). The sentence was twelve months in prison and a flogging for the third offense. Dolly, who appears to have been a well-known practitioner, had been found in possession of the instruments of Obeah, which included several articles, "largely composed of skulls, of portions of skulls, human bones, brass charms, with pieces of bone attached, silver coins, pieces of chalk, piece of looking-glass, horse-hair, turpentine and asafoetida" (Udal 1915, 271). A piece of skull with a cross chalked on it had been found concealed under the bolster of his bed, and another human skull was found with a cloth wrapped around it, with a horsehair and tin band plaited around its front. In his confession to the court, Dolly the Obeah Man, as he was known, explained how if one used "asafoetida smoked from a pipe through openings or crevices in a dwelling-house, the occupants would be rendered unconscious" (Udal 1915, 272).

In September 1904, at Charleston, Nevis, Charles Dasent was tried at a special sitting of the magistrates' court for the trial of Obeah cases. He had been found in possession of the instruments of Obeah, which were, according to the police:

> a tin canister containing two pieces of bone, three pieces of chalk, and other things. A quart tin containing sundry bones and bluestone. A calabash with bones, hard bread, orange peel and cassava roots. A parcel containing powdered leaves. A parcel of ashes tied up and put in a cup. Small tin cans containing "jumby" beads and old blue glass. Parcel containing what looked like Epsom salts—alum, rosin, etc. in a broken glass cup. Calabash with dried "bird-pepper" (*Pyper methysticum*). Parcel of what looked like "grave dirt." Bag containing cassava. Pack of playing cards. Small calabash cup. Large black helmet or hat. Pint of vinegar (gin). Small bottle of oil. [A jumby bead is a small, red, oval-shaped bead with a black spot at one end, used as an apotropaic charm against jumbies, or ghosts.] (Udal 1915, 273)

A relative, Theophilus Dasent, was prosecuted for Obeah in the following month. The instruments of Obeah found by the police were listed as "a keg containing white lime and hair. Bottles containing carbolic oil, and something white like—but—a fruit salt. Kerosene oil and quicksilver. In a locked-up room were found phials of Florida Water, turpentine, oil, and parcels of Epsom salts, and of sulphur. Also bottles of carbolic oil and turpentine; and in the defendent's own chamber a tusk and some asafoetida." (Florida water is one of the substances sold for use by hoodoo practitioners in the United States.)

Searching Theophilus Dasent's house for evidence of Obeah, the police found what they called letters: "Nearly all the letters were covered with hieroglyphics in pencil, very similar in character, representing plain short strokes in regular lines, as if scoring in a cricket score-book, finishing up each line with a couple of o's. Thus: /////////////00. They extended over a period of four years. Some asked for protection against the machinations of other persons, and for means of attacking or injuring them in return." Theophilus Dasent was convicted of practicing Obeah and was sentenced to twelve months' hard labor with two years subsequent police supervision (Udal 1915, 276–78).

West Indian Obeah was known in Great Britain from the eighteenth century, and items found in the possession of arrested Obeah men were exhibited and traded as curios there. A figure confiscated from Alexander Ellis, arrested for Obeah in Montserrat Bay, Jamaica, and subsequently tried in 1887, was exhibited in Jamaica and subsequently shown in England, and a report was published in the journal *Folk-Lore* in 1893 (Robinson and Walhouse 1893, 211). The references to "black men" visiting English witches are often presented as though they were not literal descriptions of real happenings. Was the black man who called at that house in Horseheath in 1928 (see chapter 10, page 106) an Obeah man bringing the woman the instruments of Obeah? After that, her neighbors believed her to have powers, and many people visited her to obtain cures (Robbins 1963, 556). The link between magical practices in Great Britain and those in her colonial possessions is a subject that would repay further research.

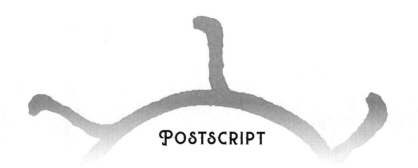

Operative Witchcraft and the Emergence of Wicca

The 1735 Witchcraft Act remained on the United Kingdom statutes until 1951, when the Fraudulent Mediums Act repealed it and brought in new offenses unrelated to witchcraft, which, by then, was seen as an extinct relic of a superseded world. Subsequent to the repeal of the Witchcraft Act, and influenced by Margaret Murray's books *The Witch Cult in Western Europe* and *The God of the Witches* (Murray 1921; 1933), Gerald Gardner set up a new religious form of pagan witchcraft that he called Wicca. In her popular books, Murray had argued that witchcraft was an ancient religion that had continued intact from ancient times as a secret practice. She claimed that it was even part of British royalty's mythos, with several medieval kings of England in Christian times having been human sacrifices to the old gods. There is one documented instance of this in pagan Sweden, when King Dómaldi was assassinated during a sacrificial ritual as a deliberate human sacrifice (Sturluson 1964, 15); this was the subject of an art controversy in Sweden in the second decade of the twentieth century in which this sacrifice was portrayed in a painting that was to be hung in a public building, then denied exhibition because of its scandalous pagan subject matter. It was finally allowed after many years (Moynihan 2007). Margaret Murray in turn had been influenced by the folklorist Charles Godfrey Leland's *Aradia, or the Gospel of the*

Fig. P.1. A traditional charm against evil

Witches, published in 1899, Leland himself being well versed in Romani folk magic.

Gerald Gardner, who was born in 1884, had claimed in 1939 that he possessed Matthew Hopkins's magical objects against witchcraft,

(Gardner 1939, 188–90). He took the opportunity of the old law's repeal in 1951 to publicize his group of witches, which, of course, attracted attention from the sensationalist Sunday newspapers that gave him further publicity and made him notorious. The press could never have enough of the titillating naked witches' sabbats, "sex worship," orgies, and "unspeakable rites" that an undercover journalist witnessed before he customarily "made his excuses and left" before having to join in. Gardner, who had been a functionary of the British Imperial regime in the colonies of Borneo and Malaya, was a Freemason, and the Wiccan rituals that he wrote about along with Doreen Valiente in his *Book of Shadows* showed influence from Malaysian folklore and Masonic rites and ceremonies as well as other contemporary currents of ritual magic, such as the writings of Éliphas Lévi and Aleister Crowley, Arthur Edward Waite's *The Book of Ceremonial Magic* (1911), and contemporary English literature. He claimed his rituals were ancient, and subsequently, his more enthusiastic followers made extravagant but unsupportable claims about continuity over thousands of years. Gardner said that he had been initiated into a group of witches in the New Forest in the 1930s, but his contribution to the journal *Folklore* in 1939 about Matthew Hopkins's supposed artifacts made no allusion to this.

In his books *Witchcraft Today* and *The Meaning of Witchcraft,* Gardner promoted his modern version of witchcraft, which benefited from the techniques of modern publicity. His new speculative witchcraft paralleled the development of Freemasonry, where the rites and ceremonies of the operative freemasons who worked with stone for a living were transmuted into a primarily ceremonial and spiritual organization whose members performed the rites but not the practical work of stonemasonry. The functional distinction between the operative masons and speculative Freemasonry still exists. Because of Gardner's popularization of speculative witchcraft as Wicca, by the 1960s various versions of Wicca proliferated, started by individuals whose practices had little connection with the documented activities of historical operative witches (as opposed to the accounts given at witch trials). But in

1964, following on the publicity surrounding Gardner and his death in that year, people from other currents of witchcraft had already outed themselves publicly by forming the Witchcraft Research Association. Some of the members claimed that the "old religion," a term formerly used by Protestants to describe Roman Catholicism in Britain but now appropriated to mean paganism, had been carried on in secret by groups of loyal adherents who perpetuated their knowledge hereditarily, carrying on the teachings to the present (Gwyn 1999, 206).

In November 1964, Doreen Valiente reported in *Pentagram* magazine that the group had contacted people from witchcraft traditions—the "old craft"—that had nothing to do with Wicca but which had survived in fragments all over the British Isles. Each group, Valiente asserted, had its own version of the tradition, and its own ideas of practice and ritual (Valiente 1964). The Witchcraft Research Association was wound up in 1967 because of internal schisms and external arguments with practitioners of Gardnerian Wicca, as it had become known. In 1969 it was considered that "the upsurge of interest in psychic phenomena—be they flying saucers or extrasensory perception—is conducive to the revival of witchcraft" (Johns 1969, 119). So by 1969, Alex Sanders could be described as "a professional white witch" who was said to be "the elected 'King of the Witches' and probably the most powerful witch in Europe" (Johns 1969, cover blurb). Sanders had already admitted to having performed acts of ritual magic that included the conjuration of demons for wealth, riches, and power before he assumed the mantle as the self-styled King of the Witches (Johns 1969, 35). He called his version of Wicca Alexandrian witchcraft, a name derived from Alex Sandrian but inferring connections with ancient Alexandria in Egypt.

In opposition to those who claimed traditional knowledge transmitted hereditarily, Sanders claimed that the classical text of Judaeo-Christian magic, *The Key of Solomon,* was "one of the few storehouses of witchcraft to have come down through the ages very much in its original form" (Johns 1969, 61). It was this text that he used as the basis of his rituals (Johns 1969, 62–63). Subsequently, he published his own

Book of Shadows, which has the authoritarian tone of Crowley's writings about it. It has dire warnings that for anyone who breaks the laws, even under torture, "the Curse of the Goddess shall be upon them" (*Laws* 35, 50, 123; quoted in Johns 1969).

In 1971, John Score, a Gardnerian Wiccan, founded the Pagan Front, which later published the *Wiccan* magazine, which was printed for the Front by the present author on his duplicating machines in the same room where this book was later written. Later, the Front changed its name to the Pagan Federation. Some members of the two kinds of Wicca, Gardnerian and Alexandrian, like those adherents of any other schismatic religion, long held sectarian hatred for one another, as indeed some of both persuasions did with those who practiced solitary Wicca and other currents—traditional, hereditary, and modern. By the early twenty-first century, the religion of Wicca had splintered into a proliferation of sects, currents, traditions, and lineages.

> *While Fates permit us, let's be merry;*
> *Passe all we must the fatall Ferry:*
> *And this our life too whirles away,*
> *With the rotation of the day.*
> ROBERT HERRICK, "TO ENJOY THE TIME"

FINIS

Glossary

biddie: An old woman, but one who has the power of "bidding" animals and people (and possibly spirits) to do her will.

black witch: A practitioner of malevolent witchcraft, bringing evil on others.

bor: East Anglian expression meaning "friend, farmer, comrade, or neighbor."

cardinal directions: North, east, south, and west. Between each are the intercardinal directions (q.v.).

charter: An unwritten code of conduct, such as the Fenman's Charter or the Old Charter, concerning the license for Plough Monday.

Devil's Plantation: A piece of uncultivated ground at the corner of a field or road, like a no-man's-land (q.v.), belonging to the otherworld. Also (in Scotland) Gudeman's Croft, the Old Guidman's Ground, the Halyman's Rig, the Halieman's Ley, the Black Faulie, or Clootie's Croft and (in England) Gallitrap or the Devil's Holt.

doctor: To doctor something is either to lay a spell on it or to add some substance to food or drink without the knowledge of the recipient; to fix up (q.v.).

electional astrology: Working out the optimal inceptional horoscope for a project in advance and founding the venture at that moment; punctual time (q.v.).

fane: A pagan sanctuary.

farthest beacon: Distant landmark, used in lining up the first rig in ploughing and shepherds' (witches') dials.

fix up: To alter an object magically, either to lay a spell on it or to add some substance to food or drink without the knowledge of the recipient; to doctor (q.v.).

foundation: The act of marking the beginning of a building by laying a stone with rites and ceremonies.

gallitrap: A magical circle made by a conjuring parson to entrap spirits or a criminal. Also, when used to refer to land, it can be the entrance to the underworld or an uncultivated plot of land given over to spirits or the devil.

gast: A piece of ground bound magically to be unproductive; a piece of land from which all the spirits have been banished.

geomancy: The art of location for buildings and other structures holistically in recognition of the site and the prevailing conditions—physical and spiritual.

gray witch: A witch who uses her power for ill or good.

hokkiben: Romani term meaning "deception or confidence trick.

hoodoo: African American folk magic.

inceptional horoscope: The horoscope of a project at its beginning (q.v., electional astrology).

instruments of Obeah: The materia magica (q.v.) of West Indian Obeah as defined by Jamaican antiwitchcraft laws.

intercardinal directions: The directions lying at 45 degrees to the cardinal ones: northeast, southeast, southwest, and northeast.

invultation (invultuation): The practice of making and using images or effigies of people or animals for magical purposes.

lock: The interlocking pattern of swords used by traditional sword dancers.

materia magica: The materials, paraphernalia, and such used in the performance of magic.

mell: A hammer.

nail down his (or her) track, to: To hammer a nail into a footprint made by an ill-wisher to nullify his or her magic.

no-man's-land: A triangle of ground at a trifinium (q.v.) belonging to no individual but rather to the spirit world, sometimes called a Cocked Hat. Closely related to the Devil's Plantation (q.v.) and other such terms.

Obeah: The West Indian equivalent of witchcraft, combining African and European elements.

obi: A magical object empowered by Obeah.

omphalos: Navel of the World, spiritual center point, depicted as an egg-stone.

orientation: The alignment of a building toward the east.

pentacle/pentagram : A five-pointed equal-sided star.

plumpendicular: Vertically perpendicular as verified by a plumb line.

punctual time: The exact moment for a foundation according to electional astrology (q.v.).

puss-skin wallet: A receptacle for the "instruments of obeah."

trifinium: Junction of three roads.

put a pin in for someone, to: To stick a pin into an image, a pincushion, an onion, or other similar object to magically harm someone.

put the toad on, to: To use toad magic to affect someone.

rempham: An alternative name for a pentagram.

rig: A straight line, as in ploughing.

teir nos ysbrydion: Welsh term meaning "a three-spirit night."

three holy names, the: Many traditional spells in British witchcraft use the three epithets of God from the Christian trinity as names of power—the Father, the Son, and the Holy Ghost.

trifinium or trivium: A junction of three roads, sometimes enclosing a triangular piece of ground that is a no-man's-land (q.v.).

witch men: Guisers or mummers who go about on Plough Monday with their faces darkened.

witches' church: In the Cambridgeshire Fens, an outside toilet.

white witch: Witch who employs countermagic against black witchcraft, charging clients money so to do.

Bibliography

Adams, William Henry Davenport. 1895. *Witch, Warlock and Magician: Historical Sketches of Magic and Witchcraft in England and Scotland*. London: Chatto & Windus.

Addy, Sidney Oldall. 1888. *A Glossary of Words Used in the Neighbourhood of Sheffield*. London: English Dialect Society.

———. 1907. "Guising and Mumming in Derbyshire." *Journal of the Derbyshire Archaeological and Natural History Society* 29: 31–42.

Adler, Margot. 1986. *Drawing Down the Moon*. New York: Beacon.

Agrippa, Heinrich Cornelius (1531–1533). *De occulta philosophia libri tres*. Translated by J. F. [John French], 1651. As *Three Books of Occult Philosophy*. London: printed by R.W. for Gregory Moule.

Aldred, Wags. n.d. *Stories from Wags Aldred: Suffolk Stallion Leader*. Helions Bumpstead, England: Neil Lanham.

Allen, Andrew. 1995. *A Dictionary of Sussex Folk Medicine*. Newbury, England: Countryside Books.

An Act For The Better Ordering of Slaves. 1684. In *The Laws of Jamaica, passed by the Assembly and confirmed by His Majesty in Council, April 17, 1784*. London: Government publication 140–48.

Andrews, William. 1898. *Bygone Norfolk*. London: William Andrews.

Annand, Kenneth Fraser, and Ann Butcher. 1994. *Remedies and Reminiscences*. St. Day, England: Tredinnick Press.

Ashmole, Elias. 1652. *Theatrum Chemicum Britannicum*. London: John Grismond.

Ashton, John. 1896. *The Devil In Britain and America*. London: Ward and Downing.

Atkinson, Rev. J. C. 1891. *Forty Years in a Moorland Parish: Reminiscences and Researches in Danby in Cleveland.* London and New York: Macmillan and Co.

Bächtold-Stäubli, Hanns, ed. 1927–1942. *Handwörterbuch des Deutschen Aberglaubens.* 9 vols. Berlin: Koehler und Amerlang.

Bales, E. G. 1939. "Folklore from West Norfolk." *Folklore* 50, no. 1 (March): 66–75.

Banbury, Thomas. 1895. *Jamaica Superstitions, or The Obeah Book.* Kingston: Mortimer C. DeSouza.

Banks, M. M., and M. A. Hardy. (1902) 1913. "The Evil Eye in Somerset." *Folk-Lore* 24, no. 3 (September): 382–83.

Bannerman, John. 1986. *The Beatons: A Medical Kindred in the Classical Gaelic Tradition.* Edinburgh: Humanities Press.

Barrell, John. 1980. *The Dark Side of the Landscape.* Cambridge, England: Cambridge University Press.

Barrett, Francis. (1801) 2007. *The Magus, or Celestial Intelligencer.* Stroud, England: Non Such Publishing.

Barrett, Walter Henry. 1958. "A Cure for Witches." *East Anglian Magazine,* March, 295–90.

———. 1963. *Tales From the Fens.* London: Routledge & Kegan Paul.

Barrett, Walter Henry, and Enid Porter, eds. 1964. *More Tales from the Fens.* London: Routledge & Kegan Paul.

Bärtsch, Albert. 1993. *Holz Masken: Fastnachts- und Maskenbrauchtum in der Schweiz, in Süddeutschland und Österrech.* Aarau, Switzerland: AT Verlag.

Baskervill, C. R. 1924. "Mummers' Wooing Plays in England." *Modern Philology* 21, no. 3 (February): 241–45.

Baudrillard, Jean. 1993. *The Transparency of Evil: Essays on Extreme Phenomena.* Translated by James Benedict. London and New York: Verso.

Bayliss, Peter. 1997. "Secrets of the Horse Whisperers." *Tradition* 3 (September–October): 12–13.

Becker, Howard. 1963. *The Outsiders: Studies in the Sociology of Deviance.* Glencoe, Scotland: Free Press.

Bendix, R. 1997. *In Search of Authenticity: The Formation of Folklore Studies.* Madison: University of Wisconsin Press.

Bennett, Gillian. 1993. "Folklore Studies and English Rural Myth." *Rural History* 4, no. 1: 77–91.

Bettis, Joseph Dabney, ed. 1969. *The Phenomenology of Religion.* New York: Harper and Row.

Bevis, Trevor. 1994. *Hard graft for Old-Time Fenmen.* March, England: privately published.

Bishop, Peter. 1998. *The Sacred and Profane History of Bury St. Edmunds.* London: Unicorn.

Black, George Fraser, and Whitridge Thomas Northcote. 1903. *Examples of Printed Folklore Concerning the Orkney and Shetland Islands.* London: David Nutt.

Black, William George. 1893. *Folk Medicine.* London: Elliott Stock.

Blécourt, Willem de. 1994. "Witchdoctors, Soothsayers, and Priests." *Social History* 19: 285–303.

Bouget, Henri. 1608. *Discours des Sorciers.* Lyon, France: Pillehote.

Bovet, Richard. 1684. *Pandæmonium, or, The Devil's Cloyster.* London: J. Walthoe.

Braekman, Willy L. 1997. *Middeleeuwse witte en zwarte magie in het Nederlands taalgebied.* Ghent, the Netherlands: Koninklijke Academie voor Nederlandse Taal-en Letterkunde.

Braithwaite, Edward. 1971. *The Development of Creole Society in Jamaica.* Oxford, England: Oxford University Press.

Briggs, Katharine Mary. 1962. *Pale Hecate's Team.* London: Routledge & Kegan Paul.

Brill, Edith. 1990. *Life and Traditions on the Cotswolds.* Stroud, England: Alan Sutton Publishing.

Broadwood, Lucy, and J. A. Fuller Maitland. 1893. *English County Songs.* London and New York: Charles Scribner's Sons.

Brockie, William. 1886. *Legends and Superstitions of the County of Durham.* Sunderland, England: B. Williams.

Bronner, S. J. 1992. *Creativity and Tradition in Folklore: New Directions.* Logan: Utah State University Press.

Brown, Calum G. 2001. *The Death of Christian Britain.* London: Routledge.

Brown, Carleton F., and John George Hohman. 1904. "The Long Hidden Friend." *Journal of American Folklore* 17, no. 65 (April–June): 89–152.

Brown, Theo. 1958. "The Black Dog." *Folklore* 69, no. 3 (September): 175–92.

———. 1962. "The Dartmoor Entrance to the Underworld." *Devon and Cornwall Notes & Queries* XXIX: 6–7.

———. 1966. "The Triple Gateway." *Folklore* 77, no. 2 (Summer): 123–31.

———. 1970. "Charming in Devon." *Folklore* 81, no. 1 (Spring): 37–47.

Browne, Thomas 1658. *Hydriotaphia. Urne-Buriall, or, A Discourse of the Sepulchrall Urnes lately found in Norfolk*. London, Hen. Brome.

Bunn, Ivan. 1975. "Mummified Cats!" *Lantern* 12 (Winter): 9.

———. 1977a. "Black Shuck. Part One: Encounters, Legends, and Ambiguities." *Lantern* 18 (Summer): 3–6.

———. 1977b. "Black Shuck. Part Two." *Lantern* 19 (Autumn): 4–8.

———. 1982. "A Devil's Shield . . . Notes on Suffolk Witch Bottles." *Lantern* 39 (Autumn): 3–7.

Burdett, William. 1800. *The Life and Exploits of Mansong, Commonly Called Three-Fingered Jack, The Terror Of Jamaica*. Sommers Town, Jamaica: n.p.

Burgess, Michael W. 1978. "Crossroad and Roadside Burials." *Lantern* 24 (Winter): 6–8.

Burn, Ronald. 1914. "Folk-Lore from Newmarket, Cambridgeshire." *Folk-Lore* 25, no. 3 (September): 363–66.

Burne, Charlotte Sophie, and Georgina F. Jackson. 1883. *Shropshire Folk-Lore*. London: Trübner.

Burton, Robert. (1621) 1926. *The Anatomy of Melancholy*. 3 vols. London: Bell and Sons.

Butcher, D. R. 1972. "The Last Ears of Harvest." *East Anglian Magazine* 31: 463–65.

Canney, Maurice A. 1926. "The Use of Sand in Magic and Religion." *Man*, January, 13.

Carrouges, Michel. 1974. *André Breton and the Basic Concepts of Surrealism*. Birmingham: University of Alabama Press.

Chambers, Edmund Kerchever. 1933. *The English Folk Play*. Oxford, England: Clarendon Press.

Charters, Samuel. 1973. *Robert Johnson*. New York: Oak Publications.

Cheape, Hugh. 1993. "The Red Book of Appin: Medicine as Magic and Magic as Medicine." *Folklore* 104, no. 1/2: 111–23.

Chumbley, Andrew. 2000. *Grimoire of the Golden Toad*. London: Xoanon Publishing.

———. 2001. *The Leaper Between: An Historical Study of the Toad Bone Amulet*. Privately published and circulated.

Cielo, Astra. 1918. *Signs, Omens, and Superstitions*. New York: George Sully.

Clabburn, Pamela, ed. 1971. *Working Class Costume from Sketches of Characters by William Johnstone White, 1818*. London: The Costume Society.

Clark, Stuart. 1980. "Inversion, Misrule and Meaning of Witchcraft." *Past and Present* 87: 98–127.

Cohen, Stanley, and Laurie Taylor. 1992. *Escape Attempts: The Theory and Practice of Resistance to Everyday Life.* London: Routledge.

Cohn, Norman. 1975. *Europe's Inner Demons.* New York: Basic Books.

Coles, William. 1650. *Nature's Paradise.* London: n.p.

Connel, John. 1901. *Confessions of a Poacher.* London: Lilliput Press.

Conway, Moncure Daniel. 1879. *Demonology and Devil Lore.* London: Chatto & Windus.

Cooper, Emmanuel. 1994. *People's Art: Working-Class Art from 1750 to the Present Day.* Edinburgh and London: Mainstream Publishing.

Cooper, Thomas. 1617. *The Mystery of Witchcraft: Discovering the Truth, Nature, Occasions, Growth, and Power Thereof.* London: Nicholas Okes.

Cotta, John. 1616a. *The Triall of Witchcraft.* London: Samuel Rand.

———. 1616b. *A Treatise of Witchcraft.* London: Samuel Rand.

———. 1625. *The Infallible and Assured Witch.* London: R. H.

Couch, Thomas Quiller. 1871. *The History of Polperro.* Truro, England: W. Lake.

Courtney, Margaret Ann. 1886. "Cornish Feasts and 'Festen' Customs." *Folk-Lore Journal* 4, no. 2: 109–32.

Cowper, Henry Swainson. 1899. *Hawkshead.* London: Bemrose and Sons.

Crombie, James E. 1895. "Shoe-Throwing at Weddings." *Folk-Lore* 6, no. 3 (September): 258–81.

Crooke, W. 1909. "Burial of Suicides at Crossroads." *Folklore* 20, no. 1 (March): 88–89.

Crossing, William. 1911. *Folk Rhymes of Devon.* Exeter, England: James G. Commin.

Crowley, Aleister. 1991. *Magick in Theory and Practice.* New York: Castle Books.

Crowley, Vivianne. 1989. *Wicca: The Old Religion in the New Age.* Wellingborough, England: Aquarian.

———. 1992. *Principles of Wicca.* London: Aquarian.

Crowther, Patricia. 1998. *One Witch's World.* London: Hale.

Dacombe, Marianne R., ed. circa 1935. *Dorset Up Along and Down Along.* Dorchester, England: Longmans.

Daily, Mary. 1973. *Beyond God the Father: Towards a Philosophy of Women's Liberation.* Boston: Beacon.

Dalyell, John Graham. 1834. *The Darker Superstitions of Scotland.* Edinburgh: Waugh & Innes.

Daniel, George. 1842. *Merrie England in the Olden Time.* 2 vols. London: Richard Bentley.

Davenport, John. 1646. *The Witches of Huntingdon.* London: n.p.

Davidson, Thomas. 1956. "The Horseman's Word: A Rural Initiation Ceremony." *Gwerin* 1: 67–74.

Davies, Jonathan Ceredig. 1908. "Ghost-Raising in Wales." *Folklore* 19, no. 3 (September): 327–31.

Davies, Owen. 1996. "Healing Charms Used in England and Wales 1700–1950." *Folklore* 107: 19–32.

Day, Brian. 1998. *A Chronicle of Fen Customs.* London: Hamlyn.

Day, George. 1894. "Notes on Essex Dialect and Folk-Lore, with Some Account of the Divining Rod." *Essex Naturalist* 8: 71–85.

Debus, Allen G. 1982. "Scientific Truth and Occult Tradition: The Medical Works of Ebenezer Sibly (1751–1799)." *Medical History* 26: 259–78.

De Casseres, Benjamin. 1909. "Pamela Colman Smith." *Camera Work* 27 (July): 20.

De Laurence, William Lauron. 1904. *The Book of Magical Art: Hindu Ritual and Indian Occultism.* New York: The De Laurence Co.

Denham, Michael Aislabie. 1892. *The Denham Tracts.* London: David Nutt. Reprinted from the original tracts and pamphlets printed by Mr. Denham between 1846 and 1859.

Dewey, John. 1922. "Realism without Monism or Dualism." *Journal of Philosophy* 19: 13.

Ditchfield, Peter Hampson. 1896. *Old English Customs Extant at the Present Time: An Account of Local Observances, Festival Customs, and Ancient Ceremonies Surviving in Great Britain.* London: G. Redway.

Dowson, Warren R. 1932. "A Norfolk Vicar's Charm against Ague." *Norfolk Archaeology* 24: 233–39.

Drake, Mavis R. 1989. *A Potpourri of East Anglian Witchcraft.* Royston, England: Sylvana Publications.

Drechsler, Paul. 1903. *Brauch und Volksglaube in Schlesien.* Leipzig, Germany: B. G. Teubner.

Drury, Susan. 1991. "Plants and Wart Cures in England from the Seventeenth to the Nineteenth Century: Some Examples." *Folklore* 102: 1, 97–100.

Durant, John. 1997. *Art and Nature Joyn Hand in Hand, or, the Poor Man's Daily Companion.* London: Sam Clark.

Dyer, Thomas Firminger Thistleton. 1878. *English Folk-Lore.* London: Bogue.

———. 1881. *Domestic Folk-Lore.* London: Cassell.

———. 1889. *The Folk-Lore of Plants*. London: Chatto & Windus.

———. 1905. *Folk-Lore of Women*. London: Elliot Stock.

Eddrup, Rev. Canon. 1885. "Notes on Some Wiltshire Superstitions." *Wiltshire Archaeological and Natural History Magazine* 22: 330–34.

Egidius. 1935. "Magic in Norfolk." *East Anglian Magazine* 1, no. 2 (August): 93–95.

Ellis-Davidson, Hilda. 1993. *The Lost Beliefs of Northern Europe*. London: Routledge.

Elworthy, Frederick Thomas. 1895. *The Evil Eye*. London: John Murray.

Emerick, Abraham J. 1915. *Obeah and Duppyism in Jamaica*. Woodstock: privately published.

———. 1916a. *Jamaican Duppies*. Woodstock: privately published.

———. 1916b. *Jamaica Myalism*. Woodstock: privately published.

Ettinger, Ellen. 1943. "Documents of British Superstition in Oxford." *Folklore* 54, no. 1 (March): 227–49.

Evans, E. Estyn. 1957. *Irish Folk Ways*. London: Routledge & Kegan Paul.

Evans, George Ewart. 1965. *Ask the Fellows Who Cut the Hay*. London: Faber and Faber.

———. 1971. *The Pattern under the Plough*. London: Faber and Faber.

Evans-Wentz, W. Y. 1911. *The Fairy Faith in Celtic Countries*. Oxford, England: Oxford University Press.

Farrar, Janet, and Stewart Farrar. 1981. *Eight Sabbats for Witches*. London: Hale.

———. 1990. *The Witches' Way*. London: Hale.

Finnegan, Ruth. 1991. "Tradition, but What Tradition and for Whom?" *Oral Tradition* 6: 104–24.

Flaherty, Robert Pearson. 1992. "Todaustragen: The Ritual Expulsion of Death at Mid-Lent: History and Scholarship." *Folklore* 103: 1, 40–55.

Forbes, Thomas R. 1966. *The Midwife and the Witch*. New Haven, Conn.: Yale University Press.

Forby, Robert. 1830. *The Vocabulary of East Anglia*. 2 vols. London: J. B. Nichols and Son.

Forrest, James T. 1951. "Folk 'Medicine.'" *Midwest Folklore* 1, no. 2 (Summer): 121–23.

Foster, J. J. 1917. "Goat and Cows." *Folklore* 28, no. 4 (December): 451.

Fox, Adam. 1999. "Remembering the Past in Early Modern England: Oral and Written Tradition." *Transactions of the Royal Historical Society* 9: 233–56.

Frazer, Sir James George. 1922. *The Golden Bough*. Abridged edition. London: Macmillan.

Frazier, Paul. 1952. "Some Lore of Hexing and Powwowing." *Midwest Folklore* 2, no. 2 (Summer): 101–7.

Friedman, J. 1992. "The Past in the Future: History and the Politics of Identity." *American Anthropologist* 94, no. 4: 837–59.

G. B. 1644. *A Dog's Elegy*. London: n.p.

Gallup, P. W. 1985. "The Ceremony of the White Cock in Winchester." *Folklore* 96, no. 1: 112–14.

Gardner, Gerald Brosseau. 1939. "Witchcraft." *Folk-Lore* 50: 188–90.

———. 1954. *Witchcraft Today*. London: Rider.

———. 1959. *The Meaning of Witchcraft*. London: Rider.

Gardner, Phyllis. 1933. "Billy-Goats." *Folklore* 44, no. 2 (June): 218.

Gaster, M. 1910. "English Charms of the Seventeenth Century." *Folk-Lore* 21, no. 3 (September): 375–78.

Gent, F. P. 1956. "Witches and Other Foul Fiends." *East Anglian Magazine*, March, 255–57; June, 471–72; August, 587; December, 119.

Gellner, E. 1992. *Postmodernism, Reason and Religion*. London: Routledge.

Gerish, William Blyth. 1892. *Norfolk Folk-Lore*. London: n.p.

———. 1895. "A Churchyard Charm." *Folk-Lore* 6, no. 2 (June): 200.

———. 1911. *The Folk-Lore of Hertfordshire*. Bishop's Stortford, England: n.p.

Gettings, Fred. 1981. *Dictionary of Occult, Hermetic, and Alchemical Sigils*. London: Routledge & Kegan Paul.

Gifford, George. 1607. *A Dialogue Concerning Witches and Witchcraft*. London: n.p.

Gilbert, William. 1911. "Witchcraft in Essex." *Transactions of the Essex Archaeological Society* n.s., XI: 210–18.

Gill, W. W. 1944. "The One-Night House." *Folklore* 55, no. 3 (September): 128–32.

Ginzburg, Carlo. 1983. *The Night Battles: Witchcraft and Agrarian Cults in the Sixteenth and Seventeenth Centuries*. London: Routledge & Kegan Paul.

———. 1990. *Ecstasies: Deciphering the Witches' Sabbath*. London: Hutchinson.

Glanvil, Joseph. 1681. *Saducismus Triumphatus, or Full and Plain Evidence Concerning Witches and Apparitions*. London: Thomas Newcombe.

Glyde, John, Jr. 1872. *Norfolk Garland: A Collection of the Superstitious Beliefs and Practices, Proverbs, Curious Customs, Ballads, and Songs of the People of Norfolk, as well as Anecdotes Illustrative of the Genius or Peculiarities of Norfolk Celebrities*. Norwich, England: Jarrold and Sons.

———. 1976. *Folklore and Customs of Suffolk*. Originally published in 1866 as *A New Suffolk Garland*. Norwich, England: EDP Publishing.

Gomme, Alice B. 1909. "Folk-Lore Scraps from Several Localities." *Folklore* 20, no. 1 (March): 72–83.

Goodrich-Freer, A. 1899. "The Powers of Evil in the Outer Hebrides." *Folk-Lore* 10, no. 3 (September): 259–82.

Gossett, A. L. J. 1911. *Shepherds of Britain: Scenes from Shepherd Life Past and Present from the Best Authorities.* London: Constable and Co.

Graves, Robert. 1948. *The White Goddess.* London: Faber & Faber.

Green, Arthur Robert. (1926) 1978. *Sundials: Incised Dials or Mass-Clocks.* London: Society for Promoting Christian Knowledge.

Green, Thomas. 1832. *The Universal Herbal.* Liverpool, The Caxton Press.

Gregor, Walter. 1881. *Notes on the Folk-Lore of the North-East of Scotland.* London: Folk-Lore Society.

Gregory, Annabel. 1997. "Witchcraft and Politics and 'Good Neighbourhood' in Seventeenth-Century Rye." *Past and Present* 133: 31–66.

Grey, William. 1975. *The Rollright Rituals.* London: Helios.

Grieve, M. 1931. *A Modern Herbal.* Edited and introduced by C. F. Leyel. London: Jonathan Cape.

Griffinhoofe, H. G. 1894. "Breeding Stone." *Essex Review* III: 144.

Groves, Derham. 1991. *Feng-Shui and Western Building Ceremonies.* Lutterworth, England: Tynron Press, and Singapore: Graham Brash.

Gundermann, G. 1901. "Die Namen der Wochentage bei den Römern." *Zeitschrift für deutsche Wortforschung* 1: 175–80.

Gurdon, Camilla. 1892. "Folk-Lore from South-East Suffolk." *Folk-Lore* 3, no. 4 (December): 558–60.

Gurdon, Lady Evelyne C. 1893. *County Folk-Lore of Suffolk.* London: David Butt.

Gutch, Mrs., and Mabel Peacock. 1908. *Examples of Printed Folk-Lore Concerning Lincolnshire.* London: David Nutt.

Gwyn. 1999. *Light from the Shadows: A Mythos of Modern Witchcraft.* Chieveley, England: Capall Bann Publishing.

Gypsy Queen. 1901. *The Zingara Fortune Teller: A Complete Treatise on the Art of Predicting Future Events.* Philadelphia, Pa.: David McKey.

Hadow, Grace E., and Ruth Anderson. 1924. "Scraps of English Folk-Lore IX (Suffolk)." *Folk-Lore* 35, no. 4 (December): 346–60.

Harland, John, and Wilkinson, T. T. 1867. *Lancashire Folk-Lore.* London: Frederick Warne and Co.

Harley, David. 1990. "Historians as Demonologists: The Myth of the Midwife-Witch." *Social History of Medicine* 3: 1–26.

Heanley, Rev. R. M. 1902. "The Vikings: Traces of Their Folklore in Marshland." *Saga Book of the Viking Club* III, part I (January) 13–17.

Helm, Alex. 1981. *The English Mummers' Play.* London: D. S. Brewer and Rowman and Littlefield for the Folklore Society.

Henderson, William. 1866. *Notes on the Folk-Lore of the Northern Counties of England and the Border.* London: Longmans, Green and Company.

Hennels, C. E. 1961. "The Broomstick Dancers of the Fens." *East Anglian Magazine* 21: 188–89.

———. 1972. "The Wild Herb Men." *East Anglian Magazine* 32: 79–80.

Herrick, Robert. (1648) 1902. *The Poems of Robert Herrick.* London: Grant Richards.

Hetherington, Kevin. 2000. *New Age Travellers: Vanloads of Uproarious Humanity.* London: Cassell.

Hewison, R. 1987. *The Heritage Industry.* London: Methuen.

Hewett, Sarah. 1900. *Nummits and Crummits: Devonshire Customs.* London: Thomas Burleigh.

Hickey, Sally. 1990. "Fatal Feeds? Plants, Livestock, and Witchcraft Accusations in Tudor and Stuart Britain." *Folklore* 101: 131–42.

Hissey, James John. 1898. *Over Fen and Wold.* London: Macmillan.

Hobsbawm, Eric, and George Rudé. 1969. *Captain Swing.* London: Lawrence and Wishart.

Hochschild, Arlie Russell. 1983. *The Managed Heart: Commercialization of Human Feeling.* Berkeley: University of California Press.

Hole, Christina. 1977. "Protective Symbols in the Home." In *Symbols of Power,* edited by H. R. Ellis-Davidson. London: The Folklore Society.

Holmes, Clive. 1993. "Women: Witnesses and Witches." *Past and Present* 140: 45–78.

Hone, William. 1827–1828. *The Every-Day Book.* 2 vols. London: Hunt and Clarke.

Hopkins, Matthew, the Witchfinder General. 1647. *The Discovery of Witches.* London: n.p.

Howard, Margaret. 1951. "Dried Cats." *Man* 61: 149–51.

Howard, Michael. 1987. *Traditional Folk Remedies.* London: Century Hutchinson.

Howe, Bea. 1952. "Witches over the Crouch." *East Anglian Magazine,* November, 21–24.

———. 1956. "James Murrell, Last of the Essex Wizards." *East Anglian Magazine,* January, 138–41.

Hudleston, N. A. n.d. *Lore and Laughter of South Cambridgeshire.* Cambridge, England: St. Tibbs Press.

Huelsenbeck, Richard. 1918. *Dadaistisches Manifest.* Berlin: n.p.

Humphries, John. 1995. *More Tales of the Old Poachers.* Newton Abbot, England: David and Charles.

Hurston, Zora N. 1931. "Hoodoo in America." *Journal of American Folklore* XLIV: 317–417.

Hyatt, Harry Middleton. 1970–1978. *Hoodoo, Conjuration, Witchcraft, Rootwork.* 5 vols. Memoirs of the Alma Egan Hyatt Foundation.

J. B. 1886. "Superstitions and Customs of Leicestershire." *Nottingham Guardian,* January 13, no. 9344, 3.

J. E. P. 1937. "Witches I Have Known." *East Anglian Magazine,* July, 450–52; August, 507.

Jarman, Neil. 1998. "Material of Culture, Fabric of Identity." In *Material Cultures: Why Some Things Matter,* edited by Daniel Miller, 121–146. London: UCL Press.

Jekyll, Gertrude. 1904. *Old West Surrey.* London: Longmans, Green and Company.

Jobson, Allan. 1966. *A Suffolk Calendar.* London: Robert Hale.

Johns, June. 1969. *King of the Witches: The World of Alex Sanders.* London: Peter Davies.

Johnson, Walter. 1912. *Byways in Archaeology.* Cambridge, England: Cambridge University Press.

Jonas, M. C., J. B. Partridge, Ella M. Leathers, and F. S. Potter. 1913. "Scraps of English Folk-Lore." *Folk-Lore* 24, no. 2 (July): 234–51.

Jones, Prudence. 1979. "Broomsticks." *Albion* 4: 8–10.

———. 1982. *Eight and Nine: Sacred Numbers of Sun and Moon in the Pagan North.* Fenris-Wolf Pagan Paper 2. Bar Hill, England: Fenris-Wolf.

Jones, Prudence, and Nigel Pennick. 1995. *A History of Pagan Europe.* London: Routledge.

Jones-Baker, Doris. 1977. *The Folklore of Hertfordshire.* London: B. T. Batsford Ltd.

Jonson, Ben. (1609) 1816. *The Works of Ben Jonson.* 9 vols. Notes and memoir by W. Gifford. London: W. Bulmer & Co.

Kamp, Jens. 1877. *Danske folkeminder, Æventyr, folkesagen, gaader, rim, og folketro.* Odense, Denmark: R. Nielsens Forlag.

Kandinsky, Wassily. 1912. *Über das Geistige in der Kunst.* Munich: Piper.

Karpeles, Maud. 1932. "English Folk Dances: Their Survival and Revival." *Folk-Lore* 43: 123–43.

Kelly, J. T. 1977. *Practical Astronomy during the Seventeenth Century: A Study of Almanac-Makers in America and England*. Ph.D. thesis, Harvard University.

Keverne, Richard. 1955. *Tales of Old Inns*. London: Collins.

Kieckhefer, Richard. 1976. *European Witch Trials: Their Foundation in Learned and Popular Culture, 1300–1500*. London: Routledge & Kegan Paul.

"King of the Norfolk Poachers, The." (1935) 1974. In *I Walked by Night*, edited by Lilias Rider Haggard. Woodbridge: Boydell Press.

Kirk, Robert. 1691. *The Secret Commonwealth of Elves, Fauns, and Fairies*. Edinburgh: n.p.

Kittredge, George L. 1922. *Witchcraft in Old and New England*. Cambridge, Mass.: Harvard University Press.

Klaits, Joseph. 1985. *Servants of Satan: The Age of the Witch-Hunts*. Bloomington: Indiana University Press.

Knight, C. 1859. *The Popular History of England: An Illustrated History of Society*. London: Bradbury and Evans.

Kramer, Heinrich, and Jacob Sprenger. 1971. *Malleus Maleficarum*. Translated in 1928 by M. Summers. New York: Dover.

Lambert, Margaret, and Enid Marx. 1989. *English Popular Art*. London: Merlin Press.

Latham, Charlotte. 1878. "Some West Sussex Superstitions Linger in 1868." *Folk-Lore Record* 1: 1–67.

Laver, Henry. 1889. "Fifty Years Ago in Essex." *Essex Naturalist* III (January–June): 27–35.

Law, Robert. 1818. *Memorials*. Edinburgh: Archibald Constable.

Lawless, Elaine J. 2003. "Woman as Abject: 'Resisting Cultural and Religious Myths that Condone Violence against Women.'" *Western Folklore* 62, no. 4 (Autumn): 237–69.

Lawrence, Robert Means. 1898. *The Magic of the Horse Shoe*. Boston and New York: Houghton Mifflin.

Leather, Ella Mary. 1912. *The Folk-Lore of Herefordshire*. Hereford: Jakeman and Carver; London: Sidgwick and Jackson.

———. 1914. "Foundation Sacrifice." *Folk-Lore* 24: 110.

Lecouteux, Claude. 2013. *The Tradition of Household Spirits*. Rochester, Vt.: Inner Traditions.

Lee, Rev. Frederick George, ed. 1875. *Glimpses of the Supernatural*. 2 vols. London: Henry S. King and Co.

Leland, Charles Godfrey. 1891. *Gypsy Sorcery and Fortune Telling: Illustrated by*

Numerous Incantations, Specimens of Medical Magic, Anecdotes and Tales. London: T. Fisher Unwin.

———. 1897. "The Straw Goblin." *Folk-Lore* 8, no. 1 (March): 87–88.

———. 1899. *Aradia, or the Gospel of the Witches.* London: David Nutt.

Lip, Evelyn. 1979. *Chinese Geomancy.* Singapore: Times Books International.

Locke, John. 1715. *A Compleat History of Magick, Sorcery, and Witchcraft.* London: E. Curll.

Lovett, Edward, F. Barry, J. G. Frazer, and F. N. Webb. 1905. "Veterinary Leechcraft." *Folk-Lore* 16, no. 3 (September): 334–37.

Lucas, John. 1990. *Hertfordshire Curiosities.* Wimborne: The Dovecote Press.

Lugh [E. W. Liddell]. 1982. *"Old George" Pickingill and the Roots of Modern Witchcraft.* London: Wiccan Publications.

M. G. C. H. 1936. "On a Hardle." *East Anglian Magazine,* June, 507.

MacCulloch, Mary Julia. 1923. "Folk-Lore of the Isle of Skye." *Folk-Lore* 34, no. 1 (March): 86–93.

MacFarlane, Alan. 1970. *Witchcraft in Tudor and Stuart England.* London: Routledge & Kegan Paul.

———. 1978. *The Origins of English Individualism.* Oxford, England: Blackwell, Oxford.

Mackinnon, John. (1825) 1881. *Account of Messingham in the County of Lincoln.* Edited in 1881 by Edward Peacock. Hertford: n.p.

MacPherson, Joseph McKenzie. 1929. *Primitive Beliefs in the North East of Scotland.* Edinburgh: Longman Green and Co.

Manning, Percy. 1902. "Stray Notes on Oxfordshire Folk-Lore." *Folk-Lore* 13, no. 3 (September): 288–95.

Maple, Eric. 1960. "The Witches of Canewdon." *Folklore* 71, no. 4 (December): 241–50.

———. 1965a. *The Dark World of Witches.* London: Pan.

———. 1965b. "Witchcraft and Magic in the Rochford Hundred." *Folklore* 76, no. 3 (Autumn): 213–24.

March, H. Colley. 1899. "Dorset Folk-Lore Collected in 1897." *Folk-Lore* 10, no. 4 (December): 478–89.

Marett, Thomas J., and Edith F. Carey. 1927. "Channel Islands Folk-Lore III." *Folk-Lore* 38, no. 2 (June): 178–82.

Marshall, Sybil. 1967. *Fenland Chronicle.* Cambridge, England: Cambridge University Press.

Martinengro-Cesaresco, Countess. 1887. "Negro Songs from Barbados." *Folk-Lore Journal* 5, no. 1: 5–10.

Massey, Alan. 1999. "The Reigate Witch Bottle." *Current Archaeology* 169: 34–36.

Mathers, Samuel Liddel MacGregor. *The Goetia: The Lesser Key of Solomon the King.* Edited by Aleister Crowley. York Beach, Maine: Samuel Weiser, 1997.

McAldowie, Alex. 1896. "Personal Experiences in Witchcraft." *Folk-Lore* 7, no. 3 (September): 309–14.

McIntosh, David S. 1951. "Blacksmith and Death." *Midwest Folklore* 1, no. 1 (April): 51–54.

McNeill, F. Marian. 1957–1968. *The Silver Bough.* 4 vols. Glasgow: William MacLellan.

Mehring, Walter. 1951. *The Lost Library: An Autobiography of a Culture.* New York:

Merrifield, Ralph. 1954. "The Use of Bellarmines and Witch Bottles." *Guildhall Miscellany* 3.

———. 1987. *The Archeology of Ritual and Magic.* London: Guild.

Miller, William Marion. 1944. "How to Become a Witch." *Journal of American Folklore* 57, no. 226 (October–December): 280.

Mitchell, Arthur. 1860–1862. "Superstition in the North-West Highlands and Islands of Scotland, Especially in Relation to Lunacy." In *Proceedings of the Society of Antiquaries of Scotland* 4: 251–88.

Moffatt, Adelene. 1891. "The Mountaineers of Middle Tennessee." *Journal of Midwest Folklore* 4, no. 15 (October–December): 314–20.

Monter, E. W. 1983. *Ritual, Myth, and Magic in Early Modern Europe.* Brighton, England: Harvester.

Moor, Edward. 1823. *Suffolk Words and Phrases.* London: J. Loder.

Morgan, Prys. 1983. "A Welsh Snakestone: Its Traditions and Folklore." *Folklore* 94, no. 2: 184–91.

Morgan, W. E. T. 1895. "Charms." *Folk-Lore* 6, no. 2 (June): 202–4.

———. 1895. "Charms." *Folk-Lore* 6, no. 3 (September): 304.

Morley, George. 1917. "The Wart Charmers of Warwickshire." *Occult Review* 26: 226–30.

Mortimer, Bishop Robert. 1972. *Exorcism: The Report of a Commission Convened by the Bishop of Exeter.* Edited by Dom Robert Petitpierre. London: The Society for Promoting Christian Knowledge.

Moynihan, Michael. 2007. "Carl Larsson's Greatest Sacrifice: The Saga of *Midvinterblot.*" *Tyr* 3: 215–46.

Murray, Margaret. 1921. *The Witch Cult in Western Europe.* Oxford, England: Oxford University Press.

———. 1933. *The God of the Witches.* London: Sampson Low.

———. 1952. *The Divine King in England.* London: Sampson Low.

Neat, Timothy. 2002. *The Horseman's Word.* Edinburgh: Birlinn.

Newall, Venetia. 1966. "Folklore and Male Homosexuality." *Folklore* 97, no. 2: 123–47.

———. 1973. *The Witch-Figure.* London: Routledge & Kegan Paul.

———. 1978. "Some Examples of the Practice of Obeah by West Indian Immigrants in London." *Folklore* 89, no. 1: 29–51.

———. 1987. "The Adaptation of Folklore and Tradition (Folklorismus)." *Folklore* 98, no. 2: 131–51.

Newman, L. F., and E. M. Wilson. 1952. "Folklore Survivals in the Southern 'Lake Counties' and in Essex: A Comparison and Contrast." *Folklore* 63, no. 2 (June): 91–104.

Newman, Leslie F. 1940. "Notes on Some Rural and Trade Initiations in the Eastern Counties." *Folklore* 51, no. 1 (March): 33–42.

———. 1946. "Some Notes on the Practise of Witchcraft in the Eastern Counties." *Folk-Lore* 57, no. 1 (March): 12–33.

———. 1948a. "Some Notes on the Pharmacology and Therapeutic Value of Folk-Medicines I." *Folklore* 59, no. 3 (September): 118–35.

———. 1948b. "Some Notes on the Pharmacology and Therapeutic Value of Folk-Medicines II." *Folklore* 59, no. 4 (December): 145–56.

Nöldeke, T. 1901. "Die Namen der Wochentage bei den Semiten." *Zeitschrift für deutsche Wortforschung* 1: 161.

Olsen, Olaf. 1966. *Hørg, Hof og Kirke.Historiske og arkælogiske vikingtidsstudier.* Copenhagen: G.E.C. Gad.

O'Neill, John. 1895. "Straw." *Journal of American Folk-Lore* 8, no. 31 (October–December): 291–98.

Ord, John. 1920. "The Most Secret of Secret Societies. Ancient Scottish Horsemen." *Glasgow Weekly Herald,* November 13.

———. (1930) 1995. *Ord's Bothy Songs and Ballads of Aberdeen Banff and Moray Angus and the Mearns.* Reprinted by John Donald Publishers, Edinburgh, 1995.

Ordish, T. Fairman. 1893. "English Folk-Drama II." *Folk-Lore* 4, no. 2 (June): 149–75.

Otto, Rudolf. 1973. *The Idea of the Holy.* New York: Oxford University Press.

Palmer, Roy. 1992. *Folklore of Hereford and Worcester.* Woonton, Almeley, England: Logaston Press.

———. 2004. *The Folklore of Shropshire.* Woonton, Almeley, England: Logaston Press.

Palmer, William. 1974. "Plough Monday 1933 at Little Downham." *English Folk Dance,* Spring, 24–25.

Papworth, Cyril. n.d. "The Comberton Broom Dance." Unpublished typescript.

Parker, B, and Raymond Unwin. 1901. "The Art of Building a Home." *Architect's Magazine* 1, no. 12 (October).

Parsons, Catherine E. 1915. "Notes on Cambridgeshire Witchcraft." *Proceedings of the Cambridge Antiquarian Society* XIX, no. LXVII: 31–52.

———. 1952. "Horseheath: Some Recollections of a Cambridgeshire Parish." Unpublished manuscript. Little Abingdon.

Parsons, Elsie Clews. 1934. "Ashanti Influence in Jamaica." *Journal of American Folklore* 47, no. 106 (October–December): 391–95.

Parsons, Melinda Boyd. 1987. "The 'Golden Dawn,' Synaesthesia, and 'Psychic Automatism' in the Art of Pamela Colman Smith." In *The Spiritual Image in Modern Art,* compiled by Kathleen J. Regier. Wheaton, Ill.: Theosophical Publishing House.

Pattinson, G. W. 1953. "Adult Education and Folklore." *Folklore* 64, no. 3 (September): 424–26.

Peacock, Edward. 1877. *A Glossary of Words Used in the Wapentakes of Manley and Corringham, Lincolnshire.* London: The Dialect Society.

Peacock, Mabel Geraldine W. 1896. "Executed Criminals and Folk Medicine." *Folk-Lore* 7, no. 3 (September): 268–83.

———. 1897. "Omens of Death." *Folk-Lore* 8, no. 4 (December): 377–78.

———. 1901a. "The Folk-Lore of Lincolnshire." *Folk-Lore* 12, no. 2 (June): 161–80.

———. 1901b. "Notes on Professor Rhys's Manx Folklore and Superstitions." *Folk-Lore* 2, no. 4 (December): 509–13.

Peacock, Mabel Geraldine W., Katherine Carson, and Charlotte Burne. 1901. "Customs Relating to Iron." *Folk-Lore* 12, no. 4 (December): 472–75.

Peesch, Reinhard. 1983. *The Ornament in European Folk Art.* New York: Alpine Fine Arts.

Pennick, Nigel. 1980. *Sacred Geometry: Symbolism and Purpose in Religious Structures.* Wellingborough, England: Aquarian Press.

———. 1985a. *The Cosmic Axis.* Bar Hill, England: Runestaff.

———. 1985b. *Daddy Witch and Old Mother Redcap*. Cambridge, England: Cornerstone Press.

———. 1985c. "Geomantic Reflections." *Practical Geomancy* 1, no. 1 (Winter): 13–14.

———. 1986. *Skulls, Cats, and Witch Bottles*. Bar Hill, England: Nigel Pennick.

———. 1987a. "The Subterranean Kingdom. Part One: Secret Rites in Secret Places." *Supernatural* 1, no. 12 (July): 49–53.

———. 1987b. "The Subterranean Kingdom. Part Two: Darkness and Light." *Supernatural* 1, no. 13 (August): 33–37.

———. 1989. *Practical Magic in the Northern Tradition*. Wellingborough, England: Thorsons.

———. 1992a. *The Pagan Source Book: A Guide to Festivals, Traditions, and Symbols of the Year*. London: Rider.

———. 1992b. "The Reality Censors: The World as Real Estate." *Fortean Times* 62 (April): 45–46.

———. (1995) 2004. *Secrets of East Anglian Magic*. London: Robert Hale. Second edition. Milverton, England: Capall Bann Publishing.

———. 1996. *Celtic Sacred Landscapes*. London and New York: Thames and Hudson.

———. 1998. *Crossing the Borderlines: Guising, Masking, and Ritual Animal Disguises in the European Tradition*. Chieveley, England: Capall Bann Publishing.

———. 1999a. *Beginnings: Geomancy, Builders' Rites, and Electional Astrology in the European Tradition*. Chieveley, England: Capall Bann Publishing.

———. 1999b. "Regarding the Ooser." *3rd Stone* 35 (July–September): 39–40.

———. 2002. *The Power Within: The Way of the Warrior and the Martial Arts in the European Tradition*. Chieveley, England: Capall Bann Publishing.

———. 2003–2004. "Heathen Holy Places in Northern Europe: A Cultural Overview." *Tyr: Myth-Culture-Tradition* 2: 139–49.

———. 2004. *Threshhold and Hearthstone Patterns*. Bar Hill, England: Old England House.

———. 2005a. *Natural Magic*. Earl Shilton, England: Lear Books.

———. 2005b. *The Sacred Art of Geometry: Temples of the Phoenix*. Bar Hill, England: Spiritual Arts & Crafts Publishing.

———. 2005c. "Vom Fortbestehen alter Grenzen." *Hagia Chora* 20: 103.

———. 2006a. *The Eldritch World*. Earl Shilton, England: Lear Books.

———. 2006b. *Folk-Lore of East Anglia and Adjoining Counties*. Bar Hill, England: Spiritual Arts & Crafts Publishing.

———. 2006c. *The Spiritual Arts and Crafts.* Bar Hill, England: Spiritual Arts & Crafts Publishing.

———. 2010a. "Pines On The Horizon, or, Seeing What We Want To See." *Silver Wheel Annual* 2: 97–101.

———. 2010b. *The Toadman.* Hinckley, U.K.: The Society of Esoteric Endeavour.

———. 2011. *In Field and Fen.* Earl Shilton, England: Lear Books.

———. 2015a. *The Book of Primal Signs.* Rochester Vt.: Destiny Books.

———. 2015b. *Pagan Magic in the Northern Tradition.* Rochester Vt.: Destiny Books.

———. 2017. *The Ideal Tower.* Hinckley, U.K.: The Society of Esoteric Endeavour.

Pennick, Nigel, and Sheila Cann. 1980. *Mother Shipton (Ursula Sontheil 1488–1561): Her Life and Prophecies.* Megalithic Visions Antiquarian Papers 15. Bar Hill, England: Fenris-Wolf.

Pennick, Nigel, and Paul Devereux. 1989. *Lines on the Landscape: Leys and Other Linear Enigmas.* London: Robert Hale.

Pennick, Nigel, and Helen Field. 2003. *A Book of Beasts.* Milverton, England: Capall Bann Publishing.

Perkins, William. 1608. *A Discourse of the Damned Art of Witchcraft.* Cambridge, England: O. Legge.

Petrie, Sir Flinders. (1930) 1990. *Decorative Patterns of the Ancient World.* London: Studio Editions.

Peukert, Will-Erich. 1961. *Deutsche Sagen.* Berlin: E Schmidt.:

———. 1963. *Ostalpensagen. Europäische Sagen Band III.* Berlin, E.Schmidt.

Porteous, Crichton. 1976. *The Ancient Customs of Derbyshire.* Derby, England: Derbyshire Countryside.

Porter, Enid. 1958. "Some Folk Life of the Fens." *Folklore* 69, no. 2 (June): 112–22.

———. 1961. "Folk Life and Traditions in the Fens." *Folklore* 72, no. 4 (December): 584–98.

———. 1969. *Cambridgeshire Customs and Folklore.* Fenland material provided by W. H. Barrett. London: Routledge & Kegan Paul.

———. 1974. *The Folklore of East Anglia.* London: Batsford.

Pringle, Patrick. 1951. *Stand and Deliver: The Story of the Highwaymen.* London: The London Museum.

Puhvel, Martin. 1976. "The Mystery of the Cross-Roads." *Folklore* 87, no. 2: 167–77.

Radcliffe, John Netten. 1854. *Fiends, Ghosts, and Sprites. Including an account of the origin and nature of belief in the supernatural.* London: L.R. Bailey.

Rampini, Charles Joseph Galliari. 1873. *Letters from Jamaica: The Land of Streams and Woods*. Edinburgh: Archibald Constable, Edmonton and Douglas.

Randall, Arthur. 1966. *Sixty Years a Fenman*. Edited by Enid Porter. London: Routledge & Kegan Paul.

Ranke, K. 1969. "Orale und literale Kontinuität." In *Kontinuität? Geschichtlichkeit und Dauer als volkskundliches Problem. Festschrift Hans Moser*, edited by H. Bausinger and W. Brückner. Berlin: E. Schmidt.

Ransom, Arthur. 1907. *Bohemia in London*. London: Chapman and Hall.

Rawlence, E. A. 1914. "Folk-Lore and Superstition Still Obtaining in Dorset." *Proceedings of the Dorsetshire Natural History and Antiquarian Field Club* 35: 81–87.

Rayson, George. 1865a. "East Anglian Folk-Lore, No. 1. 'Weather Proverbs.'" *East Anglian, or, Notes & Queries on Subjects Connected with the Counties of Suffolk, Cambridgeshire, Essex, and Norfolk* I: 155–62.

———. 1865b. "East Anglian Folk-Lore, No. 2. 'Omens.'" *East Anglian, or, Notes & Queries on Subjects Connected with the Counties of Suffolk, Cambridgeshire, Essex, and Norfolk* I: 185–86.

———. 1865c. "East Anglian Folk-Lore, No. 3. 'Charms.'" *East Anglian, or, Notes & Queries on Subjects Connected with the Counties of Suffolk, Cambridgeshire, Essex, and Norfolk* I: 214–17.

Read, D. H. Moutray. 1911. "Hampshire Folk-Lore." *Folk-Lore* 22, no. 3 (September): 292–329.

Regardie, Israel. 1977. *How To Make and Use Talismans*. Wellingborough, England: Aquarian Press.

Rennie, William, et al. 2009. *The Society of the Horseman's Word*. Hinckley, U.K.: The Society of Esoteric Endeavour.

Report of the Jamaica Royal Commission. 1866. London: n.p.

Reuter, Otto Sigfrid. 1987. *Skylore of the North*. Translated by Michael Behrend. Bar Hill, England: The Earthlore Institute.

Richter, Hans. 1965. *Dada: Art and Anti-Art*. London: Thames & Hudson.

Robbins, Rossell Hope. 1963. "The Imposture of Witchcraft." *Folklore* 74, no. 4 (Winter): 545–62.

Robinson, May, and M. J. Walhouse. 1893. "Obeah Worship in East and West Indies." *Folk-Lore* 4, no. 2 (June): 207–18.

Roper, Charles. 1893. "On Witchcraft Superstition in Norfolk." *Harper's New Monthly Magazine* 87, no. 521 (October): 792–97.

Rosen, Barbara, ed. 1991. *Witchcraft in England, 1558–1618*. New York: Taplinger.

Ross, Frederick. 1892. *Bygone London*. London: Hutchinson.

Roud, Steve. 2003. *The Penguin Guide to the Superstitions of Britain and Ireland*. London: Penguin.

Rudkin, Ethel. 1933. "Lincolnshire Folk-Lore." *Folk-Lore* 44, no. 3 (September): 189–214, 279–95.

———. 1934. "Lincolnshire Folk-Lore: Witches and Devils." *Folk-Lore* 45, no. 3 (September): 249–67.

———. 1936. *Lincolnshire Folklore*. Gainsborough: EP Publishing.

Russell, J. 1972. *Witchcraft in the Middle Ages*. Ithaca, N.Y.: Cornell University Press.

Russett, Vince. 1978. "At the Gallows Pole." *Picwinnard* 7 (November): 15–20.

Sadler, Ida. 1962. "Fifty Years of Working with Horses." *Cambridgeshire Local History Council Bulletin* 18 (Summer): 10–16.

Salmon, L. 1902. "Folk-Lore in the Kennet Valley." *Folk-Lore* 13, no. 4 (December): 418–29.

Sartori, Paul. 1898. "Ueber das Bauopfer." *Zeitschrift für Ethnologie* 30: 1–54.

Saunders, W. H. Bernard. 1888. *Legends and Traditions of Huntingdonshire*. London: Simpkin Marshall, Elliot Stock; Huntingdon, England: Geo. C. Caster.

Sawyer, Frederick E. 1884. "'Old Clem' Celebrations and Blacksmiths' Lore." *Folk-Lore Journal* 2, no. 11 (November): 321–29.

Schmitz, Nancy. 1977. "An Irish Wise Woman: Fact and Legend." *Journal of the Folklore Institute* 14, no. 3: 169–79.

Schwitters, Kurt. 1919. *Anna Blume: Dichtungen*. Hanover, Germany: P. Steegmann.

Scot, Reginald. (1584) 1886. *The Discoverie of Witchcraft*. Annotated by Brinsley Nicholson. Limited edition of 250. London: Elliot Stock.

Scott, Mackay Hugh Baillie. 1906. *Houses and Gardens*. London: George Newnes.

———. 1909. "Ideals in Buildings, False and True." In *The Arts Connected with Building*, edited by R. Weir Schulz. London: Batsford.

Scott, Sir Walter. 1885. *Letters on Demonology and Witchcraft*. 2nd ed. London and New York: George Routledge & Sons.

Seymour, St. John D. 1913. *Irish Witchcraft and Demonology*. Dublin: Hodges Figgis.

Sharp, Cecil. n.d. *The Sword Dances of Northern England*. Vol. 1. London: Novello.

Simper, Robert. 1980. *Traditions of East Anglia*. Woodbridge, England: The Boydell Press.

Simpson, Jacqueline. 1994. "Margaret Murray: Who Believed Her, And Why?" *Folklore* 105: 89–96.

———. 1996. "Witches and Witchbusters." *Folklore* 107: 5–18.

Singer, William. 1881. *An Exposition of the Miller and Horseman's Word, or the True System of Raising the Devil*. Aberdeen, Scotland: James Daniel.

Sinclair, A. T. 1909. "The Secret Language of Masons and Tinkers." *Journal of American Folklore* 22, no. 86 (October–December): 353–64.

Sly, Rex. 2003. *From Punt to Plough: A History of the Fens*. Slough, England: Sutton Publishing.

Smedley, Norman. 1955. "Two Bellarmine Bottles from Coddenham." *Proceedings of the Suffolk Institute of Archaeology* XXVI: 229.

———. 1967. "More Suffolk Witch Bottles." *Proceedings of the Suffolk Institute of Archaeology* XXX: 88–93.

Smith, Georgina. 1981. "Chapbooks and Traditional Plays: Communication and Performance." *Folklore* 92, no. 2: 196–202.

Smith, Pamela Colman. 1899. *Annancy Stories*. New York: R. H. Russell.

Speth, G. W. 1894. *Builders' Rites and Ceremonies*. Margate, England: Keeble's Gazette.

Spufford, Margaret. 1994. "The Pedlar, the Historian, and the Folklorist: Seventeenth Century Communication." *Folklore* 105: 13–24.

Starhawk. 1979. *The Spiral Dance*. New York: Beacon Press.

———. 1982. *Dreaming the Dark*. New York: Beacon Press.

Steiner, Rudolf. 1914. *An Outline of Occult Science*. Chicago and New York: Rand McNally.

Sternberg, Thomas. 1851. *The Dialect and Folk-Lore of Northamptonshire*. London: John Russell Smith; Northampton, England: Abel & Sons, G. N. Wetton; Brackley, England: R. Todd, Oundle, A. Green.

Stone, Alby. 1998. *Straight Track, Crooked Road: Leys, Spirit Paths, and Shamanism*. Wymeswold, England: Heart of Albion Press.

Street, Sean, ed. 1994. *A Remembered Land: Recollections of Life in the Countryside 1880–1914*. London: Michael Joseph.

Stuart, James (King James VI and I). (1587) 1603. *Demonologie: In Forme of a Dialogue*. London: Robert Waldgrave.

Sturluson, Snorri. 1964. *Heinskringla: History of the Kings of Norway*. Translated by Lee M. Hollander. Austin: University of Texas Press.

Taylor, Mark R. 1929. "Norfolk Folk-Lore." *Folk-Lore* 40, no. 2 (June): 113–33.

———. 1934. "Some Witchcraft Tales." *Folk-Lore* 45, no. 2 (June): 169–70.

Tebbutt, C. F. 1941. *History of Bluntisham cum Earith*. Bluntisham, England: privately published.

———. 1942. "Huntingdonshire Folk and Their Folklore." *Transactions of the Cambridgeshire and Huntingdonshire Archaeological Society* VI: 119–54.

———. 1950. "Huntingdonshire Folk and Their Folklore." *Transactions of the Cambridgeshire and Huntingdonshire Archaeological Society* VII: 54–64.

———. 1984. *Huntingdonshire Folklore*. St. Ives, England: Norris Museum.

Thiesen, Karen. 1979. *Country Remedies*. London: Pierrot Publishing.

Thomas, Val. 2002. *A Witch's Kitchen*. Chieveley, England: Capall Bann Publishing.

Thompson, C. J. S. 1934. *The Mystic Mandrake*. London: Rider.

———. 1993. *The Quacks of Old London*. New York: Barnes and Noble.

Timbs, John. 1907. *Something for Everybody, and a Garland for the Year*. London: Elliot Stock.

Tonkin, E. 1992. *Narrating Our Pasts: The Social Construction of Oral History*. Cambridge, England: Cambridge University Press.

Townshend, Dorothea. 1898. "May-Day in Lincolnshire." *Folk-Lore* 9, no. 3 (September): 276.

Tregelles, J. A. 1908. *A History of Hoddesdon in the County of Hertfordshire*. Hertford: Stephen Austin.

Trevelyan, Marie. 1909. *Folk-Lore and Folk Stories of Wales*. London: E. Stock.

Trubshaw, Bob. 1995. "The Metaphors and Rituals of Place and Time: An Introduction to Liminality." *Mercian Mysteries* 22 (February): 1–8.

Tusser, Thomas. 1577. *July's Husbandry*. London: Richard Tottel.

Udal, J. S. 1889. "Dorsetshire Children's Games, Etc." *Folk-Lore Journal* VII (July–September): 202–64.

———. 1915. "Obeah in the West Indies." *Folklore* 26, no. 3 (September): 255–95.

Valiente, Doreen. 1962. *Where Witchcraft Lives*. London: Aquarian.

———. 1964. "Fifty at Pentagram Dinner." *Pentagram* 2 (November).

———. 1989. *The Rebirth of Witchcraft*. London: Hale.

Vickery, Roy. 1991. "The Use of Broad Beans to Cure Warts." *Folklore* 102, no. 2: 230–40.

Villiers, Elizabeth. 1923. *The Mascot Book*. London: T. Werner Laurie.

Waite, Arthur Edward. 1911. *The Book of Ceremonial Magic: Including the Rites and Mysteries of Goëtic Theurgy, Sorcery, and Infernal Necromancy.* London: Rider.

Wales, F. L. 1920. "The History of the Shelfords—Great and Little." Great Shelford, England: manuscript.

Wall, J. Charles. 1905. *Shrines of British Saints.* London: Mathuen.

Walsh, Martin W. 2000. "Mediaeval English *Martinmesse:* The Archaeology of a Forgotten Festival." *Folklore* 111, no. 2 (October): 231–54.

Walvin, James. 1973. *Black and White: The Negro and English Society, 1555–1945.* London: Allen Lane.

Warrack, Alexander. (1911) 1988. *The Scots Dialect Dictionary.* Poole, England: New Orchard Editions.

Wartburg, W. von. 1956. *Von Sprach und Mensch.* Bern, Switzerland: Francke Verlag.

Watt, Tessa. 1991. *Cheap Print and Popular Piety.* Cambridge, England: Cambridge University Press.

Webb, Denzil. 1969. "Irish Charms in Northern England." *Folklore* 80: 262–65.

Webster, D., ed. 1820. *Collection of Rare and Curious Tracts on Witchcraft.* Edinburgh: T. Webster.

Wentworth-Day, James. 1973. *Essex Ghosts.* Bourne End, England: Spurbooks.

Wheeler, W. H. 1868. *History of the Fens of South Lincolnshire.* Boston: J. M. Newcomb; London: Simpkin, Marshall and Co.

Wherry, Betrix, and Hermione L. F. Jennings. 1905. "A Cambridgeshire Witch." *Folk-Lore* 16, no. 2 (June): 187–90.

Whittick, Arnold. 1971. *Symbols: Signs and Their Meaning and Uses in Design.* London: Leonard Hill.

Widnall, Samuel Page. 1875. *History of Grantchester.* Grantchester, England: privately published.

———. 1892. *Gossiping through the Streets of Cambridge.* Grantchester, England: privately published.

Wilby, Emma. 2000. "The Witch's Familiar and the Fairy in Early Modern England and Scotland." *Folklore* 111: 283–305.

Wilgus, D. K. 1973. "The Text Is the Thing." *Journal of American Folklore* 86: 241–52.

Williams, F. Kemble. 1936. "The Sign of the Stallion's Tail." *East Anglian Magazine* 1, no. 11 (August): 587–88.

Williams, John (Ab Ithel), ed. 1861. *The Physicians of Myddfai.* Translated by John Pughe. The Llandovery, Wales: Welsh Manuscripts Society.

Williams, Joseph J. 1932. *Voodoos and Obeahs: Phases of West Indian Witchcraft.* New York: Dial Press.

Williams, Thomas, and Kate Pavitt. 1922. *The Book of Talismans, Amulets, and Zodical Gems.* 2nd ed. London: Rider.

Willock, Colin. 1962. *Kenzie: The Wild Goose Man.* London: Deutsch.

Wood, Juliette. 1999. "Margaret Murray and the Rise of Wicca." *3rd Stone* 34 (April–June): 18–22.

Wood-Martin, W. G. 1902. *Traces of the Elder Faiths of Ireland.* 2 vols. London: Longmans, Green and Company.

Woods, Barbara Allen. 1958. "The Norwegian Devil in North Dakota." *Western Folklore* 17, no. 3 (July): 196–98.

Wordsworth, Rev. Christopher. 1903. "Two Yorks Charms or Amulets: Exorcisms and Adjurations." *The Yorkshire Archeaological and Topographical Journal* XVII: 376–412.

Wortley, Russell. 1972. "Traditional Music in and around Cambridge." Unpublished typescript.

Wright, A. R., and T. E. Lones. 1936. *British Calendar Customs I. Movable Festivals.* London: William Glaisher Ltd.

———. 1938. *British Calendar Customs II. Fixed Festivals, January–May, Inclusive.* London: William Glaisher Ltd.

———. 1940. *British Calendar Customs III. Fixed Festivals, June–December, Inclusive.* London: William Glaisher Ltd.

Wright, A. R., and E. Lovett. 1908. "Specimens of Modern Mascots and Ancient Amulets of the British Isles." *Folk-Lore* 19, no. 3 (September): 288–303.

———. 1912. "Seventeenth Century Cures and Charms." *Folk-Lore* 23, no. 2 (June): 230–36.

Wright, A. R., and W. Aldis Wright. 1912. "Seventeenth Century Cures and Charms." *Folk-Lore* 23, no. 4 (December): 490–97.

Index